A Rural Diversion

Ray Hobbs

Wingspan Press

Published in the United States and the United Kingdom by WingSpan Press, Livermore, CA

The WingSpan name, logo and colophon are the trademarks of WingSpan Publishing.

ISBN 978-1-59594-640-9 (pbk.)
ISBN 978-1-59594-955-4 (ebk.)

First edition 2019

Printed in the United States of America

www.wingspanpress.com

1 2 3 4 5 6 7 8 9 10

This book is dedicated to returned service personnel and prisoners of conflict and to those who help them make the inevitable adjustment.

ACKNOWLEDGEMENTS

I wish to thank my wife Sheila for her unfailing encouragement during the writing of this book, and my faithful companion Phoebe for the cover illustration. I am also indebted to my brother Chris, whose idea it was to revisit Freddy and Sylvia, and who acted, as ever, both as soundboard and as a ready source of ideas from planning to final draft, whilst helping to fuel my enthusiasm throughout.

RH

GLOSSARY FOR READERS OUTSIDE THE UK

WRNS (Wrens): The Women's Royal Naval Service

Magistrate/Justice of the Peace: a minor justice

Picts: early Lowland Scottish tribe

Petrol: gasoline

Pink (dyed) petrol: the extra ration for essential users

Women's Institute: community-based organisation

'Kriegie' (*Kriegsgefangener*): prisoner-of-war

Tack shop: saddlery

Waistcoat: vest

Lorry: truck

At HM Pleasure: (archaic) a prison sentence

Tennis Shoes: sneakers

Queue: line

Lords (cricket ground, St John's Wood, London): the home of cricket

Dispensing chemist: pharmacist, druggist

Auxiliary Territorial Service: women's army

Borstal: young offenders' institution

'Old lag': ex-convict

Chip: fried potato

Nappy, napkin: diaper

The Green Howards: North Riding infantry regiment

Grammar School: a selective high school

Festival of Britain: national expo/celebration in 1951

Town Clerk: legal executive to a town council

ENSA (Entertainments National Service Association): entertainers of troops in WW2

Author's Note

I t must seem incredible to many that rationing remained in force in Britain for nine years after the war, but that was nevertheless the case. Meat, the last foodstuff to be rationed, became freely available on the 4th July, 1954.

The reasons for the extended rationing were both economic and political. In those days, Britain was far from self-sufficient, and relied heavily on imported goods. Such purchases had to be paid for, and Britain's reserves of foreign currency were severely limited.

The First World War of 1914-1918 had left Britain almost bankrupt, so that, when war returned in 1939, it was necessary to borrow heavily from the USA and Canada. Then, in 1945, the US Government terminated the Lend-Lease Agreement. To tide Britain over, they granted a loan of $4.33 billion, one condition being that sterling was made convertible. Within a month, nations with sterling balances had withdrawn almost $1 billion, leaving British dollar reserves dangerously depleted. With what remained, Britain had to make repayments to the US whilst feeding the home population and the British sector of West Germany as well.

Imports had to be financed by exports, and controls were placed on the domestic sale of manufactured goods, such as motor cars. New vehicles were impossible to acquire because they were reserved for the export trade.

In some cases, food quality was also subject to government controls. In 1942, the government decreed that, to preserve stocks of white flour, the only bread to be baked would be The National Loaf, made from wholemeal flour with added salt, calcium and vitamins. It looked and tasted unappetising but was not abolished until after the end of rationing.

Another food to be standardised was cheese. Manufacture of regional cheeses was forbidden, and the milk previously used in their manufacture was now reserved for Government Cheddar, the only cheese available throughout rationing. When the control was finally lifted, manufacture of regional cheeses had to be planned and developed from scratch, and was therefore extremely slow to recover.

On the 31st December 2006, Chancellor of the Exchequer Gordon Brown wrote the final cheque in repayment of Britain's war debt. For such an important milestone, the news announcement seemed to pass almost without notice, coming as it did on New Year's Eve, with its attendant distractions. By contrast, however, I am sure I am not alone in remembering the 4th July, 1954. In particular, I recall my mother's reaction on sending me on an errand to the corner shop, when I asked for the ration book.

'You don't need it,' she told me. 'Rationing is over.' It was a great day, even for a boy of seven.

RH

A RURAL DIVERSION

1

May 1950

A North Riding Town

It seemed to Freddy that horses were very much like people. There were those who were inclined to take life seriously; others had a childlike sense of fun. Some, it had to be said, could be sly, whilst others were endearingly transparent. Most of them, however, were basically friendly, and that was just as well, he felt, considering their size and strength.

His current interest was in Mandy, a brown cob of fifteen hands, who had taken friendliness to its ultimate conclusion and was due to foal in the next month or so, hence Freddy's interest in her. That she was unfazed by the sound of the camera shutter was a bonus.

'It's not loaded,' Freddy told her owner. 'I just want her to get used to having it pointed at her.'

'I didn't think it would worry her at this stage,' said Mrs Cresswell. 'It takes a lot to unsettle her but I still think you should wait at least a couple of days after the foaling before you come. She'll be very protective at first.'

'All right, you know best.' He liked the mare's owner. She was older than him, maybe in her forties, but friendly and sociable. She'd been among the first to welcome Sylvia and him to the town and introduce them to her friends, although being a photographer with a particular interest in animals must have given him a head start. He suspected that most of the local equestrian population would have their horses photographed before their children.

He felt obliged to ask, 'Will this be Mandy's first foal?'

'Yes.' She looked at him strangely and said, 'She'll know exactly what to do when the time comes, Freddy. They do it by instinct, you know.'

'Of course.'

'You were looking worried.' It seemed to amuse her.

'I'm sorry.'

'Oh, I appreciate your concern, but there's really nothing to worry about.'

'Fine, I'll stop worrying.'

'You should.' Then, possibly to assist him in the process, she changed the subject and asked, 'How's Sylvia? I haven't seen her for a while.'

'She's fine, thank you.'

'She's a lovely girl. I'm glad you two got together.'

'I'm quite pleased about it myself, Mrs Cresswell.'

She was smiling when she asked, 'What's that pet name you have for her?' Then she hesitated. 'Maybe I shouldn't ask.'

'Oh, there's no secret. It's "SP", short for "Sugar Plum Fairy". She was in a ballet presentation when she was very young. She told me about it in a letter when I was in Poland. I suppose the name just stuck.'

'I still think it's lovely that you got together through writing to each other.' Changing the subject, she asked, 'How's that dance band of yours? "The Dalesmen", isn't it?'

'That's right. It's going well, thank you. At least, I've had no complaints so far. I suppose time will tell.'

'You're far too modest, Freddy.' She pulled out Mandy's mane with a grooming brush and began tidying it.

'To be honest,' he confided, 'I've been criticised about the name, basically because I'm a foreigner from the East Riding. I can't really understand what the problem is, because we're billed as "Freddy Hinchcliffe *and* The Dalesmen". I'm not pretending to be anything I'm not.'

'You're ours by adoption, Freddy. Take no notice of them. As far as I'm concerned you're bringing a little enjoyment to a community that's coping, like the rest of the country, with rationing, shortages and austerity, and if that doesn't make you one of us, I don't know what does.'

⁂

Sylvia dried the last of the cutlery, hung up the towel and looked at the kitchen clock. It was almost six-fifteen.

'If you're interested,' she said, 'Geraldo's on the Light Programme in fifteen minutes.'

'Is he?' Freddy dried his hands and rolled down his shirt-sleeves. He wasn't terribly keen on the style Geraldo had adopted in recent times.

They went into the sitting room and he joined her on the sofa.

'You're sitting on my deaf side, Freddy.'

'I'm sorry, SP. I should have learned by now.' He swapped sides of the sofa with her and adopted a look of penitence.

She patted his knee. 'You're forgiven.'

Physically they were very different. She was slightly built with medium-brown hair and a light complexion enhanced by a genuine smile that was seldom absent for long. He, on the other hand, was taller and stocky, and his hair, which at one time had been dark, was largely grey, unusually so for a man of thirty. In other respects, however, they were the ideal match, which was surprising, considering their courtship had been conducted largely at a distance of a thousand or so miles when he was a prisoner-of-war and she was serving in the WRNS.

'I was at the Cresswells' place this morning,' he said.

'Were you?' She looked up with new interest. 'Mandy must be near her time.'

'She's due to foal in about a month.'

'As much as that? I have to say, though, you're improving, Freddy.'

'Am I?'

'You said "foal" like a true countryman.'

'Well, that's something at least.' It was an uncomfortable reminder of another minor embarrassment. 'My equestrian clients must think I'm an awful townie,' he said.

'Did something happen this morning?' She was adept at reading his discomfiture.

'I asked Mrs Cresswell if it was going to be Mandy's first foal. I just wondered if she'd had some experience or if it was all going to be an awful shock for her.'

'Oh, Freddy.' She tried to maintain a straight face.

'I know. She thought it was funny too.'

'I'm sorry. It's not really funny.' She became properly serious. 'The main thing is – and I'm sure Mrs Cresswell would agree with me – that you care. Anyone can learn about horses but no one can learn to care. That's something you do quite naturally, just as animals calve, lamb and foal.' She seemed to dwell on that for a while, and then said, 'Animals do it naturally, don't they? It's just some of us who struggle.'

'It'll happen, SP.' He put his arm round her and gave her shoulder a squeeze. 'We just need to give it every opportunity.'

'Spoken like a man.' Then, as abruptly as only a woman can, she changed the subject. 'It's half-past six. Do you want to listen to Geraldo?'

'Not really.'

'So what are we going to do instead?'

'We could go upstairs and have another go at starting a family.' He adopted a hopeful pose. 'It's just a suggestion.'

'Not at half-past six, Freddy. It's still light.'

'When's lighting-up time?'

'About eight-thirty, I think.'

He made his lower lip tremble until her resolve weakened.

'I suppose we could reach a compromise.'

His pout gave way to a beaming smile.

'Freddy, you're impossible.'

'Not entirely. Mrs Cresswell paid me a compliment this morning. She told me that the Dalesmen and I brought entertainment to a deprived community.'

'She's absolutely right.'

'Very loyal of you, SP. As a matter of fact I've been thinking about the community.' He sat upright to explore the subject properly. 'What activities did people get up to around here before the war?'

4

'Oh, the usual things. There were agricultural shows, horse shows, sheepdog trials, racing, harvest suppers and that kind of thing. Of course, everyone's getting back into the swing of things but it all takes time.'

'I was thinking more along the lines of music and entertainment.'

That seemed to prod her memory. 'Oh, there were the Yoredale Players as well. I'd forgotten about them.'

'The who?'

'It was an amateur society. "Yoredale" was the old Viking name that became "Uredale" and then "Wensleydale".'

'Fascinating, but were they good?'

'Some of them were. You find good, not so good and downright awful in most societies, although I don't remember anyone really awful in the Players.' She thought about that briefly. 'Actually,' she said, 'I was in their last production before the war.'

'What was that?'

'*Rosemarie.*'

'What part did you play?'

'A Red Indian girl. It was a dancing part, and a very small one at that.'

'I bet you stole the show. I wish I'd been there.' With some difficulty, he left the mental picture behind him and said, 'This is the first I've heard of the Yoredale Players. I take it they're defunct?'

'Not so much defunct as mothballed. My dad could tell you more. He was chairman and treasurer.' She thought quickly. 'Aren't you going fishing with him on Sunday? If you're really interested you can ask him about it then.'

2

Freddy's conversation with his father-in-law turned out to be informative if not immediately encouraging. To the best of Walter Charlesworth's recollection, the society had little more than one pound in its bank account, and that was unlikely to go far. Problems, however, were there to be overcome, and several other members had recently hinted that they would like to see the dormant society revived, so, at Walter's suggestion, an extraordinary general meeting was called for the following Friday in the function room of the Fox and Hounds.

⊷⊶⊰⊱⊱⊷

Freddy had hoped to see a reasonable number at the meeting. In the event, twenty-two turned up, which meant that, allowing for natural wastage, the meeting was at least quorate. He was pleased also that Walter lent a measure of authority to the proceedings. He was a man of military bearing, having held a commission in the Green Howards until 1916, when he was invalided out of the army with a shattered kneecap. He bore his injury well, however, and was invariably smartly turned out. On this occasion, he wore a lovat tweed suit and a plum red bow tie. He had sported a pencil moustache throughout the thirties and the war years, but had lately cultivated an immaculately-groomed chevron.

The first item on the agenda was Apologies for Absence. There were none, from which Freddy surmised that the only interested members were those present.

The Election of Officers followed and Walter was unanimously re-elected Chairman and Treasurer. No one else wanted either post, and neither was the office of Secretary contested. Everyone was happy to re-elect Emma Crawshaw, who had held the post in 1939 to everyone's satisfaction.

'The next item,' announced Walter, 'is the Treasurer's Report, and I have to tell you that the Society's assets amount to exactly one pound and nine shillings.'

'Is that all?' The question came from one of the erstwhile chorus members. There was a hint of accusation in her tone.

'It was somewhat less before hostilities intervened,' said Walter. 'I placed the balance on deposit shortly after war was declared, and I can report that interest amounting to eight shillings has been earned.'

Another member raised his hand and said, 'I'd like to propose a vote of thanks to our Treasurer for his foresight and timely intervention.'

'Don't worry about that.' Walter dismissed the matter with a discreet wave of his hand. 'I appreciate your thanks but it's still a very tiny sum and we have more important matters to discuss.'

'But what are we going to do with only twenty-nine bob in the kitty?' It was Edith Foster, the woman who'd queried the bank balance.

'That's what I'm about to tell you if you'll all be patient.' He looked around the room and began. 'I had a very useful discussion about it with my son-in-law Freddy Hinchcliffe on Sunday.'

'We saw you down at Redmire Falls,' said Ernie Holmes the greengrocer. 'How many did you catch, Walter?'

'It was a good day, Ernie, but hear me out, if you please.'

'All right.' Then to no one in particular Ernie said, 'I see them two down there many a time. It's a wonder there's any trout left in that river.'

'Ernie, please.'

'Sorry, Walter.'

'Good. Now, as I was saying, Freddy and I discussed the possibility of resurrecting the Players, and he advanced a few ideas that he'd like to put to you.' With a nod in Freddy's direction, he sat down.

Freddy rose uncertainly to his feet. 'You're possibly wondering,' he said, 'what a newcomer to the area knows about the Yoredale Players, and the answer is that I only know what I've been told.' In contrast with his father-in-law, he'd dressed casually in a navy-blue jumper, grey flannels and brown Oxford brogues. He was happy for

Walter to be the authority figure. He was an accountant and a magistrate, and it was what he did best.

'I know something else, though,' he went on, 'something that's very important. I know that, as things stand, The Yoredale Players are in no position to pay for performing rights, music scores and scripts, band parts or musicians, and that rules out any existing musical play.'

'We know all that,' said Edith Foster. 'What are you saying?'

'We could always do a straight play,' someone suggested.

'No,' said Edith sharply, 'we've always done musicals. It wouldn't be right to change now.'

'I'm not suggesting that at all,' Freddy told them. 'I'm as keen on music as you are. Some of you know that I have a dance band called "The Dalesmen", but maybe you don't know that I've had some success as well at writing music and lyrics. What I'm asking is that you let me write a musical. It won't cost you anything and I'm fairly certain I can persuade the band, or at least some of them, to lend their services free of charge.'

There was silence, which Freddy found unsettling, until someone asked, 'What will the show be about?'

'I have in mind a musical comedy set in Wensleydale's Viking past. I should tell you, however, that the Vikings won't be as we usually think of them.'

Another hand went up. Its owner asked, 'Are you trying to tell us that the Vikings danced the foxtrot and the waltz?'

'No, I'm not, but you mustn't expect historical accuracy either. It would be a comedy after all.'

'So will they have to dance the tango?'

'No. Please forget dance music if you can, and accept my assurance that I can write in other musical styles, and the musicians can play anything I write. Does that help?' He was rewarded by a murmur of approval, and then a heavy-browed individual with the look of one who would countenance nothing improper, said, 'It seems to me, Walter, that the Charlesworth family has more than a stake in this affair.'

'Sit down, Herbert,' said Edith Foster. 'You're making a fool of yourself as usual.'

'No, Edith.' Walter was quick to overrule her. 'Let Herbert have his say.' Turning to the speaker, he said, 'Go on then, Herbert. Tell us what's bothering you.'

Herbert shifted uncomfortably before saying, 'Well, you're Treasurer as well as Chairman, and now you want to give your son-in-law another top job. That's all I'm saying.'

'He just has to say something,' said Edith. 'He can't go two minutes without stickin' his oar in.'

'Well, let's take a sounding.' Walter addressed the meeting. 'You elected me unanimously to both offices. Have any of you changed your minds since you voted?'

The only response was from that voice of common sense, the redoubtable Edith Foster. 'Nay, Walter, it's just that some folk are so full of their own importance they have to make a fuss, no matter what.' She gave the offending Herbert a foul look.

'All right,' said Walter, 'Does anyone else fancy writing a show?' The silent chorus of embarrassed looks provided the welcome answer. 'Very well, I think that clears things up. Are you satisfied, Herbert?'

'I suppose so. I just thought it was worth mentioning.'

'Well, I think it sounds like a good idea,' said another member, 'and it's very good of Frankie to offer his services.'

Walter corrected him gently. ' "Freddy",' he said.

'Yes, I meant "Freddy". Sorry, Freddy.'

'Don't worry about it. You were close.' He was encouraged by the nods and other encouraging signs but he was still grateful when Walter spoke.

'Are there any more questions? No? In that case, may we have a proposal that we ask Freddy to write our next show?'

The motion was proposed, seconded, and carried unanimously, and Freddy was appointed Artistic Director, all of which caused him enormous relief after the embarrassment. All he had to do now was write the show. According to Irving Berlin, writing a musical was easy, but Freddy reasoned that anything was easy for those who knew how, and it was therefore important for him to acquire that knowledge. Before that, though, he had to recruit an orchestra.

3

The trouble with rehearsing at Easingthorpe Village School was that the chairs were designed for young children, and that meant that the Dalesmen were obliged to sit on the sloping desks instead. Second Reed George Clay was unimpressed.

'I'm getting a permanent ridge across my arse,' he complained, 'and it's bad for the concentration.'

'Bring a cushion,' Derek Littlewood advised him. 'I never leave home without mine.' The others nodded knowingly. Derek's inflatable ring and the condition that made it necessary were no secret.

Forgetting his ridge for the moment in the interest of debate, George said, 'So what you're saying, Freddy, is you want us to do the job for nowt.'

'That,' Freddy had to admit, 'is what I'm asking. It's just a way of bringing a bit of fun into people's lives.'

'Aye, you said so, an' it certainly sounds like fun. You can count me in.'

'Me an' all,' said Derek. 'As I see it, if I'm not playin' somewhere, the wife will only find me jobs to do at home.' He added sadly, 'She's good at that.'

There was a general murmur of accord, prompting Freddy to test the waters. 'Who else is prepared to give it a go?' He'd been hoping to persuade a few, confident that he could fill in as necessary on the piano, but he was delighted to see the entire band volunteering.

'Derek's right,' said Wilf Bennett the bass player. 'We'd rather play for fresh air than sit at home twiddling our thumbs.'

'Well, I'm grateful to you all. Thanks, all of you.'

'Aye, well,' said Wilf, 'you'll need us there to keep an eye on you. Have you done much pit conducting?'

'None at all. The only pit I've ever known was a salt mine in Poland.'

'We'll look after you,' Derek told him. 'We won't let you make a fool of yourself, not while folk associate you with us, anyroad.'

'That's big of you, Derek.' He told himself he would get used to their rough-hewn camaraderie in time.

❧◦❊◦❧

He had a different question for Sylvia and he put it to her that night.

'Have you ever thought of having a dog, SP?'

'A dog?' She had to stop brushing and remove her toothbrush to articulate the question. 'I'm not having much success providing you with a baby, never mind a dog.'

'Be sensible, SP. How would I find the name of a dog breeder?'

'I suppose you could write to the Kennel Club.' She frowned at the idea. 'Surely you've done it before. What about the dog you told me about, the one who was a good listener and a keen swimmer?'

'Arthur? I'm surprised you remember him. I grew up with him, though. I don't remember anything about where he came from.'

Sylvia finished rinsing her mouth and said, 'Anyway, why do you suddenly want a dog?'

'It's not a sudden thing, SP. I've been thinking about it for some time. I mean to say, your dad has Rainbow. She comes fishing with us and she's lovely, but she's your dad's dog when all's said and done. I can't bring her home.'

'My mum would have let you have her for good that time she stole the bacon ration.'

'That doesn't count. Humour me, SP. I'd really like a dog, and so would you if you'll only admit it.'

'All right.' She slipped into bed and pulled up the covers. 'What kind of dog would you like?'

'An Aberdeen terrier.'

'A Scottie?' We've never had one. What's the appeal?'

11

'The life I left behind, I suppose.' He took his place beside her and drew her closer. 'I spent my formative years, as you did, in the thirties. We were children of the Art Deco age, and the Aberdeen terrier is the Art Deco dog. It's geometric and fun and totally appealing and, by the way....'

'What?'

'I love it when you taste of toothpaste.' He kissed her to make his point.

'All right,' she said, collecting herself, 'you've won me over but you do need to know more about the breed. If I were you I should be inclined to talk to Mr Helliwell.'

'Who?'

'The vet who looks after Rainbow. He might know who's likely to have a litter. He'll give you some advice about breed characteristics as well.'

He nodded. 'So that I don't look like a complete chump with dogs as well as horses?'

'Don't be like that, darling. You take beautiful animal pictures and you're not a chump. I only suggested it to make life easier for you when you get a dog.'

'Okay, I know there's a lot to take into consideration. There's exercise – he'll need regular walking, and if he's going to come to work with us he'll have to get used to travelling in the van. He'll have to be trained as well.'

'Lots and lots to think about,' she agreed, snuggling closer, 'and important decisions to be made.'

'What decisions?'

'Oh, Eton or Harrow, Oxford or Cambridge, cricket or rowing....'

'Mock me if you like, SP, but I'm taking this seriously.'

'This and the show, Freddy. I'm impressed.'

❦❧❦

Jessie Charlesworth was also impressed but with reservations, which she voiced at the breakfast table a few hours later.

'I admire the way you've taken this thing on, Walter, but I can see lots of problems.'

12

'There are challenges, I agree, but so far I've seen nothing that can't be overcome.' He buttered a piece of toast and said, 'This isn't best butter, is it?'

'It's a mixture of butter and margarine, one of the challenges I've had to overcome.'

'You manage these things so well, Jessie.'

'Thank you, but how is Freddy going to produce scripts and music without paper?'

'There's a mountain of official documents of one kind or another at the office, and many of them printed on one side only. He can use them for a start.' He took a spoonful of marmalade and spread it on his toast, hoping it would mask the taste of margarine.

'All right, but what about costumes? Clothing's only been off the ration a year, if that.'

'Blackout material, Jessie. Freddy and I were discussing it only yesterday. If it's treated with a weak solution of bleach, it'll come out brown, which was apparently the predominant colour in Viking times.' He raised a finger to make his point. 'Now that's authenticity for you.'

'You have an answer for everything.'

He shrugged good-naturedly. 'It's essential in my job, Jessie.'

Freddy hung the 'Closed' sign on the studio door and went upstairs to join Sylvia for lunch.

'You'll have to go fishing again,' she told him, putting a cheese and pickle sandwich in front of him, 'because until they take meat off the ration it's the only way you're going to get a hearty meal.'

'That's true.' But the sandwich was no less welcome. Five years had passed since Freddy's liberation but he still regarded food of almost any description with a level of appreciation that bordered on reverence.

'One day,' said Sylvia, eyeing the cheese in her sandwich, 'we'll have Wensleydale again instead of this awful Government Cheddar.'

'I've heard of Wensleydale Cheese,' said Freddy, like someone recalling a half-forgotten legend. 'I gather it was rather special.'

' "Special" isn't the word, Freddy. 'It was *exquisite*. It was creamy and crumbly and it had a smooth, delicate taste that lingered on the tongue like....' She paused for want of an adequate simile.

'Like a fond recollection?'

'Something along those lines,' she agreed, 'but you get the idea.'

'Without actually tasting it, yes.'

'That's a treat in store,' she promised. Then, as one thought followed another, she asked, 'How are you getting on with the show?'

'It's forming gradually,' he told her, 'in my head. I have lots of ideas. I just need to organise them.'

'Tell me about your ideas.'

'I shouldn't.'

'Why not?'

'They say it's counter-productive to talk to anyone about work in progress.'

She gave him a challenging look. 'Are you calling me "anyone"?'

'Of course not. No, on reflection, I think I can make an exception in your case.'

'I should think so.'

'Right, the action takes place towards the end of the ninth century in a settlement in Wensleydale.'

'It wasn't called that in those days.'

'Okay, it's a half-formed idea. I'll tidy it up later. Just pay out some slack for now.'

'All right.'

'Right. Raids by Vikings and marauding Picts have left the settlement short of able-bodied men, thus making the women somewhat vulnerable, or at least as vulnerable as a collection of spirited Daleswomen can ever be. However, what they don't realise is that the latest boatload of Vikings is commanded by a rather unusual chieftain with a guilty secret.' He sat back in his chair, enjoying her interest.

'Go on, Freddy. Don't keep me in suspense.'

'All right. He comes with an impressive pedigree; his father was the great warlord Erik the Ready. Unfortunately, our hero is

Erik the Not Quite Ready, and his secret is that he's not the classic Viking bully. He cares not a goose egg for burning, looting, pillaging, and carrying away nubile maidens. He's more the aesthetic kind of Norseman. I'm sure they existed. I mean someone had to write the sagas, so yes, he's a reluctant hero of the best and most wholesome kind. The trouble is I need a really good bass to play the part, and so far there's no sign of one.'

'Why does he have to be a bass?'

'I want the ironic contrast between the aesthetic persona and the masculine voice.'

She nodded appreciatively. 'I like it, and you never know, as word gets about and new members come forward, you may find this bass singer.'

'You continue to be a comfort to me, SP.' He looked at the clock. 'I must get back to work. I have a Pekingese portrait session at one-thirty.'

'And not every photographer can say that.'

'True.' He drained his coffee cup and stood up.

'Oh, Freddy?'

'Yes?'

'Did you speak to Mr Helliwell?'

'I did. He doesn't know of any local breeders. Everyone round here breeds sheepdogs.' He added, 'And Pekingese, apparently.'

'And you don't fancy either of those breeds, I take it?'

'Not much. As I see it, Pekingese are so inscrutable, I'd always feel that the dog was keeping something from me, and I couldn't live with that.'

'Or a Border collie?' Sylvia shook her head as she spoke.

'No, I gather they're excellent at herding sheep and chasing ramblers, but a Border collie wouldn't be the ideal dog for a photographer.'

'I agree. They're very specialised.'

'I'm looking for a dog that can adapt to changing situations, SP, just as I have to from time to time.'

Nodding with mock solemnity, she said, 'Good luck, Freddy.'

'What's the joke, SP?'

'Only that you're expecting an awful lot from a dumb animal.'

'I have to find the animal yet.'

It seemed that Freddy's dream of dog ownership was not to be realised, at least for the time being, although he hadn't given up on the idea. In the meantime, though, he had a show to write.

4

Freddy had the merest skeleton of a synopsis in his head and he wanted to get it down on paper while it was still clear in his mind. The nearest paper to hand was the back of a spoiled four-and-a-half by seven-inch print, which was quite large enough for his miniscule handwriting. He was sketching Act 1, Scene 2 when Sylvia opened the studio door and interrupted him.

'You'll never guess,' she said, sounding breathless.

'Don't tell me. They've found Hitler, alive and disguised as the rear half of a pantomime horse.'

'No.'

'The King wants me to photograph his racehorse. I knew it would happen eventually, SP. I've lived for this moment.'

'No, Freddy, listen!'

'All right, but it had better be good.'

'It is.' She was struggling to contain herself. 'Petrol rationing is over! No more pink petrol, no more planning our journeys to the nearest mile; in fact, lots of marvellous things!'

'That's good news, SP. It's going to make life a lot easier.'

'Oh, Freddy!' It seemed that words almost failed her. 'How can you be unmoved? People have been waiting for this since nineteen-forty. It's the best news since clothes came off the ration.'

Freddy laid down his pen. He hadn't intended to sound dismissive. 'I'm sorry,' he said. 'I'm sure it's a big thing for most people.'

'But not for you?'

'As I said, it'll make life much easier for all of us, and that's a welcome development. I'm pleased, just not excited.'

'It's that prisoner-of-war thing again, isn't it?' She perched on the edge of his desk, facing him. 'Somehow, it makes you play everything down.'

'I'm afraid so,' he said, taking her hands. 'When we were liberated and I came here, all the talk was about food rationing. It was a major preoccupation, but I was just grateful I was no longer existing on cabbage water and compressed sawdust. This is the same kind of thing. It's a matter of perspective, that's all.'

'It's so awful, Freddy. That was five years ago.'

'I don't think there's a time limit.' Releasing her hands, he drew her on to his lap. 'But I've experienced things that have excited me beyond belief, some more than the rest.'

Intrigued, she asked, 'What things?'

'There was the time we reached the camp at Seigenheim and learned that the guards had deserted us; there was liberation itself, a grand event, and then there was that day in Trafalgar Square, when I peered through the murk and drizzle and saw you walking towards me. My postal Sugar Plum Fairy had taken human form at last and we were about to meet face to face. That was the greatest moment of my life and I'll never forget it.'

Her eyes were moist. 'Better than our wedding day?' It was more a genuine question than a challenge.

'I'd say it wins by a short head. Anyway, our wedding day was ever so slightly overshadowed by the... well, the anti-climax.'

'Do you mean that night? I couldn't help it, Freddy. Nerves can play havoc with a woman's natural rhythm.'

'I'm not blaming you. Mother Nature must shoulder the blame entirely, and anyway, some things are worth waiting for.'

'That's not what you said at the time.' She smiled involuntarily at the memory. 'As I recall, you were so disappointed, you lost your appetite, possibly for the only time since the war.'

'I still say it was tactless of you to eat my share as well as yours.'

'I can't abide waste.'

'That's what you told me at the time.' He mustered a smile and said, 'It was a good honeymoon, though. We found plenty to do, didn't we?'

'Yes, we did.' Suddenly distracted, she picked up Freddy's notes and asked, 'What's this?'

'Act One, Scene Two,' he told her, 'where the Viking chief confides in his men that he's no brigand but a softy at heart.'

'How do they react?'

'They're relieved. They've been dreading the looting, burning, pillaging and snatching of eligible maidens. Suddenly they're a much happier crew now that they're no longer expected to behave like cads.'

She pondered the information and said, 'Only you could invent a situation like that, Freddy.'

'I could struggle to meet your expectations, SP. One thing I must say, however, is that you and I should celebrate the end of fuel rationing as soon as possible.'

'Don't feel that you have to, I mean, because of what I said. It really doesn't matter.'

'No, SP, it's a landmark event that warrants celebration.' He patted the desktop with the flat of his hand to emphasise his point.

'But how will we celebrate?'

He said nothing but rolled his eyes in an upward direction.

'Oh, Freddy.' She gave him an admonishing look. 'It's eight-thirty in the morning.'

'You're obsessed with time, SP.'

'Can't you wait 'til later?'

'I have an appointment at ten o'clock.'

Her expression betrayed her impatience. 'I meant tonight.'

'Tonight,' he said, 'we shall be at our usual eating and dancing place in Harrogate. That's what I really had in mind, now we have the petrol to get there and back. I was only joking about the other.'

'I might have known it was a leg-pull.'

'A matter as serious as today's news, SP, calls for something more profound than a spot of you-know-what.'

She regarded him as if he'd claimed supernatural powers. 'I'm surprised you of all people think anything can compete with that,' she said.

He adopted a sheepish pretence. 'I wish you wouldn't look at me like that.'

'Like what?'

'Leading Wren Charlesworth. I feel intimidated.'

'Nonsense. Anyway,' she said, brightening, 'yours is a nice idea.'

'It seems appropriate,' he agreed, giving her a sideways look as he added, 'I suppose the other thing can wait just a little longer.'

His ten o'clock appointment was with a Jack Russell terrier, a small, mainly-white dog with brown and black markings largely about the face and ears. After a discreet glance to ascertain the animal's sex, he asked, 'What's his name, Mrs Woolliscroft?

'Tigger.'

'Is that after the character in *The House at Pooh Corner*?' As he spoke he realised it was a silly question. Within the confines of the studio, the dog was already making repeated bids to become airborne, and apparently for no reason other than for the undoubted joy of it.

His owner nodded slowly; it was as if she were forcing herself to remain calm. 'It was my husband's idea to get a Jack Russell,' she explained, 'only I'm the one who has to look after him. He comes home from work and plays rough games with him, and then I have the job of calming him down and making him act right in his head.' It was difficult to tell which of them Mrs Woolliscroft regarded as the greater menace.

'What kind of picture do you have in mind?'

'If you can get him to stand still long enough, I'd say any kind you can get.'

'What size?'

'No bigger than that.' She described a rectangle with her hands.

'Ten by eight. Excuse me for a moment, Mrs Woolliscroft.' He disappeared into the darkroom, returning with a different camera.

'What's that, then?' Mrs Woolliscroft viewed the camera with suspicion.

'It's a camera with a fast lens and shutter, ideal for photographing jet-propelled Jack Russells.'

She was still suspicious. 'It looks expensive,' she said.

'It would have been expensive to buy,' he agreed, 'but the fee is just the same whichever camera I use.'

'Oh.' She looked relieved but then asked, 'What do you mean, "It *would* have been expensive"?'

'I didn't buy it,' he said. 'I acquired it by barter when I was in Germany. You see, the Americans who liberated us were very generous with things like cigarettes and chocolate. Now, I'd given up smoking by that time, and I didn't need the cigarettes, but they came in very useful as currency in a country that was starved of just about everything.'

Mrs Woolliscroft eyed him warily. 'I've heard about that sort of thing,' she said. 'Some of them German women had no shame, not that it excused our lads for taking advantage of them.'

'Well, I exchanged cigarettes for two cameras. It was a stroke of luck for me, and the owner was happy enough to part with them. There was no film to be had in Germany anyway.'

'I see.' She appeared to be satisfied of his innocence. Then, in an impromptu change of subject, she asked, 'Do you play cricket?'

'Cricket? I haven't played since I was at school.'

'Oh, that's no problem. You'll soon get back into the way of it. Even my husband's taking part and he hasn't played for ever such a long time.'

It seemed to Freddy that Mrs Woolliscroft was taking something for granted. 'Your husband is taking part in what, Mrs Woolliscroft?'

'The charity cricket match.' Her tone suggested that he should have known about it all along. 'The WI is organising a match between Easingthorpe Cricket Club and a team of local challengers. It's to fund a Christmas party for the kiddies. There's some as wouldn't get much for Christmas as things stand, and we want to do what we can for them.' Her gaze was unwavering. 'Well,' she asked, 'are you game?'

'When is it going to happen?'

'We've pencilled in the twenty-third of July. We can have the cricket field and the pavilion. We just need a team of challengers.'

'I don't know how much use I'm going to be, Mrs Woolliscroft, but all right, I'll do it. Put me down as a medium-pace bowler and late-order batsman.'

'Oh, that'll be for the captain to sort out.'

'Who is he?' It all sounded very disorganised.

'We don't know yet. We've asked the Rector of St Jude's, but he hasn't replied yet. Anyroad, we'll keep you informed.'

'Thank you.' He wasn't sure he had much to thank her for. 'Shall we get started with these pictures?' Tigger had grown tired of aerobatics and was now curled up on the sofa, so he stroked him and tickled him behind one ear. 'Are you going to let me take some pictures, Tigger?' He knelt on the studio floor, as the dog jumped off the sofa, and took a series of exposures. There was a limit to how many he could afford in the light of current shortages, but he reckoned he had some good shots. He would work on them later. Then he would sketch the rest of 'Viking High Jinks.'

⸎⸎⸎

More than three hundred miles away and oblivious to Freddy's problems, a tall, well-groomed man, possibly in his mid-thirties, sat writing a letter.

My dear old thing,

How the years have flown by, but I hope this letter finds you and the fair lady of the house in the very pinnacle of health.

Now, straight to the point, I wonder if I might prevail upon you for a couple of nights' board and lodging. If such a favour is possible, I shall be eternally grateful. The fact is, Messrs Blackwell Brothers of Northallerton, purveyors of superior motor vehicles to the discerning, have summoned me for interview on Friday, 16th instant. I entertain high hopes for the outcome and feel therefore inclined to report on the said date, washed, groomed, pressed and polished for the event. Therefore, if my company is agreeable on the nights of the 15th and 16th, I thank you in advance.

Looking forward to hearing from you, to seeing you again and to making the acquaintance of your lovely lady, I remain yours as ever

He signed the letter and addressed the envelope to F. Hinchcliffe Esquire, c/o Mr and Mrs W. G. Charlesworth. He would find the address later. It was the only one he had for Freddy, and he hoped the letter would find him.

5

The letter was dated 6th June, written in an ornate hand and in a language that Freddy found instantly and pleasingly familiar. 'Your dad must have put it through the letter box on his way to the office,' he said.

'Who's it from?' Sylvia had been watching his amused expression as he read the letter, and could contain her curiosity no longer.

'It's from my fellow-kriegie Bailey,' he said, handing the letter across the table. 'You remember his connivance on our part that night in London, don't you?'

'Of course I do. It was the perfect evening.' She read the letter, sharing his amusement. 'He refers to me as "the fair lady" and "your lovely lady", but not by name. D' you think he's forgotten it?'

'I think he's being delicate. He has no way of knowing that things worked out for us the way they did. For all he knows, you and I might have parted company after that night in London.'

'How awful.'

'If you remember, I tried contacting him when we were organising the wedding, but he'd disappeared without leaving a clue.'

'Yes, I remember now.' She looked at the letter again and said, 'His style is very flowery.'

Freddy nodded. 'He adopted bullshit as his first language a long time ago.'

'Oh, Freddy.'

'I'm sorry, but at Niwka we all knew him as "Bullshit Bailey." He was famous for it.'

Ignoring her husband's vulgarity for the moment, she said, 'It'll be interesting to meet him after all this time.'

'Oh yes, I can guarantee that.'

'Well,' she said, checking the contents of the teapot before pouring, 'a couple of nights' hospitality is little enough to ask after all he did for us in London; in fact, he could spend the weekend with us.'

'Agreed, SP. It'll be good to see him again, and if all goes according to plan we may well have him for a neighbour.'

'We'll just have to wait and see.'

It was a pleasing thought, and one that Freddy took with him to the studio.

It was a morning for good news, because the phone rang after about five minutes and, surprisingly, the caller turned out to be Mr Helliwell, the vet.

'You were asking me about Aberdeen terriers,' he reminded Freddy.

'That's right.' Freddy had almost given up on that one.

'I still don't know of a breeder hereabouts – the nearest that's registered with the Kennel Club is in Northumberland – but I do know of a Scottie who needs a good home. The only problem is that you were talking enthusiastically about "him" and "he", whereas this dog is... well, her name is Thea and she's a lovely animal but not remotely masculine.'

⋙◦⊱◦⊰◦⋘

'Tell me again where we're going.' Sylvia climbed into the passenger seat of the van and closed the door.

'Have you forgotten already?'

'I was chopping onions when you told me. Tears can be a distraction, you know.'

'Okay, you're forgiven. We're going to Hawes, where the daughter lives. I told you she was looking after the dog, didn't I?'

'Probably, but tell me again.'

'Those onions must have been very strong, but never mind. The dog's owner is Mr Womersley, an old man who's become very frail and he's gone to live with his daughter and her husband. To cut a long story short, he can't look after the dog now because his son-in-law doesn't want her in the house. He doesn't like animals.'

'How awful. We fought a war against people like him, didn't we?'

'As a matter of fact, I believe Hitler was quite kind towards animals. He was vegetarian, you know.'

'Well, that just shows what a horrible man this son-in-law must be.' She watched the countryside for a while before asking, 'How old is she?'

'Thea? She's six. Oh, and Mr Helliwell told me she's been spayed. He did the job himself, apparently. He told me her whole history.'

'She has a history?'

'Yes, a history of being rescued. Mr Womersley gave her a home two years ago, when her previous owner died.'

'Poor little scrap.'

'Well, hopefully we'll be the last entry in her log book.'

Sylvia was thoughtful for a while, and then she said, 'She was honoured, being spayed by Mr Helliwell. He doesn't do much with small animals; in fact, he only looks after Rainbow because my dad does his books.'

Freddy slowed down behind a horse trailer. 'Accountants get all kinds of perks, don't they? I think I'm in the wrong job.'

'I'm sure the perks will come in time, Freddy. My dad's been collecting them for years, but it didn't happen immediately.'

As they approached Hawes, Sylvia asked, 'What's the address we're going to?'

'Just a minute.' He felt in his shirt pocket and took out a slip of paper, which he handed to her. 'It's better if you take care of this, SP.'

'Very likely.' They were both conscious of Freddy's woeful sense of direction.

'This is the street after the tack shop on the left.'

'If you say so, SP.'

'Steady now.' They were entering the Main Street. 'It's about a hundred yards ahead.'

'I'm impressed.'

'Okay. Slow down and take the next left.'

They entered a narrow street and stopped outside a stone cottage with a dark-green door and Georgian window frames. At first sight, it looked modest but well cared-for. The paintwork was clean and the stone doorstep had been recently holystoned. It was almost seven o'clock, and the sounds that carried loudly from within suggested that Dick Barton, Special Agent, was making way for the news and sport on the Light Programme. Freddy knocked on the door, prompting a barrage of enthusiastic barking. If he had to compete with the family's evening listening, he had an ally, and an effective one, because just then the door opened.

'Mrs Jagger?'

'Yes.' She was a slight, nervous-looking woman, possibly in her fifties. 'You must be Mr Hinchcliffe.'

'That's right. This is my wife.'

She nodded. 'You'd best come in then.' She led them into a small room where a man in shirtsleeves but no collar sat trying to listen to the BBC news. 'Mr and Mrs Hinchcliffe have come about the dog,' she told him.

'Good. I've had enough of that damned barking.' He returned his attention to the news, so Freddy turned away, and that was when he saw the old man in an armchair by the fire. Thea sat at his knee, now emitting only a tentative and half-hearted 'woof' now and again. In contrast to Mr Jagger, the old man wore a suit with a waistcoat, collar and tie, and his shoes were polished and well kept. He tried to stand up.

'Don't get up, Mr Womersley,' Sylvia told him, helping him back into his seat. He was clearly distressed.

Freddy stroked Thea, awkwardly conscious of the old man's misery. 'She'll be well cared-for,' he promised him.

Sylvia was holding Mr Womersley's hand. 'She's coming to a very loving home,' she told him gently. Freddy was grateful to her for that. Some things sounded better from a woman, and Sylvia had a gift for that sort of thing.

'My dad's come to live with us,' said Mrs Jagger. 'He can't manage on his own any more but we can't keep the dog.' She added quietly, 'My husband won't have her in the house any longer than he has to.'

Mr Jagger evidently had no difficulty in hearing his wife even over the wireless. 'I'll be glad to be rid of it,' he told them.

Sylvia was more interested in Mr Womersley. She asked him, 'Would you like us to bring her to see you sometimes? We could do that.'

The old man opened his mouth to speak but his tears answered for him.

'You'll have to do it when my husband's at work,' said Mrs Jagger.

'Aye,' he agreed, muttering, 'it's one thing 'avin' him here but I can do without his bloody dog an' all.'

Mr Womersley tried to get up.

'No,' said Sylvia, 'don't get up. Just take it easy.' She could see what an effort it was for him. 'And don't forget what I said. We'll bring Thea to see you.' Her assurance earned her a look of disdain from Mr Jagger.

Freddy had been studying him. 'You know,' he said, 'you remind me very strongly of someone I knew a few years ago in Poland.'

'I've never been to Poland.'

'He's never been abroad at all,' said his wife. 'He had a reserved occupation in the war, working for the council.'

'I'm not saying it was you. You just remind me of him, that's all.'

'Oh, who was he, this bloke?'

'He went by the name *Feldwebel* Vogel.'

'A German?' For a man of little expression his response was almost theatrical. 'You were mates with a Jerry?'

'Not exactly mates. As a matter of fact, he was lucky to escape being hanged as a war criminal.'

The man was consumed with curiosity. 'How did he manage that?'

'They shot him instead.'

⚊⚌⚍⚎⚏⚊

'Would you like me to drive so you can get acquainted with Thea?'

'Thank you, SP. That's very accommodating of you.' He gave her the key and took Thea to the passenger side.

'I'm intrigued,' she said, starting the engine and waiting for him to position the dog between his feet. 'How do you know they shot that man Vogel?'

'An American officer who turned up at the camp told me as

much. Vogel had a letter from me, detailing his crimes, only he thought it was his passport to freedom. He couldn't read English.'

After a moment Sylvia said, 'What a grisly business.'

'War crime? It certainly is.'

'I mean what happened just then at the house,' she explained, changing the subject in her usual way, and clearly still affected by the scene at the cottage. 'That poor old man. You know, that's only the second time I've seen a man cry.'

'I'm sorry I let you in for that, SP.' He gave Thea another stroke in case she also had been affected by the scene.

'Oh, I can cope.'

'You're a great coper,' he said, stroking Thea's ears. He thought he'd better ask. 'You said the second time?'

'Oh yes, the first was a German prisoner, an airman. The RAF picked him up in the Channel. He was wounded and waiting to be taken to hospital. I spoke to him and gave him a cigarette, and a horrible flight-sergeant called me a stupid bitch.'

'And I thought the RAF were cultured.'

'His officer sent him about his business. He was very nice. His daughter had recently joined the Wrens and she was training to be a telegraphist. He explained why I was wrong to speak to the prisoner. Apparently, although I didn't realise it at the time, I was fraternising with the enemy.'

'Well, I'm glad you did it, SP, although you'd have surprised me if you hadn't, and there's someone here who agrees with me. He was stroking Thea behind her ears while she gazed at him more in ecstasy, he guessed, than in comprehension. Even so, she seemed the kind of dog he could rely upon to respect his judgement in most things.

━━◦◦◦━━

He was returning from a walk with her a few mornings later, when Sylvia met him at the door. She seemed agitated, and there were tears in her eyes.

'Mrs Cresswell's been on the phone,' she told him.

'Has Mandy foaled?' He imagined it would be about that but he couldn't see why it might make Sylvia tearful, unless it had gone terribly wrong.

Sylvia nodded wretchedly. 'Mandy's all right but the foal was stillborn.'

It was as he'd feared, and it explained Sylvia's distress. It was inevitable that she should be vulnerable to stories of frustrated motherhood, regardless of species. He closed the door behind them and put his arms round her. 'Poor old Mandy,' he said.

'And Mrs Cresswell,' sniffed Sylvia. 'The vet's been on the grapevine, looking for an orphaned foal. She should hear something quite soon.'

'Oh?'

'There's a foal somewhere,' she explained, 'that needs her milk. At the same time, after all those months, her instinct is telling her very forcefully that she needs to nurse a foal.'

'Let's hope the vet can find one.'

'And that she can accept it.'

'I hadn't thought of that.'

Sylvia looked down and saw Thea still with her lead clipped to her collar. 'Did you have a nice walk?'

'Are you asking Thea or me?'

'I'm not going to get much of a response from her, am I?' She unclipped the lead and handed it to him.

'She's actually a good listener. You should try talking to her some time.' He drew her into a hug. 'I find it soothing.'

'Oh yes?' She sounded unconvinced.

'Absolutely, although there's one area in which she's a little too forthcoming.'

'Don't tell me she interferes in your musical activities.'

'Actually, she does. Each time I play the piano, she sings lustily; at least, I imagine she regards it as singing.'

'Do you mean howling?'

'No, not howling. You know that extended vocabulary she uses when she wants something?'

'I have heard it once or twice.'

'Well, she goes right through the gamut when I'm playing, even when I'm just trying out an idea, and she's not complaining either, because she wags her tail the whole time. I think she's joining in.'

'You have some funny ideas.'

'Yes, it comes from being an air-gunner. Alone in the after cockpit for long periods, I resorted after a while to strange fancies and eccentric notions. It prevented me from going completely potty.'

'I thought you shared the after cockpit with someone else.'

'The observer? He was forever fiddling with his instruments and plotting courses and doing clever things with numbers. I didn't like to distract him in case he got us lost.'

She looked at him through narrowed eyelids and said, 'You told me all that to cheer me up, didn't you?'

'Guilty as charged.'

'I thought so.' After a moment, she asked, 'What do you do when you're down in the dumps? I mean it doesn't happen very often, does it?'

'It does sometimes, but I'm quite philosophical really.'

'You're going to tell me it comes of being an air-gunner, aren't you?'

'Not now you've guessed it,' he admitted.

'But what do you really do?'

'When I'm feeling down? I think back to nineteen-forty-two and forty-three, the worst period of my life, when I was at rock bottom, and then I remember getting a letter from a girl in Dover, and it lifts my spirits just as it did then.'

'You really mean that, don't you?'

'Of course I do.' He continued to hold her close. 'I've just remembered what a wonderful girl I married,' he said. 'It was clever of me, wasn't it?'

'You didn't do it all on your own, and stop getting ideas. It's not nine o'clock yet. You have work to do.'

'This morning,' he agreed. 'I'm free this afternoon.'

'That's when you can help me sort out the spare room for Bailey.'

'It shouldn't take all afternoon,' he said hopefully.

On Saturday morning, there was a phone call from Mrs Cresswell.

'Freddy, I'm glad I caught you in. Is there any chance you can come over some time in the next few days?' Considering recent events, she sounded remarkably cheerful.

'I could come this afternoon if you like. Sylvia told me about the foal. I really am sorry.'

'Thank you, Freddy, but the orphaned foal arrived yesterday and Mandy accepted him without a problem. He's an Arab, so they look very odd together, but Mandy doesn't care. As far as she's concerned he's hers.'

It was the best possible news, and he shared it with Sylvia as soon as Mrs Cresswell had put the phone down.

'One thing puzzles me,' he said. 'Why would an Arab look odd with Mandy?'

'They couldn't look more different. Mandy's stocky, as you know, with a broad head and body, but an Arab looks altogether more delicate. It has a dished body and a face that's almost wedge-shaped. Oh, and it carries its tail high. That's another of its characteristics. They have their champions and their critics, but I can't wait to see this one.'

⊕⊷⊰⊱⊹⊱⊱

They spent some time following a slow lorry but picked up speed again and arrived soon after three. Mrs Cresswell came out as she heard the van in the yard and lost no time in taking Freddy and Sylvia to the paddock.

Freddy had a ninety millimetre lens on the Leica so that he could get in fairly close without distorting the perspective. He could see Mandy at the far side of the paddock, and he waited as Mrs Cresswell called her, the all-important bowl of oats in her hand. Mandy lifted her head and came straight towards them, and it was then that Freddy saw the foal for the first time, tiny, stilt-legged and vulnerable beside the mare's familiar, solid frame. They were the perfect mismatch.

Mrs Cresswell held out the bowl and Mandy shoved her nose

into it, so Freddy moved around to get a better view of the foal. Mandy turned her head, instantly protective, but Mrs Cresswell cajoled her. 'Come on, Mandy, show us your baby.' She handed the bowl to Sylvia, still talking to Mandy. 'You know Freddy and Sylvia. Come on, let's all have a look at him.' She motioned to Sylvia to bring the bowl towards her so that both mare and foal were in sunlight, and Freddy started shooting. As Sylvia and Mrs Cresswell backed away, he took frame after frame, with Mandy occasionally showing some fleeting interest in what he was doing, but keeping her attention mainly on the foal, nuzzling at his shoulder or just keeping a maternal eye on him. Freddy was vaguely conscious that Mrs Cresswell and Sylvia were talking to her, encouraging and reassuring her, but he could hear nothing they said, because for a short time the world belonged to the mare, the foal and him. It was as if by some special consent that he was included for that spell and they seemed somehow happy to indulge him. On that sunny afternoon in June, he was able to capture their two heads together, the mare's, wide and honest, and the foal's with its characteristic delicate, curved face. He knew that if he could get the development right he would have the picture he wanted: twin tragedies that could never be reversed, but out of them this small, touching consolation.

Then, without warning, like a manager bringing a celebrity photo call to a close, Mandy turned and walked away with the foal beside her. For the first time Freddy was aware of the sun on the back of his neck and he turned up his shirt collar to shield it.

'That's all you're going to get,' Mrs Cresswell told him. 'They've had enough for now.'

Freddy said, 'I think I've got all I need.' He'd taken the best part of a cassette of film and he was sure he had some very promising pictures. He'd also experienced something he would never forget.

6

The man who stood by the entrance to Leyburn Station was tall and powerfully built, but with finely-drawn, aesthetic features and, whilst the hair that showed beneath his immaculate trilby was greyer than Freddy remembered, he had no difficulty in recognising him.

'Bailey,' he said, extending his hand.

'Freddy, my dear old chum.'

The two men shook hands and, after the usual polite enquiries, Freddy led the way to the van.

'A humble chariot,' he admitted, 'but it's functional.'

'Breathe not a word of apology, old man. I'm grateful for the ride.' Bailey had evidently noticed the signwriting on the exterior, because he said, 'So you're back in the photography business, then.'

Freddy left the station forecourt and turned left to leave Leyburn. 'Yes, I've been doing this since I was demobbed.'

'Business brisk, is it?'

'It's steady.'

Bailey stirred uncomfortably and said, 'Do tell me, old man, before we reach the Hinchcliffe homestead and I put my size twelve in it, did the thing with Sylvia meet all expectations? I mean did you and she...?'

'Yes, we were married three years ago. We'd have invited you to the wedding, but you seemed to have done a disappearing act.'

'I am delighted, old chap. Felicitations and all that.'

'Thank you.'

'Actually, before you ask, my absence at that time was absolutely above board. As I told you in London, I'm a reformed character.'

'Such a thing never crossed my mind.' Freddy slowed down

behind the inevitable horse-drawn cart, and remained patient. After all, it was good to catch up on things with Bailey, especially now he knew that his friend's absence had not been at His Majesty's Pleasure.

'I was in Boston, Massachusetts, actually. It's in America, you know.'

'I suspected it might be.'

'Yes, I was rather successful in selling cars to appreciative Americans. They seemed quite taken with my urbane English persona.'

'If they'd only known, Bailey.' The horse and cart were turning into a farm entrance and Freddy was able to pick up speed. 'Anyway, why did you come back?'

'Visas are fleeting things, Freddy, and the automobile trade is very conscious of the need to employ home-grown talent. It was good while it lasted, but it's pleasant to be home as well.'

'And speaking of home,' said Freddy, pulling up outside the cottage, 'we have arrived.'

'How perfectly charming.' Bailey admired the cottage and its surroundings while Freddy took his suitcase from the back of the van and carried it to the door. 'Thea,' he called, opening the door, 'your lord and master has returned.'

There was a barrage of enthusiastic, throaty sounds such as only an Aberdeen terrier could enunciate, and Freddy responded by stroking her behind her ears, a gesture that was always well received.

He beckoned Bailey inside. 'Thea's a recent addition to the family,' he told him.

Thea greeted the visitor in her usual way.

'She's quite harmless,' Freddy told him, 'and she's good company.'

'Thea,' said Bailey a little formally, 'I'm naturally delighted to meet you, but you'll have to make allowances. You see, I'm what you might call a newcomer to the canine kingdom, but you'll find me a quick learner.'

'I think you've won her over, Bailey,' said Freddy. 'By the way, Sylvia must have nipped out to the village shop. I'm sure she'll be back soon. In the meantime, would you like a cup of tea?'

'That would be most acceptable, Freddy. Thank you.'

Freddy waved him towards an armchair. 'Take a seat. Thea will keep you company.'

He returned with the tea things to find Bailey and Thea now on familiar terms. Bailey was delighted with his new relationship.

'This dog thing is quite easy once you get the hang of it,' he said, with the air of an expert playing down a particularly arcane skill.

His triumphal moment was interrupted when the outer door opened and Sylvia walked in.

'SP, come and meet Bailey,' said Freddy, relieving her of her shopping basket to facilitate the process.

'My dear lady,' said Bailey, taking her hand, 'you can have no idea how delighted I am to make your acquaintance.'

'I'm delighted too, because now I can thank you for everything you did for us that night in London.'

'It was the work of a moment, and as rewarding for me as for you.'

'There's just one little thing, though. I can hardly call you "Bailey". It's your surname, after all.'

Bailey held up a dismissive hand. ' "Bailey" is the only name to which I answer, dear lady. Freddy will tell you that, and he and I were close friends for two years.'

Freddy nodded his agreement. 'I've just made tea, SP. Would you like me to pour you a cup?'

'Just let me put the shopping away and then I'll join you.'

'I'll come and help. Back in a moment, Bailey.'

'Don't mind me, old man.'

In the kitchen and out of Bailey's earshot, Sylvia said, 'My mother's given us some rabbits she had to spare. Do you think Bailey will eat rabbit pie?'

'Bailey's an ex-kriegie, SP. He'll eat anything, especially if you've cooked it.'

'Do you think so?'

'He's besotted. I know the signs.'

'There's just one thing,' said Sylvia, putting the last of her purchases away. 'I wish he'd use my name. When he calls me "dear lady" I feel like a character in an Oscar Wilde play.'

'Tell him. He's very adaptable.'

They returned to the sitting room, where Freddy poured tea for Sylvia and replenished Bailey's cup. Meanwhile, Sylvia made her request.

'I'd like you to call me "Sylvia", Bailey, if you don't mind,' she said.

'Nothing would please me more, Sylvia.'

'Good, and on the subject of names, I'd better explain, in case you're wondering, that "SP" is Freddy's pet name for me. It's a reference to a ballet performance, when I involuntarily turned 'The Sugar Plum Fairy" into a burlesque act.'

'I remember Freddy telling me that long ago. At least, it seems a long time ago. I believe we were in a stable in Germany at the time.' It seemed his memory was becoming clearer, because he said, 'Didn't you tell us it was where Beethoven was born, Freddy?'

'It was J S Bach, actually.'

'I knew it was one of those classical johnnies.'

Sylvia said, 'I'll serve dinner at about seven if that's all right, Bailey.'

'That sounds wonderful, Sylvia. Before we eat, however, I wonder if I might be allowed a bath.'

'Of course. I've kept a fire going in the kitchen, so there'll be ample hot water. Freddy will show you to your room and the bathroom, won't you, Freddy?'

'With pleasure.'

When he came downstairs, Sylvia was in the kitchen preparing dinner, so he pulled up a chair and sat at the table. 'Can I do anything?'

She handed him a knife. 'You can peel some carrots if you like.' Then, more conversationally, she said, 'He's unbelievable. I could hardly credit your description of him, but he's everything you said.'

The water stopped running through the pipes. It seemed that Bailey's bath was ready.

'He's "Bullshit" Bailey right enough,' confirmed Freddy, 'but in a strange sort of way he's the most genuine posturer you can imagine.'

'I like him.' She was about to say more, when from upstairs came a deep, sonorous voice.

' *"How say you, maiden, will you wed*
A man about to lose his head?
For half an hour you'll be a wife,
And then the dower is yours for life." '

Sylvia looked questioningly at Freddy, who said, 'It's from *The Yeomen of the Guard*.' The singing continued.

' *"A headless bride-groom why refuse?*
If truth the poets tell,
Most bride-grooms, ere they marry,
Lose both head and heart as well!" '

Then, switching to a high *falsetto*, he continued.

' *"A strange proposal you reveal,*
It almost makes my senses reel.
Alas! I'm very poor indeed,
And such a sum I sorely need." '

'You know,' said Freddy, suddenly excited, 'I do believe we've found our Viking chieftain.'

'Don't tempt Providence,' Sylvia cautioned him. 'He hasn't got the job in Northallerton yet.'

'He'll get it,' said Freddie confidently. 'Bailey could talk his way into a sultan's harem.'

Later, at dinner, Bailey let them in on some of the events of his post-war life.

'I thought at one time of treading the boards,' he said, 'but it's not all that easy to get started. I put a great deal of effort into it, you know. I took acting and singing lessons. Apparently I'm a bass-baritone.' He sounded as if he were still surprised at that development.

'We know,' said Sylvia.

'And a closet soprano,' added Freddy.

37

'You heard me in the bath, I suppose. Ah well, I was only filling in the missing parts.' He shrugged off the embarrassment and continued with his reminiscence. 'You know,' he said, 'the part of Lieutenant of the Tower is little more than a cameo. I was looking for a meatier part altogether. I auditioned for Sergeant Meryll and Wilfred Shadbolt, but I think those parts were cast before the auditions began.'

'Freddy's writing a show,' Sylvia told him.

'Oh? Of course, you're rather good at that sort of thing. I remember now. What's it about?'

'It's a musical comedy set in the ninth century; Vikings, Anglo-Saxons and that sort of thing.' Freddy told him a little about 'Viking High Jinks', which made him eager to hear more.

Finally, and after a full synopsis, Bailey said, 'I really must get that job tomorrow. You know, I mean to audition for the part of Erik.'

<hr />

'No, Freddy,' she whispered, 'I can't do it with Bailey in the next room.'

'I don't want you to do it with Bailey in the next room. I want you to do it with me in this room.'

'You know what I mean. What if I make a noise?'

'Ecstatic whispering,' he told her, kissing her enticingly, 'will be a new challenge, but you can do it.' He tried a new approach. 'I need to celebrate, you see.'

'It's the first time I've heard it called that. Anyway, what have you got to celebrate?'

'Finding our Viking chieftain.'

'You're counting chickens again.'

'They say a man with a lovely wife always has something to celebrate,' he said, kissing her neck softly.

'*All right*,' she whispered, clearly aroused by his attentions, '*but don't make me noisy.*'

<hr />

As prophesied, Bailey was offered the post of Sales Manager and consequently the part of Erik, so that Freddy had even more to celebrate. After that, he had to attend the Easingthorpe Agricultural Show.

7

The Brass Band was a welcome feature at the Easingthorpe Show. Its current repertoire included gems from light opera, and the showground was filled with the strains of well-known numbers from *The Pirates of Penzance* and *The Gondoliers*.

As Freddy and Sylvia walked through the entrance and showed their tickets, they received a welcoming nod from Derek Littlewood, seated on his faithful inflatable ring and in his alternative capacity as Principal Solo Trombonist with the Easingthorpe Band.

'He says if he wasn't out playing with one band or another,' said Freddy, 'his wife would only find him jobs to do at home.'

'That's not what I've heard.' Sylvia smiled nevertheless and waved to Derek. 'She's only too glad to have him out of her way.'

'Why is that?'

'She's one of those people who make housework a kind of religious observance. Anything that gets in the way of cleaning, dusting and polishing is an unholy nuisance, and that includes Derek.'

'In that case he's probably doing the right thing.'

They stopped outside the Women's Institute tent. A bouquet of appetising aromas issued from within, and Freddy, a staunch admirer of the WI and all that it produced, inhaled longingly.

'I'll see you here at one o'clock for lunch,' Sylvia reminded him, more to shake him out of his epicurean trance than to jog his memory.

'I'll be here,' said Freddy confidently. Then, reminding himself of his professional duty, he went in search of Nathan Parker, one of the local farmers, who had left a message that he wanted to see him.

He found several men of bucolic appearance in the beer tent.

One of them noticed him in the entrance, and said, 'You're looking lost, lad. Who are you after?'

'I thought I might find Mr Parker in here.'

The man jostled his neighbour and said, 'Hey up, Nathan, thy reputation's gone before thee.' He laughed. 'This chap thought he'd find thee in t' beer tent. He were right an' all.'

Nathan Parker put his beer down and looked up. He was lean, quite short and maybe in his fifties, or possibly sixties. His most noticeable features, however, were a narrow face and a sharply-pointed nose that gave him an uncompromising appearance. He asked, 'Are you t' photographer, then?'

'That's right.'

'Aye well, I have a Wensleydale tup being judged at half-past two, an' he stands a good chance of winning t' First Prize. If he does, I'll be wanting a photo of him for t' breeders' magazine. Can you do that?'

'Yes, I can do that.' He had no idea what a tup was, but he suspected that revealing his ignorance in the company of sheep farmers would do his reputation no good at all. Instead, he asked, 'Where will the judging be done?'

'That ring,' said Mr Parker, pointing through the opening of the tent, 'just out there. You can see t' programme on t' fence.'

'Very good, Mr Parker. I'll be there.'

Parker merely nodded and resumed drinking, a gesture Freddy took to be one of dismissal. He decided to make a tour of the showground, beginning with the enclosure where the tups were to be judged.

He found the programme pinned to the fence, just as Mr Parker had said, but it told him no more than he already knew, that Wensleydale tups would be judged at two-thirty. It was fairly obvious from the name 'Wensleydale' that the livestock in question were sheep of one sex or the other, but why they should be referred to as 'tups' remained a mystery. He decided that Sylvia would no doubt enlighten him over lunch and, with that cheering thought, he continued on his journey of discovery.

In one tent, a glorious array of carrots, parsnips, early potatoes and salad vegetables lay invitingly on a long table, and Freddy consulted his watch. Lunch was still an hour away, so he turned his back on the tantalising vista and went in search of a suitable distraction.

This he found in a tent devoted to birds and small, furry animals, all housed in hutches and cages of various sizes. There were pigeons, budgerigars, canaries, hamsters, guinea pigs and some animals he found difficult to identify, the enclosures being labelled only with the names of the owners. It was very puzzling, and an embarrassing reminder that, as a photographer specialising in animals, he still had much to learn about his furry, feathered and scaly subjects.

The occupant of one cage took him completely by surprise. At first glance, it resembled a rat; its piebald appearance had suggested otherwise at first, but no, there was something disturbingly rat-like about its conformation. He'd always expected them to be of the of the brown, black, grey or tawny varieties famously catalogued by Robert Browning, but this was of a different kind. He was giving the matter further consideration when confirmation came unexpectedly from behind him.

'Aye, it's a rat all right. You were wondering, weren't you?'

'That's right.' Freddy turned to face his informant, a bearded gnome of a man with a lapel badge that read *Judge*.

'A lot of folk get the wrong idea,' the gnome explained. 'That's a *fancy* rat you see there, not a common rat.'

'It's very well turned out,' agreed Freddy.

'Nay, I mean it's the kind rat fanciers keep. This 'un belongs to a little lass an' she's right fond of 'im.' He opened the cage door and picked up the animal. ''Ere, have a proper look.'

Freddy cupped his hands to receive his new acquaintance and was surprised to find its furry coat smooth and pleasant to touch. It wiggled its nose in what Freddy took to be a friendly gesture. 'I owe you an apology,' he said.

The judge looked surprised. 'Nay,' he said, 'you haven't upset me.'

'I was talking to the rat.'

'Oh well, na' then.' It seemed that such a conversation was quite acceptable.

'Yes,' said Freddy, addressing the rodent once more. 'I've only ever come across the common kind of rat, and my reaction was coloured by the experience.'

'It would be,' agreed the judge.

'Yes, I've met Italian, Polish and German rats, but I must confess there was a repellent sameness about them.'

'Oh aye? Prisoner of war, were you?'

'Yes.'

The gnome jerked his head towards the vegetables tent from which Freddy had only recently emerged, and said, 'Albert Whittaker, who's showing his parsnips next door, he were a POW an' all.' He added, 'Burma. That's where he were.'

'Poor bugger.'

'Aye.' The gnome consulted his watch and said, 'I'm judging Fancy Rats at two-fifteen, if you want to get a picture of Horace and t' little lass what owns him.'

'Horace? It's a good name.' He reckoned he could manage that before going to the tups' enclosure.

'Aye, he'll get the cup.'

'Have you judged them already?'

'Nay, he's t' only rat in t' show.'

'Right, I'll be back for that.' He took his leave of them both and made his way back to the WI tent, where several members were laying out various items for lunch. He caught the eye of one of them and asked, 'Is there somewhere I can wash my hands, please?'

The woman looked surprised and then pointed to a corner of the tent. 'There's soap and water over yonder,' she said, still regarding him strangely.

'I've been handling an animal,' he explained, 'and I'm meeting my wife here for lunch, so I thought I'd better wash my hands.'

The woman allowed her face to slip into a semblance of a smile, and addressed a colleague across the tent. 'Is this your husband, Mrs Hinchcliffe?'

'Yes.' Sylvia came over to claim him.

'I thought so. He wants to wash his hands.' She made it sound like a major event.

'Come with me, Freddy,' said Sylvia, leading him to the washing facilities.

'I've been handling a fancy rat,' he confided when they were alone. 'I thought I'd take the necessary precautions.'

'And very wise, too. I expect you'll be remembered for it.' She handed him a bar of soap and a towel.

'I believe rats have habits that are less than endearing,' he said, feeling that he should reinforce his position regarding personal hygiene. 'I'm told, for instance, that they often stroll along canal and river banks, stopping occasionally to pee into the water, and that's not healthy, whichever way you look at it.'

'No, it's not,' she agreed, 'although it doesn't happen quite like that.'

'Doesn't it?'

'No, they swim in the rivers and canals and… do it as they go.'

'Not that it makes it any more acceptable, but that's pretty clever, you know. I've never been able to do that. I mean, I can do one or the other, but not both at the same time.' He dried his hands and returned the towel to Sylvia. 'Actually,' he said, 'I'm going to photograph the rat and its owner after the judging, and then I have to photograph a tup.'

'Oh yes?'

'Just one thing worries me, SP.'

'What's that?'

'I've no idea what a tup is.'

Smiling at his discomfiture, she said, 'A tup is a ram.'

'In that case, why don't they call it a bloody ram and have done with it, instead of confusing the uninitiated?'

'It's just the dialect name for it. Actually,' she said, lowering her eyes, ' "tupping" is what the ram does to the sheep.'

'Ah, like "rutting" is to deer?'

'Yes, farmers and breeders can be very basic about these things.'

'I'm afraid so.' He inspected his fingernails, found them presentable, and said, 'Let's have lunch.'

'Yes, let's.' It appealed to Sylvia far more strongly than the earthy vernacular of reproduction.

They took a plate each and helped themselves at the buffet. As they sat down, Freddy said, 'I don't know how the WI do it. They seem to defy food rationing when they put these things on.'

'Don't ask, Freddy. Just enjoy it.'

The meal was largely vegetarian, it was true, but no less satisfying for that, and Freddy felt it was well worth the wait, although he couldn't help thinking about afternoon tea, which would also be provided by the ladies of the WI.

Eventually, duty beckoned, and he got up to leave. As an afterthought, he handed one camera to Sylvia, saying, 'Take the Leica, SP, and then if you see anything promising you'll have it to hand.'

'Gosh.' Sylvia took it from him with the look of one charged with custody of a rare and priceless object. 'This is trust on a grand scale.'

⊙┉3┉✹┆⊱┆┉⊙

When he arrived at the fur and feather tent, judging was still taking place, so he waited patiently with the handlers' families until, eventually, the results were made known.

First to emerge, possibly for the sake of convenience, was the girl with the fancy rat. She was a shy child of about eight or nine, but she held her prizewinning friend up with great pride.

'This 'ere feller's come to photograph you with Horace,' the judge told her.

'That's right,' said Freddy, taking the shot. 'If you give me your name and address I'll send you the picture.'

The idea seemed to appeal to other successful handlers, because Freddy soon found himself facing a queue, and he was working his way through the line of hamsters, rabbits and so on, when a large man in a tweed suit confronted him.

'What's all this?' The man pointed unnecessarily to the line of people with their animals. 'I'm Beresford from *The Evening Gazette*. You got in ahead of me.' He brandished a large press camera to make his point.

'Why shouldn't I? You can still take your pictures. I'm not stopping you.' He continued to photograph the successful entries and to take details from their owners. They would receive a proof free of charge, but Freddy would then sell them mounted enlargements to order.

'It's a matter of courtesy,' Beresford insisted. 'The press come first.'

'Who says? I bet you made up that rule yourself.'

'Never mind who says. It's press first, I tell you.'

'Well, you'd better make the best of a bad job, because I'm going to the tups' enclosure now, by arrangement.' Glancing at his wristwatch, he saw it was almost two-thirty-five. He would need to hurry.

When he arrived, he found Nathan Parker talking with Sylvia. The ram that accompanied him bore the winner's rosette, just as Mr Parker had prophesied. Oddly, the farmer didn't look too pleased.

'Congratulations, Mr Parker, shall we have one of you standing just there?'

'No, it's my turn.' Reddened and out of breath, Beresford was lifting his big plate camera.

'You're both too late,' said Mr Parker. 'When they finished t' judging there were nobody here 'cept this lass, so I let her take t' picture.' To Freddy he said, 'You'll have to buck your ideas up if you're going to do any good round here, lad.' He nodded to Beresford and said, 'I'll have one for t' paper, now I think of it. It won't do any harm.'

Beresford gave Freddy a triumphant look before taking the picture. Even so, his smugness evaporated when Freddy said conversationally, 'That was my assistant who got in before you.'

❦❧❦❧❦❧❦

When Freddy developed Sylvia's handiwork, he was delighted to find that it was an excellent picture. Happily, Mr Parker agreed with him, but made the stipulation that in future his animals were to be photographed exclusively by Sylvia.

8

'What's the matter, Freddy?' Sylvia placed a cup of tea on his desk. 'You're looking haunted.'

'How easily you read my moods, SP.' He tapped the part-completed score on his desk and said, 'I'm trying to cast Elga and Ardith. Basically, they need to be young and nubile, and the sometime principals of our society somehow struggle to qualify in either respect.'

'I see. Who are these characters?'

'Elga is, for want of a better description, the leading lady, in fact leader of the female population. She'll have the fascinating experience of becoming romantically involved with Erik.' He smiled at the thought of Bailey playing the lover.

'And who is the other one you mentioned?'

'Ardith? She's the soubrette, the actress who provides the comic interest.'

'I know what a soubrette is, Freddy.'

'Of course you do, darling. I'm sorry.'

'That's all right.' She looked thoughtful for a moment and asked, 'Have you spoken to my dad?'

'Not since Sunday afternoon, but honestly, I can't see him in either role. The moustache and the deep voice put him at a disadvantage from the start.'

'I meant, have you told him about your problem? He'll know what to do.'

'Will he?'

'Of course he will. It's not the first time this kind of problem has occurred, you know. He'll just send out an SOS to neighbouring societies and if we're lucky they'll suggest people.'

'What a brilliant idea. SP, you set me right as usual.'

'I also bring news, if you're interested.'

'Pour forth the news.'

She pulled a face. 'Honestly, Freddy, you're beginning to sound like Bailey. I hope it's not catching.'

'For you, dearest one, I'll try to avoid it. I imagine it's the awful tidings that the West Indies have beaten England at Lords.'

'No, it's worse than that.'

'Impossible. What could be worse than a massive defeat and the end of civilisation as we know it?'

'It depends on your point of view, Freddy. The news is that North Korea has invaded South Korea. There are urgent goings-on at the United Nations.'

'I should think there are.'

'Do you imagine there'll be another war?'

'There's always someone daft enough to start one, and why not, when the last one was so much fun?'

'Don't joke about it, Freddy. I couldn't bear it if we went to war again.'

'I'm not full of enthusiasm for it either.' He addressed his other companion, now lying beneath his desk. 'How about you, Thea?' There was no response. 'It seems Thea's no more enthusiastic than we are.' Then, returning to a happier subject, he said to Sylvia, 'I'll speak to your dad about the other thing.'

❦

With Walter's cocker spaniel Rainbow and Thea sniffing excitedly around the foxgloves and cow parsley, Freddy and Walter walked down the lane to Redmire Falls.

'I've written to the societies within easy travelling distance,' said Walter. 'We'll just have to wait and see what turns up.'

'You don't sound very optimistic, Walter.'

'Oh, I meant just what I said. We could be lucky and find the two principals we're looking for, or we could be besieged by a procession of no-hopers still looking for their first starring role. You may yet have to lower your sights.'

It all sounded very negative to Freddy. 'Lower my sights? How?'

'I mean by rewriting the difficult stuff.'

'But simplifying the music would dilute the characters. Can't you see that, Walter?'

They reached the bottom of the lane and walked along the river bank to the place they favoured when they were casting for trout.

'Of course I can. I'm just being realistic.'

'Yes, you are,' agreed Freddy. 'I get carried away.'

Walter nodded. 'You're the visionary who sees further than the rest of us, Freddy, and I'm the one with his feet on the ground. We make a good partnership, wouldn't you say?'

'I should say so.'

Walter placed his stool and bags on the ground and said, 'Forgive me for asking, but are things all right between you and Sylvia?'

The question came as a surprise. 'Yes, fine. Why do you ask?'

'I spoke to her two weeks... no, it would be three weeks ago, and she seemed rather despondent.'

'Three weeks, eh?' Freddy consulted his mental calendar. 'Yes, that would coincide with her latest disappointment.'

'Oh?'

'Tiny footsteps, Walter, or rather the absence of them.'

'Ah. It was wrong of me to pry.'

'Not at all.' Freddy opened his folding stool and unzipped his bag. 'She's your daughter after all, and it's your future grandchild who's keeping us in suspense.'

Walter nodded pensively. 'How long have you been trying?'

'A little over two years now. The specialists tell us there's no reason why it shouldn't happen, so we just have to persevere and hope for the best.'

'It's all you can do,' agreed Walter, 'but I can't help wondering if this thing runs in the family. I'm told I was reluctant to put in an appearance, and Audrey kept us waiting for a couple of years.' He stopped and thought for a moment. 'Now I think of it, Bruce wasn't exactly punctual. He had Audrey and David worried for a while. As far as the first-born is concerned, there does seem to be a pattern.' He confirmed his theory with a shrug and a smile. 'Take heart, Freddy. Your turn will come.'

'Let's hope so. Meanwhile, shall we try catching some trout?'

❦❧

By the end of the following week, Freddy was able to cast both parts. Elga would be played by Joan Curwen, an experienced singer and actress from Northallerton, and Ardith by Elaine Stafford from Thirsk. She was rather pretty, with fair hair as befitted her in her Anglo-Saxon role, and blue eyes that gave the impression, more often than not, that she was smiling. Freddy thought she was ideal for the soubrette role.

If he had a minor reservation, it was about Joan, who seemed just a little too confident, considering she was taking on an unknown part. He wondered how she would fit in with the other members.

9

July

'What time's Bailey arriving?' Sylvia had just returned from shopping.

'His train gets in at ten-past four.'

She acknowledged the information with a good-humoured nod. 'My mum and dad are going to have Thea tonight, by the way.'

'Oh, that's good of them. She'll be able to catch up on things with Rainbow. They haven't seen each other since Sunday.'

Sylvia seemed preoccupied about something. 'Freddy,' she asked, 'is it my imagination, or is Thea turning grey?'

'It's kinder not to mention it in her hearing, SP.'

'I'll try not to, but isn't it odd?'

'It's a Scottie characteristic, apparently.' Freddy had been reading up on the breed and had discovered a number of surprising facts. 'Mind you,' he said, fingering his own silvered locks, 'there's nothing wrong with premature greyness, and it can even be an advantage in mature years.'

'How do you work that out?'

'Boy scouts help us cross busy roads, and children give up their seats to us on crowded buses.'

'But you never travel by bus.'

'Nevertheless, it's a privilege I mean to enjoy one day, when I'm old and completely grey, and I could be much greyer before long.'

'Because of the show?'

'No, not that. I've been trying to train Thea to retrieve.'

Sylvia adopted her responsible grown-up look, and said patiently, 'She's a terrier, Freddy, not a retriever.'

51

'That's what she keeps telling me in her own way. She rushes after the ball, stops it, and then sits beside it and waits for me to join her. I've tried and tried, but she still hasn't grasped the essence of retrieving, which is basically to bring the damned thing back.'

She had to admit defeat. 'Tell me about tonight.'

'Okay. The dance is at Nidderdale Cricket, Bowling and Athletics Club, near Harrogate, a posh venue by all accounts, but no less welcoming for that, because they've allowed me two guests.'

'Bailey and me, presumably.'

'As usual, you presume correctly, SP. I'll have to leave you with Bailey when I'm in front of the band, but you'll be all right. He's assured me of his dancing credentials.'

'I'm sure he has, but I'll reserve judgement until tonight.'

<hr />

Out of consideration for Bailey's height and leg length, Sylvia had occupied the rear seat of the van, leaving the front seat for him, and now she was enjoying the freedom and comparative luxury of a ballroom chair. Sensuously, she stretched out her legs beneath the table simply because freedom allowed it.

'My dear la... Sylvia, I honestly had no idea of the horrors you must have endured on that back seat. I am truly mortified.'

'Please don't, Bailey. You'll have me feeling sorry for you instead of the other way round.'

'Well, I'm working on a solution to the problem.'

'Don't worry, Bailey. It's not as awful as all that, and I'm still in one piece.'

'Even so, I do believe the time has come for you and Freddy to consider a conveyance worthier of the House of Hinchcliffe.'

'You know, I thought you might, but you'll have to speak to Freddy about that.' She was wondering what had happened to Freddy. The band was on stage, its members were tuning, and she wanted to dance. She had even bought a new halter dress in French navy, with a white belt and trim. She was looking around the room to see what the others were wearing, when a burst of applause drew her attention again to the stage. Freddy had made his entrance and was briefly acknowledging the applause before turning to the band to start their signature number 'Zip-a-Dee-Doo-Dah.'

Whilst she would never say as much to anyone else, Sylvia considered he'd been particularly astute in choosing that number. It was catchy, popular and an excellent start to an evening's enjoyment.

With the brief number over, Freddy greeted the dancers and introduced the band.

'Let's begin with a waltz everyone knows,' he said. 'It's "Tenderly".' There was a general buzz of approval.

In his most gallant manner, Bailey rose from the table and offered his hand. 'May I have the pleasure?'

'Of course.' It was a lovely number, and Sylvia had been wondering what it would be like to dance with Bailey. She allowed him to lead her on to the floor.

It felt strange at first; she was used to dancing with Freddy, who was five-feet-eleven, just six inches taller than her, but Bailey stood at well over six feet. Even so, he moved well, although maybe not with Freddy's rhythmic finesse. She admitted to herself that she had been expecting an awful lot and as the rise and fall of the waltz relaxed her, she dismissed the comparison and allowed herself to enjoy the rest of the number.

When it was over, Freddy introduced the pianist, Jimmy Benson, who shared the compere's duties, and left him to carry on.

He reached the table as Jimmy was announcing the next number, 'Bewitched,' so, after a brief word with Bailey, he led Sylvia on to the floor.

'This is one of my favourite foxtrots,' she told him.

'I know. That's why I came down to dance with you. I considered leaving you with Bailey a little longer as he seemed to be doing a tremendous job, but I thought you'd like to have this one with me.'

'You're so modest, Freddy. Actually, he is quite a good dancer.'

'As a matter of fact, so are you.'

'Thank you. Have you only just realised that?'

'No, but it's been on my mind recently, because there's something I have to ask you.'

She turned her head to look at him. 'Ask away. Don't keep me in suspense.'

'I wondered if you'd like to be choreographer and dance mistress for the show.'

'Two jobs! Oh, that's a lot to ask, Freddy.'

'Yes, you do an awful lot as it is. I just thought....'

'Of course I'll do it. Mind you, I don't know what Herbert Brook will have to say.'

'Who's Herbert Brook?'

'He was the man at the meeting, who thought too many jobs were going to the Charlesworth family.'

'I'll leave your dad to deal with him.'

'That's a good idea.'

'I wonder....' He looked thoughtful.

'What do you wonder?'

'Is it "choreographer" or should it be "choreographeuse" in your case?'

'If you like, I'll wear false whiskers, and then the question need never arise.'

'Please don't.'

'All right, I shan't.' She waited until the end of the number before saying, 'You'll be relieved to know that, male or female, the word is "choreographer".'

'Then that's what I'd like you to be, SP.'

'I hope I'll give satisfaction.'

'You always do.'

They returned to their table.

The next dance was a rhumba: 'April in Portugal,' and they decided to sit it out. Bailey, however, had made the acquaintance of an attractive young woman. They were already on the floor.

'He looks rather good in the rhumba,' said Freddy. 'I suppose it's his kind of thing.'

'You dance a fair rhumba too, Freddy.'

'Thanks, SP. It's the samba that defeats me.'

'Well, they're very different.'

'Mm.' Freddy was giving the matter some thought. 'I've heard the rhumba described as a sexy dance. Who said that dancing was a perpendicular expression of horizontal desire?'

She looked at him coyly. 'I think,' she said, 'it was George Bernard Shaw.'

'You know, SP, if I were to describe it in those terms, I'd say that the rhumba suggests two people taking their time over it and enjoying it to the full, whilst the samba calls to mind an urgent and frantic knee trembler behind a bus shelter.'

'Oh, Freddy!'

'Not that I have first-hand experience of that, of course.'

'I should hope not.'

'I suppose we could try it some time, just for the novelty.'

'No.'

'Only joking, SP.'

'Good. Here comes Bailey. He looks pleased with himself.' Sylvia was grateful for the distraction.

'I'll get the drinks in, and then I'll have to take over from Jimmy.' He went to the bar, pausing briefly for a word with Bailey.

Bailey had been back at the table barely a minute, when he received a visitor. The newcomer was young and seemingly indignant.

'I think you should know,' he said, 'that the lady in the red dress is with me.'

Sylvia stiffened, sensing trouble, but Bailey seemed unruffled. He said simply, 'And a remarkable pair you make, dear boy.'

'I'd only slipped out for a minute—'

'Well, you're only human, and nature will make her demands.'

The young man was becoming increasingly exasperated. 'But I saw you dancing with her,' he insisted.

'There's no argument there, old chap.'

'The point is, she's with me.'

'Agreed, old man. Do calm yourself.'

'I'm Andrew Foster, Captain of the Cricket First Eleven. I haven't seen you here before. Who are you?'

Casually, Bailey folded his arms. 'Bailey,' he told him, 'Royal Artillery Light Heavyweight Boxing Champion, nineteen... now, when was it? It was before the Inter-Services Championships....'

For the first time, Mr Foster hesitated. 'I... I just thought I should mention it,' he said.

'Did you?' Bailey laughed and leaned forward to pat him on the shoulder. 'Take it easy, old man, and enjoy the rest of the evening.'

As the young man returned to his table and his partner, Sylvia looked at Bailey in disbelief. 'Did you really win the... what you told him?'

'The regimental championship? Yes, but not the Inter-Services, although that wasn't my fault. World War Two intervened before I could be entered for it.'

'Bailey, you're priceless.'

'What's he been telling you?' Freddy put the drinks down on the table.

'He's just seen off a jealous boyfriend by telling him about his boxing exploits.'

Freddy nodded as if it were just as he'd expected. 'You're right, SP,' he said. 'He's priceless.'

'Ah, but you see, it wasn't the boxing that did it.' Bailey leaned forward to share his wisdom. 'He backed down because he couldn't get the reaction he wanted from me, and he didn't know what to do next. It was as simple as that. I mentioned my boxing triumph merely in fun.'

'You'll come a cropper one day,' Sylvia told him, more out of concern than reproach.

'There's always that possibility,' agreed Bailey, 'but you have to remember that the ability to weigh people up is part of a salesman's stock-in-trade, not that our fiery cricket captain presented much of a challenge. He was as clear as a newly-washed windscreen.'

'May all your opponents be equally transparent,' proposed Freddy, raising his glass.

'Thank you, but I welcome a challenge.'

'We've noticed,' said Sylvia.

Freddy was reminded of something quite important. 'Bailey,' he asked, 'do you play cricket?'

'I have been known to wield the willow, old man. As a matter of fact, I was an opening batsman at one time.'

'Oh, where was that?'

'On the Isle of Wight, actually.'

'I see.' Freddy recalled that Bailey had once served a brief term of imprisonment on the Isle of Wight. It was an experience best left unprobed. 'I'm playing in a charity match at the end of the month,' he said. 'Does the prospect appeal? I mean, do you fancy a game?' The side was short of players, and Bailey might be a welcome addition, always provided his claim to batting prowess was based on reality.

'Actually, old sport, I think I'd relish a knock for old time's sake.'

'Excellent. I'll spread the word.' He looked up at the bandstand and said, 'I have to leave Sylvia in your care for a while, Bailey. Do try to live less dangerously.'

'Don't give it a moment's thought, old man. Sylvia will be safe with me.'

'Good.' Freddy finished his drink and got up. 'I think one of the pre-war masterpieces is overdue.'

'I wondered how long it would be,' said Sylvia, also wondering which number he had in mind.

She did not have long to wait, because Freddy appeared on the stand and said without hesitation, 'Let's have a foxtrot from the golden age, ladies and gentlemen: 'Love Walked In' by the late, great George Gershwin.'

'Bailey,' said Sylvia, taking his hand, 'they're playing my tune. Let's dance.'

❦

On the 15th Freddy celebrated his 31st birthday, although it would be more accurate to say that he observed it, preoccupied as he was with the show. Sylvia had knitted him a jumper for fishing. It was as much as she could manage within the constraints of the time, but Freddy was delighted, as it reminded him of the old days during the war, when she used to send him next-of-kin parcels. Nostalgia, he told her, was emotional wrapping paper: the ultimate finishing touch.

Being of a more practical turn of mind, Walter had booked the Town Hall for the week beginning the ninth of October, with a dress rehearsal on the afternoon of the eighth, so, during the remainder of July, Freddy completed the script of 'Viking High Jinks' and, with only a couple more songs to be written, addressed the daunting task of teaching the music to the cast. Mercifully, the hay harvest was now in, and he could count on most members turning up for rehearsals.

Bailey had the advantage that, living temporarily with Freddy and Sylvia, he'd been able to spend some time with Freddy, and knew his songs quite well, as he demonstrated at a rehearsal with his fellow-Vikings. It was the scene when Erik and his men found themselves sharing their respective secrets.

'I'm a Viking with a liking for the finer things in life,
Not for me the fire and pillaging, the battle-axe and knife;
Give me poetry and music, give me art and sculpture too,
And let me write a saga or perhaps an ode or two.'

The Vikings stared at him in fascination until Freddy summoned their attention.

'You really must watch me. That's the second time you've missed your cue.'

One of the Viking chorus said, 'He's good, though, isn't he?'

'He's very good,' agreed Freddy, 'and you will be too, just as long as you watch me. Now, let's try that chorus again, after "perhaps an ode or two".'

They waited for his upbeat and took up the chorus:

'He's not the kind of chieftain we expected him to be,
No broadsword-wielding warrior, no man of terror he;
But as with him we're all agreed, we ought to make it clear,
That fire and theft we, too, renounce! No going back! No fear!'

'Not bad at all,' said Freddy. 'We just need to do some work on dynamics.'

'That sounds explosive,' said one of the cast.

'It can be. In this case, the first two lines of chorus need to be softer. You're still coming to terms with Erik's secret, and then, in line three, you *crescendo* – that means becoming gradually louder – and the fourth line is *forte*, loud, that is. Let's try it again.'

And so, gradually, the show began to come together. Freddy knew there would be problems along the way, but he was generally optimistic.

His immediate preoccupation, however, was the cricket match, to be played that Saturday.

10

O n that hot, July day, Freddy would have welcomed lighter clothing, but he hadn't possessed cricket whites since 1937, when he'd last played for his school. The best he could manage for the match was a white business shirt, an old pair of grey flannel trousers and a pair of tennis shoes; not that his makeshift apparel differed much from that of the other Challengers, although there was one startling exception. Not surprisingly, Bailey had arrived in immaculate whites and a yellow silk choker knotted with studied carelessness. His boots were whitened impeccably.

'If there were a prize for style,' said Sylvia wryly, 'Bailey would win it. He's a man for the great occasion.'

'That's true,' said Freddy, 'like the Final between "D" and "E" Wings at Parkhurst Prison.'

'Was he really there?'

'You never know with Bailey. It could have been anywhere. Parkhurst may have been the name that appealed most.'

'Why would that be?'

'It's on the same island as Osborne House, home of Queen Victoria. "Wormwood Scrubs" wouldn't have quite the same ring.'

'Why,' asked Sylvia, abruptly changing the subject in her usual way, 'does the language of cricket have to be so obscure? I mean, words such as "off" and "leg" don't seem to have any meaning, yet you use them all the time.'

'They do mean something. To a right-handed batsman, "off" is his right-hand side, and "leg" is his left.'

'So do they change over when the batsman's left-handed?'

'That's right.'

'Ah.' She considered the information for a moment, and then said, 'The word "wicket" is confusing as well.'

'I suppose it can be. Sometimes it refers to the three stumps, sometimes to the prepared patch of turf, and we also talk about how many wickets a bowler has taken. I'll grant you that, SP. It might well be confusing.' He could hear the Reverend Miles Stapleton, Rector of St Jude's and Captain of the Challengers, call his team together. Quickly, he kissed Sylvia and stroked Thea. 'Wish me luck,' he said. 'I'm going to need it.'

The captain waited until everyone was assembled. Then, satisfied, he said, 'I won the toss, and we're batting first.'

Freddy made his way back to the pavilion to await his turn. He was to bat at number nine.

'Back already?'

'We're batting first,' he explained, watching the Revd Stapleton and Bailey walk out to the wicket.

'The match has drawn quite a crowd,' observed Sylvia, inevitably more interested in the cause than in the match itself.

'Yes,' agreed Freddy. 'I always say, if you're going to embarrass yourself, do it in front of a crowd.'

'What are you worried about?'

'I haven't played for a dozen years or more. I only agreed to play because it's a cause worth supporting.'

'I'm sure you're not the only reluctant hero here.'

'Maybe not,' he agreed, 'but they're about to start.'

Apparently, Bailey would receive the first ball from Dan Hirst, the local blacksmith and farrier. Freddy watched the home side's fast bowler walk back.

'He has a long run-up,' he observed.

'A long run-up to what?'

'His crease. That's the whitewashed line on the grass where he has to deliver the ball.'

The bowler was genuinely quick, but not, it seemed, always accurate, because Mr Bradley, chief bell ringer and umpire for the match, signalled 'wide.' The disgruntled blacksmith walked back again to deliver his next ball with characteristic pace. Bailey was on to it quickly, however, and the two batsmen ran two runs.

'That's two to Bailey and one extra for the wide,' Freddy explained.

'Aye, that's our first three runs on t' board,' agreed George Clay. Freddy's second reed was doubling as number six batsman for the duration of the match.

'I beg your pardon, George.' Sylvia turned her head towards him.

'You'll have to speak up, George,' Freddy told him. 'You're on Sylvia's deaf side.'

'I'm sorry, love. I'd no idea.'

'That's all right.'

'Sylvia and Bailey have that in common,' explained Freddy, 'but it was Sylvia's Blighty wound. At all events, you have to speak up for both of them.'

Sylvia sighed with the kind of heavy patience a parent reserves for an obtuse child. 'I got an infection in my ear,' she explained, 'swimming in the sea, and it perforated the ear drum. It was when I was stationed on Malta.'

'By 'eck,' said George. 'The furthest I ever got were France and Germany. Mind you, that were bad enough.' He broke off to applaud as Bailey scored two more runs. It was the final ball of the over and the Revd Stapleton took his place at the crease to face the bowling.

'This could be interesting,' said George. They say the vicar played at Cambridge University. It were game of him to fit this match in this afternoon, an' all. He's even cancelled Evensong 'til next Sunday.'

'That's dedication, George.'

Sylvia's mind was elsewhere. 'What are the "slips", Freddy? In my world, a slip is an underskirt.'

'Think of the batsman as standing in the centre of a clock face, and the slip fielders are those blokes quite close to him, at about five o'clock.'

'Ah.'

'There's sometimes a leg slip as well.'

'That was going to be my next question.'

There was a burst of applause, causing Sylvia to ask, 'What was that for?'

'It was for Reverend Stapleton. He just took four runs off the over.'

'That's another thing. What's an "over"?'

'A series of six balls. After that, they put another bowler on at the other end.'

Enlightened but not impressed, Sylvia continued to watch the mystery unfold.

The Revd Stapleton was scoring steadily. He was clearly a patient man, as Freddy imagined he would be in his particular calling. That virtue seemed to have deserted Dan Hirst however, as Bailey returned to take strike; in fact, he seemed to exude unbridled hostility as he prepared to bowl again at the upstart who had scored six off his first over. His first ball of the new over pitched in line with the off stump, and Bailey played a forward defensive shot. With his second ball, however, Dan left rather too much room for Bailey, who drove it straight to the boundary. After treating the batsman to a look of fury, Dan walked back, turning up the sleeve of his huge right arm.

'That bloke means business,' said George. 'I've seen that look before.'

Dan hurtled towards his crease and swung his arm over with such venom that even the umpire flinched. A split second later, Bailey's off stump parted company with its neighbours and, even as Dan turned to make his bloodthirsty appeal, the umpire raised his forefinger. Bailey tucked his bat beneath his arm and walked with quiet dignity to the pavilion, having scored ten runs. Freddy and the others applauded politely. 'It wasn't a brilliant innings,' he said, 'but Bailey hasn't played recently either.'

As Bailey reached the pavilion steps, George couldn't resist saying, 'Ten runs, Bailey. It were hardly worth getting dressed up for.'

'We shall see,' said Bailey, calmly taking a vacant seat. 'We may be grateful for those runs.'

'Well, I think you did all right, Bailey.'

'Thank you, Sylvia.'

'You're welcome.' Sylvia stood up, handing Thea's lead to Freddy. 'I'm going inside to help with tea,' she said. 'Will you look after Thea while I'm gone?'

'All right. I'll have to bat at some stage, but I'll pass the word when it happens.'

'I shouldn't be long.'

'Neither will I.' He wasn't looking forward to his innings.

The new batsman was Brian Makepeace, the dispensing chemist, who looked less the part than Bailey, but who went on to score twenty-three runs before being clean bowled by Dan Hirst. The Revd Stapleton meanwhile increased his score by fifteen.

Freddy and George watched with growing dismay as the Challengers lost the next two wickets cheaply. Only the Revd Stapleton offered any stability, and the time soon came for George Clay to go out and bat. With the Challengers' score on a modest sixty-eight, they needed every run they could get.

George began well, taking eight runs off two overs, but then Easingthorpe's captain made a bowling change and brought Dan Hirst back into the attack. He celebrated his second spell by catching George off his own bowling, and the unhappy clarinettist returned to the pavilion to be greeted by an impish Bailey.

'Oh, bad luck, George. Hardly worth donning the pads for that, what?'

George ignored him, preferring to speak to Freddy. 'I bet the vicar's wishing he hadn't cancelled Evensong now. At this rate, we should be finished well in time.'

'Well in time for what?' Sylvia returned from the pavilion and accepted a seat from the ever-courteous Bailey.

'I'm just sayin',' said George, 'that, at this rate, we'll be finished in time for Evensong at t' church. Leastways, I can't see us playing the full thirty overs.'

'Oh, is that good?'

George's look told her otherwise.

Again, they watched the procession of returning batsmen, and soon it was Freddy's turn at the crease, the last man having been bowled out by the last ball of the over. The Revd Stapleton would now face the gentle medium pace of Stanley Overton, garage proprietor and occasional wedding chauffeur. Freddy waited at the other end, running as his captain scored off the first four balls.

'One,' called the vicar, and he and Freddy ran the single run, which brought Freddy to the wicket to face Stanley.

It was the last ball of his over and he gave Freddy ample room to sweep it down the leg side. It brought forth two runs, which left the captain to face Dan Hirst, newly returned for another spell.

Freddy watched as the Revd Stapleton played the bowling skilfully, keeping himself on strike throughout the over. It was now Freddy's turn to face Stanley Overton and, uneasy as he'd been about playing, he was thankful he'd not yet had to face Dan.

The over produced three twos from Freddy and a single from the Revd Stapleton, which was unfortunate, because it meant that Freddy must now face the Challengers' nemesis.

'I'm sorry, Freddy,' the captain told him. 'I thought we could get a second run but I misjudged it.'

'Don't worry, Skipper.' For himself, Freddy was past worrying. He simply had to go for the runs. As the saying went, it was 'muck or nettles time'.

He watched Dan Hirst begin his run up, and waited, hands sweating inside his gloves. He'd never made any claim to batting expertise but he was determined to give as good an account of himself as luck would allow. As the ball pitched on a good length, he sent it on its way past the square leg fielder and towards deep square leg. It was a reckless shot and not what he had intended, but he managed one run before the fielder at deep square leg reached the ball and threw it to the wicket keeper.

The next ball was the captain's, and he scored two, to Dan Hirst's unconcealed disgust. The captain managed to keep the bowling to himself for the remainder of the over and, with a sense of relief, Freddy settled down to face Stanley Overton again.

It was a fruitful over for Freddy, who made six off the first three balls and, regrettably, only a single off the last ball. It meant that he must face Dan Hirst yet again.

The first ball came like a thunderbolt. Freddy swung wildly at it and missed. In a sense he was relieved, but only temporarily, because Dan was about to send down the next one.

When he did, it was probably as fast as the first, but it allowed Freddy a little more room on his leg side. It was unlikely that the stroke he played was one any cricket expert or enthusiast had ever heard of, nor yet seen, but it did what was necessary, and Freddy called for one run. Then, when he reached the other end, he saw that a fielder had misfielded the ball and was still fumbling after it. Like it or not, he had to call for a second run, which he did. It turned out to be his last as, with his next ball, Dan Hirst found the middle stump, and Freddy was out, having scored eighteen runs, exactly eighteen more than he had expected.

The last two wickets fell without increasing the score, and it was time for tea. The Challengers were all out for one hundred and forty-nine, of which the Revd Stapleton, the not-out batsman, had contributed fifty-one. His efforts apart, it was a pitiful score, and they could only hope that the inevitable humiliation would not be too great.

Within the constraints of food rationing, the Club ladies, assisted by members of the Women's Institute and the Women's Voluntary Service, had produced a commendable tea. Sylvia had taken part in two capacities, being a member of both the W I and the WVS. Freddy often claimed that her activities confused him, and that she was a member of too many clubs. On this occasion, however, her cakes were an important contribution to the meal. Even so, the atmosphere, at least among the Challengers, was muted.

George Clay waited until the Revd Stapleton had said Grace, before saying, 'By 'eck, Skipper, it's just as well you're t' vicar of St Jude's.'

'What makes you say that, George?'

'Well, isn't he Patron Saint of Lost Causes? I reckon he'll have his work cut out today.'

'He has that distinction, yes, but try not to think of this as a lost cause, George. Think of it more as a *good* cause. Remember why we're doing this.'

'All the same, Skipper, can't you put in a quick word on our behalf? Divine intervention's the only chance we've got left.'

The rector shook his head reprovingly. 'You know, you Yorkshiremen are only ever interested in winning. In any case, I'm afraid The Lord will have more pressing matters in his "In" tray than the outcome of a charity match, but today's crowd has got the

Christmas Party Fund off to a flying start, and that's what really matters.'

It was true, and possibly the only compensation the Challengers could expect as they took the field. The captain touched Freddy on the shoulder and said, 'I'd like you to field at leg slip, Freddy.'

'Very good, Skipper.' It was quite a responsibility, leg slip being behind and to the left of the right-handed batsman. Freddy would have to be particularly alert, but he was becoming increasingly fatalistic. He told himself the match would soon be over anyway, and then he would be spared further embarrassment for another year.

He watched the batsman play at the first ball and miss. It went straight to the wicket keeper. The second ball met a forward defensive shot. It seemed the batsman was playing a safe innings, until the fifth ball, which gave him room to play an attacking, if wild, stroke. Freddy watched the ball soar into the air like a startled pheasant. Keeping his eye on it, he ran backwards and took the catch. Jubilantly, he threw the ball into the air and caught it again, ignoring the stinging of his palms and fingers, and enjoying his success and the cheers of his team mates. He hoped Sylvia and Thea had been watching.

After several overs, the captain offered him the ball. 'I'm pinning my hopes on variety,' he explained. 'I don't want them to get used to one bowler and score too heavily.' It seemed he, at least, felt they still had a chance.

Freddy paced out his mark and ran in to deliver his first ball. It was quite good, and the batsman could only play a defensive shot. Feeling a little more enthusiastic, he ran in again and saw his ball remove the off stump. Elated, he swung round and made his appeal. 'How's that?'

The umpire obliged him by raising the valedictory forefinger. Again, Freddy enjoyed the congratulations of his team mates.

He conceded only one run with his first over, which meant that the Club's score stood at nine runs for the loss of two wickets, and Freddy sensed a careful but growing optimism among the Challengers.

After the first two balls of his second over, he decided to tempt the batsman into playing at a slightly wider ball on his off side. The first time, the batsman let it go through to the wicket keeper, but the next delivery brought Freddy the result he wanted. The batsman played an ambitious shot and the ball fell into the hands of the fielder at second slip. That was two wickets and a catch for Freddy, and the Club was three men down. He bowled the last ball of the over and resumed his place at leg slip. From her place beside the pavilion steps, Sylvia waved excitedly. It was harder to read Thea's mood but she seemed to be enjoying herself.

The new batsman was being extremely careful, but suddenly a loose delivery gave him the opportunity he wanted and he struck the ball past Freddy and down towards long leg. As it approached the boundary, and having evaded two fielders, it attracted Thea's notice and she responded as a terrier should. The call of the chase could not be denied, and she leapt down the pavilion steps, encouraged by the shouts and cheers of the less cricket-minded spectators, tearing after the long leg fielder. Straight as a torpedo, she reached the ball before him and, having done so, sat immediately behind it, defying all attempts to make her relinquish it. Meanwhile, the batsmen were taking full advantage of the hiatus. With a groan of embarrassment, Freddy set off towards the boundary, where Thea sat guarding the ball and emitting low-pitched growls whenever anyone tried to pick it up. He reached the scene as Sylvia arrived, lead in hand.

'Thank you, Thea,' he said. 'I was quite popular until you joined in.'

'I'm sorry, Freddy. I couldn't stop her.'

'Don't worry.' Leaving Sylvia to lead the miscreant back to the pavilion, he picked up the ball and hurled it to the wicket keeper, who swept off the bails while the batsman was still two yards out of his crease. The run-out meant that the Club was now four wickets down, and the departing batsman was clearly unhappy. 'That bloody dog distracted me,' he complained.

Freddy smiled and shrugged.

Thea's intervention was not the last surprise, as the Challengers and spectators watched a spell of stylish bowling by Bailey, who took a wicket in his first over.

Then it was Freddy's turn to bowl again. With his second over he took one wicket, and with his third, two more. The Club was now forty-two runs behind the Challengers and with only two wickets in hand. Those two went down with the addition of only three runs. The Challengers had won by thirty-nine runs, and Freddy had taken five wickets, conceding only fourteen runs. It had been a good day after all; Thea had enjoyed some of it as well as providing entertainment for the irreverent few, the Christmas Party Fund was looking healthy, and Freddy had surprised even himself with his performance. It had all been very exciting, but now it was over, he was ready more than ever to concentrate again on 'Viking High Jinks.'

11

August

Freddy woke up, conscious of the space next to him. It was still warm, so Sylvia must be in the bathroom.

Sunlight was slanting through a chink in the curtains, and birds were singing. He rubbed his eyes and looked at the clock. It was ten-past five. He heard the bathroom door being opened and, a few seconds later, the creaking stair. Five weeks had passed since the last time. It had become a familiar occurrence. He sat up and reached for his dressing gown.

He found Sylvia on the sitting room sofa, crying softly. He sat beside her and slipped an arm round her.

'Is it the unwelcome visitor again?' He couldn't remember when he'd first given it that name, but it seemed distressingly appropriate.

With her head against his chest, she nodded dumbly. After a while, she mumbled, 'I was more than a... week over... due. It was stupid... of me to think... it might have happened... at last.'

'Remember what the doctor said about anxiety. I know you can't help it, but it's bound to bugger things up.'

The sitting room door swung gently open, and Thea walked in.

'Good morning, Thea,' said Freddy. 'I'll take you out soon.'

Thea appeared to consider his offer, and then lay instead at his feet, evidently more inclined to catch up on her sleep.

'I feel... such a failure.'

'Why? You know there's nothing wrong with either of us. We just have to go on doing what comes naturally.' He stopped for a moment in reflection, and said, 'You know, there could be a lyric in there somewhere.'

'Except Irving... Berlin got there before you.' Her shudders were coming less often. It was always a good sign.

'Berlin, Kern, Porter.... It's a conspiracy.' He held her closer. 'But who cares?'

'I really want to give you a son or a daughter.'

'Yes, one or the other would be wonderful, and a family would be even better, but you have to remember that I got what I wanted most of all in nineteen-forty-five. That day in Trafalgar Square, remember?'

'I know, and you speak as a son of Kingston-upon-Hull, where the baring of souls is as rare as daffodils in December. How could I forget that?' She managed a faint smile, and said, 'I love you, Freddy.'

'Well now, that'll be a great help, because we really will have to keep on trying.'

'But not this week,' she reminded him.

'No,' he agreed, 'but you can put a big circle round next Wednesday or maybe Thursday, and even give it an exclamation mark or two.'

'I'll look forward to it.'

Thea was stirring again, so he said, 'You'd better make yourself presentable, SP, because Bailey will be down shortly. I'm going to put some clothes on and take Thea for a walk.'

He was so engaged in thought, that they were quite a way down the lane before he spoke.

'The thing is, Thea, I have to convince SP that her trouble is mine, and that I'm as keen as she is to have children. I mean, telling her I already had what I wanted must have come over as downright selfish. What do you think?' He watched her sniff her way purposefully along the grass verge. 'Of course, you were asleep, weren't you?'

It seemed, however, that confiding in Thea helped in some way, because he resolved on the way back to be completely open with Sylvia. It was all very well to jolly her out of her moments of misery but, more than anything, she needed to know that he was taking the whole thing seriously.

He realised when they reached the house that words of reassurance would have to wait their turn, because Bailey was at the breakfast table, and Sylvia was plying him with bacon and eggs. He joined him at the table, and found him remarkably chirpy for six in the morning.

'I was surprised to find you two up and about, old man.'

'Oh well, neither of us could sleep.'

'Bad luck, old thing. I must say, sleeping is never a problem for me.'

Freddy wasn't surprised.

'Here you are, Freddy.' Sylvia put a plate of bacon and eggs in front of him.

'My lovely wife, you astonish me. Despite rationing, shortages and everything else they throw at us, you still spoil me to death.'

'Mrs Fearnley at the farm let me have extra eggs. The chickens have been laying away again, but they weren't too secretive about where they'd been going.'

'In that case,' said Bailey, raising his cup, 'here's to the simple chicken. Long may it continue to give the bally game away.' He looked at his watch and said, 'I must leave you both. *Tempus* fudge it, and all that sort of thing. I'll tell you what, though; I may have just the thing for you two, something to mark my departure from the Hinchcliffe residence. I'll phone you about it later.' He picked up his briefcase. 'A thousand thanks, Sylvia, for an unexpected and sumptuous breakfast. Cheerio, souls.'

As the front door closed, Freddy asked, 'What was he talking about? Do you know?'

'This thing he's found? I've no idea.'

'Neither have I, and what did he mean about leaving?'

'Oh yes, he told me while you were out with Thea. He's found rooms in Northallerton. He's moving in at the weekend.'

Freddy shook his head. 'Everything happens so quickly with Bailey. It's difficult to keep track of his movements.'

'It'll certainly be quiet here without him.' After a moment's thought, she asked, 'Have you ever known him be less than cheerful?'

'Only when the goons gave him a beating. He had two cracked ribs and the rest of his body was one enormous bruise.'

'Why on earth did they do that?'

'Because he called *Feldwebel* Vogel a murdering bastard. He'd just shot a helpless Russian kriegie.'

'But to beat him half to death for that was awful.'

'That wasn't all. When they set about Bailey, another of the Russians, a chap we knew quite well, went berserk and attacked them. They held him while Vogel shot him in the head. I missed that, having lost consciousness just as they were leaping on Bailey.'

'Oh Freddy, I wish I hadn't asked now. I don't want you to have horrible nightmares again, like you did when you first came home.'

'Don't worry, SP.' He smiled reassuringly. 'Thanks largely to your dad and fly fishing those things are in the past.'

She nodded. 'I remember now. Redmire Falls and all that.'

'That's right, but it's important that I talk to you now about something else that occurred to me when I was out with Thea.'

⊷⊰✠⊱⊶

Bailey arrived that evening in a shiny, black Vauxhall Ten. After dinner, he handed the keys to Freddy.

'Take it for a spin, old man. See how you both like it.'

'Aren't you coming as well, Bailey?'

'Wouldn't dream of it, folks. Three's a crowd and all that.'

Sylvia opened the passenger door and gasped involuntarily as she sank into the upholstery. 'It's lovely,' she said, 'just like an armchair.'

'Very nice,' agreed Freddy, starting the engine. 'I only wish I knew what price he has in mind.'

'Just enjoy it for now. You can worry about the price later.'

'If only life were so simple. I'll drive it down the road towards Hawes, and then you can drive it back.'

'Gosh, Freddy, I'm quite overcome.'

'Well, if we decide to buy it, you'll need to drive it sooner or later.' He changed up into top gear. 'I must say, it's got a lovely feel to it.'

'Didn't Bailey say something about it being registered before the war?'

'Yes, in nineteen-thirty-nine. It was laid up throughout the war, and it's had little use since then.'

After a while, he pulled into the side of the road and reversed into an opening. 'It's all yours, SP,' he said, opening his door to get out and then, as an afterthought, moving the seat forward.

She sat in the driving seat and asked, 'Where are the gears?'

'One, two and three.' He pointed to each position. 'And reverse is here.'

'Thank you.' She engaged first gear, indicated right, and pulled out cautiously. There was nothing coming either way, so she continued up the road. 'Oh, it's lovely, and much nicer to drive than the van.'

'Oh glory. We'll have to buy it now.'

'Don't be so grumpy.' She seemed to reflect on that, because she followed it with, 'Actually you're not grumpy. You were lovely this morning.'

'Good. Now I feel better as well.'

They arrived home, and discussion naturally led to the price. Bailey consulted his paperwork and named a mark-up price, adding that the company was prepared to bargain. Incredibly, when Freddy made an offer of ninety-five pounds, Bailey would hear none of it.

'Are you serious, old man? No, let's shake hands on eighty-five.'

Freddy was happy to do that. A day that had begun badly ended more happily than either he or Sylvia could have imagined.

❧❦❧

The next morning, after Freddy had driven Bailey to work, he and Sylvia called at the Cresswells' farm. The foal had grown appreciably but his legs were still out of proportion to his body, not that it held him back at all. He was in a playful mood and in no hurry to greet his visitors. By contrast, Mandy was her usual sociable and amenable self, the disastrous foaling mercifully forgotten, and it seemed to Freddy that rural life had a remarkable and comforting way of regaining its equilibrium.

❧❦❧

Two days later, Freddy was feeling particularly cheerful.

'I just had a phone call,' he told Sylvia, 'from a young woman who wants to be in the show. She's sung principal parts, mainly Gilbert and Sullivan, but she's quite happy to join the chorus.'

'I wonder where she's been hiding.'

'She's only just moved into the village, from Skipton, I think she said.'

Sylvia smiled involuntarily.

'What's the joke?'

'There's no joke, but you were scratching around for young members a short while ago, and now one's landed on your doorstep. Let's hope she doesn't turn out to be like Joan.'

'I don't see why she should, SP. In any case, I'll know more about her after tonight. I'm auditioning her before the rehearsal.'

⚜

The new member was possibly in her twenties, dark-haired and slim, although just a little too tall to be called *petite*. She spoke to Sylvia, who pointed her in Freddy's direction.

She approached him confidently. 'Mr Hinchcliffe? I'm Marjorie Bentham. We spoke on the phone.'

'So we did. How d' you do, Miss Bentham? My name's Freddy, by the way. That looks like a score under your arm. Have you something you'd like to sing?'

'Yes.' She opened a copy of *The Yeomen of the Guard* at a book-marked page and handed it to him.

' "Were I Thy Bride",' he read. 'You know, you're the second person to audition with a song from *Yeomen*.'

'Am I?'

'Yes. Bailey, who's playing the male lead, sang "What Say You, Maiden?"'

'By himself?'

'Yes, he sang Elsie's and Jack Point's parts as well. That's what sold him to me.' He added, 'He was in the bath at our house at the time.'

'Oh,' she said, making a deliberate double-take, 'is that part of the protocol?'

'Not necessarily. If you're happy to audition now, we'll dispense with the bathtub.'

'That's a relief. Right, I'm ready when you are.'

Freddy played the gentle, staccato introduction, and Marjorie made her entry. The song was sung in the opera by Phoebe, the sergeant's daughter, whose purpose was to seduce the jailer with loving words while she stole his keys so that her father could save the life of an innocent man condemned to death.

> ' "Were I thy bride,
> Then all the world beside
> Were not too wide to hold my wealth of love
> Were I thy bride." '

She had a lovely voice, a true mezzo with a sweetness that extended into her lower register. She continued:

> ' "Upon thy breast
> My loving head would rest,
> As on her nest
> The tender turtle dove
> Were I thy bride.
>
> This heart of mine
> Would be one heart with thine,
> And in that shrine
> Our happiness would dwell
> Were I thy bride." '

The song went on with its catalogue of beguiling similes until the final stanza.

> ' "A feather's press
> Were leaden heaviness
> To my caress—" '

And then, with an impish look across the piano at Freddy, she sang:

' "But then of course, you see
I'm not thy bride!'

Freddy played out the final four bars for no better reason than that the song was one of his favourites. Then, he closed the score and handed it to Marjorie, saying, 'I wish I'd seen your Phoebe.'

'Thank you. Does that mean I'm in?'

'It does, and you're most welcome. You'll have to spend some time with me, learning the choruses, but I'm sure you're used to that.'

'It'll be a pleasure. I think it's a great thing you're doing, putting this show on.'

Freddy wondered. His next excitement would be the first principals' rehearsal.

12

Joan Curwen was eager to speak to Freddy when she arrived. She seemed agitated.

'I thought you'd call me for a principals' rehearsal nearer the performance,' she said. 'Instead of that, it seems you want me here from the start.'

'Yes, Joan, I like to do a thorough job.'

'But I know the music. I've been through it with my accompanist.'

With a feeling of unease, Freddy said, 'I'm delighted to hear it, but you have ensemble numbers to rehearse. The other cast members need to rehearse with you, and I need to hear you with them.'

She gave a deep sigh, and said, 'Oh well, if that's what you want.'

'Yes, Joan, that's what I want.' Raising his voice against the general murmur, he said, 'First, I'd like to hear Elga and Erik in "Brutes and Ravishers", please.' He played the four bars of introduction, and Joan began.

'Brutes and ravishers! Foul invaders! Yet again, you come to raid us!

Freddy thought she sounded pretty good, reminiscent of a Valkyrie, perhaps. She was on the wrong side for that, but who cared as long as she was scary?

She reached the end of her tirade, and Bailey joined the duet.

'Good lady, I implore you, let me speak and make you understand....'

It was *recitative*, a line of linking, sung dialogue that, according to the blokes in the band, added an operatic flavour to the scene.

Freddy was inclined to agree; in fact, it was just the effect he wanted. He allowed the duet to continue, and was enjoying the combination of their two voices, until Joan made a premature entry, and he had to stop the number.

'Sorry to interrupt you, folks. Joan, you have one-and-a-half beats before your entry, and then you come in on the second half of the second beat.' He demonstrated. 'One, two, *If indeed you speak the truth....*'

'I know.' She gave him a look of glowering indignation. 'I was distracted.'

⊶⊰⊱⊹⊱⊰⊷

He discussed it with Sylvia after the rehearsal. 'You should have heard her,' he said. 'She blamed the other principals for talking when she was singing.'

'What did you do?'

'I asked them to observe the usual courtesy when people were performing, but that wasn't the reason she went wrong. She just doesn't know the music as well as she would like me to believe.'

'Let's hope that's the end of it,' said Sylvia. 'The last thing we need is friction.'

'Agreed. I think she'll settle down.'

After a moment's thought, Sylvia asked, 'What's the other newcomer like? Elaine, isn't it?'

'Yes, she's picking it up well. She's a nice girl too, apparently. I haven't had much chat with her, but Bailey's quite impressed.'

That made Sylvia smile. 'How old would you say Bailey is?'

'I did know.' Freddy searched his memory. 'Yes, I remember now. He said he was twenty-two at the outbreak of war.' He did a mental calculation. 'So that makes him thirty-three.'

'In that case, don't you think it's time he settled down?'

'No, not Bailey. He'll go on philandering as he always has until the awful day dawns, when he realises he's no longer the matinee idol he thought he was.'

'What a lovely, old-fashioned description.'

'That's Bailey's world, at least as he sees it.'

'Bless him.' Sylvia glanced at the mantel clock. 'It's late,' she said. 'Yes, bedtime.'

'What are you doing in the morning?'

Freddy groaned good-naturedly. 'I've got another session with Tigger, the Jack Russell.'

'So soon after the last one?'

'His owner wants to make it a regular event, a sort of record of his development. In any case, I'm not complaining. It's what puts the butter on our National Loaf.' Correcting himself, he added, 'Well, the margarine ration, anyway.'

'That's true, and it's all good fun as well....' She stopped as she remembered something. 'I nearly forgot to tell you,' she said. 'I agreed to have the children for the weekend. You don't mind, do you?'

'Bruce and Pauline?'

'Of course. How many other children do you know?'

'I suppose it was a silly question. What's the big occasion?' It was rare for Sylvia's sister and her husband to go anywhere without the children.

'They're going to a wedding in Derbyshire. They'll be back by lunchtime on Sunday.'

'Fine, but it's just as well Bailey moved out when he did.'

'That's true. I'm borrowing the folding bed from my mum and dad, by the way.'

'I should think you'll just about squeeze it into the spare room.'

'I actually had it in mind to put it in our room. Pauline can sleep on it, and then Bruce can have the spare room to himself.'

Freddy nodded. 'He's a big lad now.'

'Six-and-a-half,' she confirmed. 'They're concerned about him. Did I tell you?'

'Yes, but you didn't say why. What's he been doing?'

'It's what he's *not* doing that worries them. He's making no headway at all with his reading; in fact, he seems to be resisting all efforts to get him to read anything. It's odd, because he's bright enough in other respects.'

It didn't seem all that odd to Freddy. 'He's a practical little soul,' he said. 'Do you remember how slow he was to start talking? I reckon he was quite happy to let Audrey do it for him. Maybe it's the same with his reading.'

'Are you saying my sister's a chatterbox?'

'Not by some people's standards.'

'But you're saying she talks a lot.'

Clearly, he'd touched a nerve. The two sisters would argue from morning until night, but neither would hear ill of the other. The situation called for diplomacy.

'Would I criticise your sister? I'm only saying that she used to speak up for Bruce an awful lot, and he's not daft; he knew he was on to a good thing, right up to the time he took a fancy to the egg on my plate, and said, "Chookie".'

'You're joking.'

'No, I'm not. It was his first word. Actually, he said, "Tookie", but we knew what he meant.'

'When did this happen?' Any suggestion of Freddy having criticised Audrey was evidently forgotten, which had naturally been Freddy's intention.

'It was when you were in Malta, and I was staying with your folks.'

'Ah.' She appeared to consider his argument. 'But reading to him shouldn't put him off doing it for himself. If anything, you'd think it would encourage him to read.'

'We'll see. I'm going into Northallerton on Friday. I'll see if I can find something that might appeal to his pragmatic values.'

⊕⊬⊰⊱⊱⊰⊱

The session with Tigger proved fruitful, even if Mrs Woolliscroft was yet to be convinced. Still, Freddy imagined the pictures would do the trick.

He took Tigger into the back garden, where Sylvia obliged him by throwing a tennis ball hard into the ground so that it soared into the air, followed enthusiastically by Tigger. The game worked well for a while, with Mrs Woolliscroft watching from a point of safety in the kitchen, but Freddy wanted to try something different. This involved Sylvia pointing the garden hose at each of the lawn's extremities, so that Tigger dashed repeatedly after the switching deluge.

After five minutes or so, Freddy declared himself confident of a number of usable pictures. All that remained was for Sylvia to fetch a towel and dry the over-excited animal before returning him to his disgruntled owner.

'He's all wet,' said Mrs Woolliscroft.

'Just a bit damp,' Sylvia assured her, giving Tigger a final rub with the towel.

'He smells horrible now.'

'He'll smell a lot sweeter when he's dry,' said Freddy, wondering if anything would ever win Mrs Woolliscroft's approval.

'Aye. Well, we'll have a look at the photos when you've developed them.'

'They'll be ready in the morning,' said Freddy.

'We'd best be off, then.' With Freddy holding Tigger still, she fastened his lead to his collar and held it firmly as Tigger hurled himself once again into the outside world.

Watching them, Sylvia said, 'He could be a lovely dog if someone would train him.'

'You're right as usual, SP, but let's go inside. I don't like the look of that black cloud.'

They had been indoors only a few minutes when the rain began to fall, gently at first, and then more heavily until the raindrops were bouncing high off the road outside.

'Tigger really is going to smell awful when Mrs Woolliscroft gets him home,' said Freddy.

13

The morning's news was dominated by the birth of a second child, a daughter, to Princess Elizabeth and the Duke of Edinburgh and, delighted though Sylvia was for the royal couple, it was yet another reminder of her on-going plight. The children's arrival was therefore a timely distraction.

At four, Pauline was a precocious parent, and her priority on crossing the threshold was to enquire about the sleeping arrangements for her two dolls, Christine and Robert.

'They have to sleep in the same bedroom,' she told Sylvia.

'Why do they have to do that?'

'Because they're twins.' Her tone suggested that the reason should have been obvious. She was a serious child, at least for much of the time, and her severe centre parting and tight plaits seemed to reinforce her air of solemnity.

'Twins don't always sleep in the same room, Pauline.'

'I know, Auntie Sylvia, but this is the first time they've been away from home.'

It made a kind of sense. 'I suppose it is rather strange for them,' she conceded. 'We'll make them a little bed next to yours.'

'Where will my bed be?'

'You're in the folding bed in our room.'

'Where you and Uncle Freddy sleep?'

'That's right.'

Pauline appeared to assimilate the information before saying, 'You'll have to be quiet and not wake up Christine and Robert.'

'Don't worry, Pauline. We shan't do anything noisy.' She glanced at Freddy, who was shaking his head in mock resignation.

Bruce was less demanding; dolls and bedrooms meant nothing

to him as long as Thea was around. She was the great attraction of the visit. Aunties and uncles were popular enough but, in a competition for Bruce's attention, they would have come a poor joint second to their pet; in fact, all the time Pauline had been organising her doll's sleeping arrangements, he had been struggling to lift the object of his affection.

'Leave her on the deck,' advised Freddy. 'She'll be happier there.' Then, sensible of the child's disappointment, he said, 'Shall we take her for a walk?'

'Yes.' The suggestion had immediate appeal. 'Can I hold her?'

'You can hold her lead, yes.' Freddy looked around for Pauline and found her explaining the arrangements to her dolls. 'Would you like to come, Pauline? We're taking Thea for a walk.'

Pauline looked up at the distraction. 'I can't leave Christine and Robert,' she said.

'That's all very well,' Sylvia told her, 'but what do you say when you don't want something?'

'What?'

'Uncle Freddy asked you if you wanted to go with him and Bruce. What should you say?'

Pauline had one finger in her mouth, a sign that she was thinking hard. Eventually, she said, 'No, thank you.'

'Good girl. That's right.'

Freddy and Bruce left her with Sylvia and set off down the road. After a short time, Bruce said in a voice filled with concern, 'Thea's got a poorly leg, Uncle Freddy. She's limping.'

'No, she's not, Bruce. That's called "carrying a leg". Terriers do it often.'

'Why?'

'Because they're happy. It's like skipping.'

After a moment's consideration, Bruce asked, 'How do you know?'

'I have a book about the Aberdeen Terrier. I read all about it in that.'

Bruce gave him a strange look, possibly the one he reserved for people with eccentric habits, such as reading, and walked on thoughtfully.

'What's on your mind, Bruce?'

'Nothing.'

'That's all right, then. I wondered if you were worrying about something.'

'Not really, but....'

'Come on, Bruce. Tell Uncle Freddy.'

'All right.' They came to a halt, and Thea busied herself by investigating a dozen tantalising scents. 'I don't want to be called Bruce anymore.'

It was not what Freddy had expected, but he held on and said, 'It's a little late for that, Bruce. You've had the name six years now. Why don't you like it?'

'Carol Bernard at school has a guinea pig called Bruce.' The words came out like a sigh of despair.

'Have you been teased about it?'

Bruce nodded mutely.

'Does it matter all that much that you share your name with a guinea pig? I mean, only a fool could find that funny.' The child's uplifted face showed his surprise. 'Are you really worried about what a fool thinks, Bruce?'

'I don't know.'

'You shouldn't be. If you show the fool you're upset, it only makes him feel clever, but we know he's not clever, don't we?'

'Mm.' Bruce was evidently giving the matter some thought. Freddy decided to give him something else to think about.

'Do you know where your name came from?'

'No.'

'I'll tell you, because it's worth remembering. You see, you're named after Admiral Sir Bruce Fraser, a very important sailor.'

'Why was he important?' Misery forgotten for the moment, there was curiosity in Bruce's eyes.

'He did something very important on the twenty-sixth of December, nineteen-forty-three.'

Bruce looked up sharply. 'That's my birthday,' he said.

'That's right.'

'What did he do?'

'He sank a ship that had been an awful nuisance. He was very popular after that. He became Lord Fraser, and your mummy and daddy named you "Bruce" after him. There's nothing funny about that, is there?'

⊛⊷⊰⊹⊱⊰⊱⊷⊛

After lunch, Bruce noticed the tartan-covered reader Freddy had placed strategically that morning. Attracted by the tartan design, he opened it and found pictures of two Aberdeen terriers.

'They're like Thea,' he said. 'Is this the book about skipping?'

'No,' said Freddy, 'that's a different book, but this one's about two Aberdeen terriers.'

'What are they called?'

'Let's see.' Freddy opened the book at the first page. 'Look,' he said, 'it tells you here.' He saw Bruce's face fall at the thought of having to read it for himself, so he gave him a start. 'When you see "t" and "h" together,' he said, 'they say "th".'

Bruce persevered and read, ' "Th-i-s i-s M-a-c." He's called Mac!'

'Good boy. What's the other one called?'

' "Th-i-s i-s T-o"....'

'When you see "s" and "h" together, they say "sh".'

' "Tosh"! He's called Tosh!'

'Mac and Tosh,' confirmed Freddy.

'Mackintosh!' Bruce recognised the pun immediately.

'Good boy.'

'That's funny.'

'Yes, and now you can read all about them.'

After a faltering start, Bruce began to make headway.

'Amazing,' said Sylvia, watching him. I'll have to look to my laurels after this.'

'Why?'

'Because you're going to be Audrey's hero now.'

'Oh, he just needed a good reason for reading, as I suspected all along. Anyway, Audrey has a lot going for her; I admire her tremendously, but she ain't got what you've got, SP.'

'And what's that?'

'I'll tell you one day when you need cheering up.'

14

B ailey knew very little about Elaine beyond the most basic particulars. He knew that she was twenty-five and employed as a secretary, that she'd served in the ATS during the latter part of the war, and that during that time she'd formed a relationship with an officer in the Parachute Regiment, who had subsequently returned from the war a changed and troubled man. She'd told him those things over the three occasions they'd been out together, and he had told her almost as much about himself as he'd told anyone. Naturally, there were episodes of his past about which he'd so far remained reticent, although he knew that sooner or later he would have to tell all. That was the way their relationship seemed to be going, and the development pleased him. He was therefore surprised, when calling for Elaine, to find her less than her usual affable self, and to encounter a young man at the cottage. He was tall, perhaps only a couple of inches shorter than Bailey, smartly dressed in a tweed jacket and grey flannels, and he seemed remarkably at home. His manner, however, was less than welcoming.

'Who are you?' It was a challenge rather than an enquiry.

'Who's asking, old man?'

Good manners prompted Elaine to intervene. 'Geoffrey, this is Bailey. We're in the show together. We're also about to go out, so I'll have to ask you to excuse us.'

'Oh, it's like that, is it?' Geoffrey ignored Bailey's outstretched hand. Instead, he said, 'You must be the second-hand car salesman I've been hearing about.' He made Bailey's occupation sound like a scurrilous activity.

'Is there any other kind of car salesman? My dear old sport, just try laying your hands on a new car nowadays. This government is making it harder than ever.'

Geoffrey appeared to ignore the challenge. Instead, he explored another facet of Bailey's existence. 'Presumably you have another name apart from... what did you say it was?'

'I didn't. That was Elaine, and my name is Bailey. It's the only one I use, so it's the only one you need to know.'

'Interesting.' Geoffrey looked him up and down, as if seeing him for the first time. 'So what brings a southerner to Wensleydale?'

'An honest crust, oddly enough.'

Geoffrey nodded for no obvious reason, and asked, 'Were you in the trade before you took this job?'

'Yes, I was.' He decided he disliked Geoffrey heartily, whatever his relationship was with Elaine. 'If you really want to know,' he said, 'I came here from Nicholl Brothers of Edgware, a company of high standing.' He felt in his pocket for his car key and looked at Elaine, who seemed equally anxious to bring the conversation to its close.

'Geoffrey,' she said, 'we really must go.'

'Very well.' He picked up his hat, pausing to say, 'You'll think about what I've said, won't you?'

'Yes, but not now.'

With a final nod in Bailey's direction, he left, leaving him to speculate.

'A friend of yours, Elaine?'

'Yes, I'll explain as we go.'

As they walked down the path to the gate, Elaine saw the car for the first time, and asked, 'What on earth are you driving now, Bailey?'

'A Rover. Lovely job.'

'I can't keep track of you and your cars.'

'I have no car of my own,' he confided, opening the door for her. 'I simply take whatever we have in the showroom as long as it has a road fund licence. The options are usually limited, but this time I was lucky, and so are you, dear lady, because tonight this is your carriage, and an appropriately splendid one, too.'

'Oh, Bailey,' she sighed, 'you're just full of it.'

'So they say, but I'm harmless.'

'Unlike some.'

'What do you mean?'

She waved her hand vaguely in the direction from which they'd driven, and said, 'That was Geoffrey, probably making a note of your car registration.'

'Why would he do that?' Bailey had heard of some strange hobbies, but this was a new one.

'Because he's jealous of you.'

'I don't see how knowing the number of this car is likely to help the dear old chilblain.' Then, suspecting that there was more to come, he touched her hand encouragingly, and asked, 'What's the story?'

For a moment, Elaine said nothing. When she did speak, it was clear that the matter had been troubling her more than Bailey realised.

'I was involved in a collision,' she said. 'It was shortly before I joined the Players. It wasn't my fault, but the other driver was hurt, so the police became involved. It was very nasty.'

Bailey squeezed her hand. 'You poor old soul,' he said. 'I'd no idea.'

'There was no way you could have known. Anyway, to cut a long, boring story mercifully short, my car was a mess, so Geoffrey drove me home.'

Sensing that it was no time for an interruption, Bailey kept his questions to himself and went on listening.

'I was grateful for the lift home, but Geoffrey couldn't leave it at that. He kept calling at odd times, checking that I was all right and wanting to do things for me. It turned out he was working up to asking me out. He lacks confidence, you see.'

'Really?'

'Oh, I know it sounds strange, but the superior act is a cover for his shyness.'

'Well, I'd never have known it, and being sensitive to that kind of thing is supposed to come easily to a chap of my calling.' He indicated right and changed down to negotiate the gateway to the restaurant.

'You only saw him for a few minutes, Bailey. I've been dodging him for some time. I've tried letting him down gently, but it's so much water off a duck's back.'

'Well, of course, if you need help in getting shot of the blighter, I'm only too happy to lend a hand. Say the word, and the Bailey brawn is at your disposal.'

'Oh no, Bailey. You must be careful.'

He drew into a convenient place and switched off the engine.

'My dear girl, you worry needlessly. I mean, he's not superhuman, so why should I have cause to be wary of this carbuncle?'

'If you haven't worked it out already,' she said, opening her door, 'he was one of the policemen who attended the accident.'

'So he's a rozzer.' Bailey slammed the car door with a flourish. 'It's not as if I'm on their list of most wanted hoodlums. I mean, what can the blighter do?'

'Oh, Bailey,' she sighed hopelessly, 'there are things he can do, dirty tricks he can resort to. He's told me about some of them, and he wouldn't hesitate to find a way of getting his own back, believe me.'

'Ah well, sufficient unto the day, I believe they say. Let's go inside and find something to take your mind off the rotten egg.'

⊕⊶3⊸⊁⊱⊰⊹⊸⊕

'Honestly, Freddy, that woman gets more difficult by the day.'

'Which woman is that, SP?'

'You haven't been listening, have you? I'm talking about Joan Curwen. She messes up the dance routines, and then when I correct her, she says I'm too bossy.'

Freddy closed the display folder he'd been working on, and gave her his full attention.

'Bossy? Leading Wren Charlesworth bossy? The very idea.'

'I wish you'd take the matter seriously. It's not just her attitude that's a problem, it's her awkwardness. She's a lovely singer, but dance just isn't her *forte*, although I'd defy anyone to tell her that.'

'I'm afraid we have to work with what we've got. I can't recruit another Elga at this stage.'

'More's the pity, and I'm not the only one who's fed up with her. Bailey finds her difficult too, and for a man who could charm an adder, that's saying a great deal.'

'It certainly is. How's the tea ration, by the way?'

Frowning at the apparent change of subject, she said impatiently, 'It's holding up.'

'I'll put the kettle on.'

'Tea isn't going to solve anything, Freddy. Honestly, I can't make Joan into a better dancer but something needs to be done about her abrasive attitude. It's affecting most of the cast.'

'I know.' He picked up the folder to return it to the studio. 'I'll speak to her.' And, being a man of his word, he fully intended to speak to Joan, although he had no idea what he was going to say to her. It was important, also, to placate Sylvia, who had put in a great deal of work on choreography and was working hard with everyone. The last thing he needed was tension at home.

15

There was something soothing about sitting on the oak settle beside the fire in the tap room of the Shearer's Arms, and the new brew, launched only that year, was going down well. The fire had been lit only that morning in response to the unseasonal cold and wet front that persisted that August.

It was a time of self-indulgence for Freddy, who reckoned he'd worked hard enough that week and had intimated as much to Sylvia before leaving the house. Happily, she had agreed.

His companion on the settle was Albert Whittaker, who sat in silence at the fireplace end. He was an habitual, solitary drinker, accepted and tolerated by the regulars, who knew better than to attempt conversation. He and Freddy had never met, although Freddy recalled a reference to his prize parsnips at the Easingthorpe Show. He was particularly surprised, then, when Mr Whittaker broke the silence.

'You're t' photographer, I fancy?'

'That's right.' Freddy did his best to hide his surprise, offering his hand. 'Freddy Hinchcliffe.'

'I know. Bert Whittaker.'

They shook hands soberly.

'I saw your parsnips at the show. I was impressed.'

'Aye?'

They sat in silence for several minutes, Freddy being reluctant to press the man into conversation. Then his neighbour spoke again.

'You were a POW, I believe.'

'That's right.' Again, Freddy was taken aback, having been told that Albert Whittaker never mentioned the subject.

'We got taken in Singapore.'

'Hell, I'm sorry.' Freddy had heard only desultory, unconnected reports of prison camp life in the Far East, but he knew that they represented horror on an unimagined scale.

'Aye, they kept us in Changi Prison while they decided what they were going to do wi' us, and that were bad enough.' He gazed down into his tankard, possibly remembering things better left untold. A series of clicks and knocks came from a nearby table, where two men sat playing dominoes, and the remains of the log on the fire ticked as if in response.

'Can I get you another, Mr Whittaker?' Freddy asked the question gently, reluctant to intrude on his recollections.

'Aye. Dark mild, if you don't mind. The name's Bert, by the way.'

'Right-oh.' Freddy took the empties to the bar. Grace, the barmaid saw him and came over.

'He's talking to you, then, Freddy?'

'Yes, I'm not pushing it. I'll just let him talk when he wants to.'

'I'm surprised he's talking at all.'

'So am I, Grace. Two pints of dark mild, please.'

Grace pulled the two drinks, and he took them back to the settle. Bert took his gratefully.

'Much obliged, Freddy.'

'You're welcome.' Again, Freddy waited patiently for his companion to speak. After a few minutes, he was rewarded as Bert spoke in what was little more than a whisper.

'They took us on a hellish voyage to Burma. Thousands crowded below and the rest of us on deck in the blazing sun. How we survived that I don't know. Some didn't. The Japs threw the bodies to the sharks.'

'If it's too much for you, Bert, don't feel you have to tell me now.'

'No, it's okay.' Bert felt in his pocket and took out a small newspaper cutting. 'This were in t' paper this morning, Freddy.' He handed it to him.

Freddy smoothed it out and read:

Japanese Commandant Found Dead in Hotel Room

The body of Colonel Takashi Osako was found yesterday in a hotel in Tokyo. Japanese police sources say that he had been shot repeatedly at close range. His killer made good his escape, and the hotel room is being searched for clues as to his identity.

The incident is thought to have been a revenge killing. Col. Osako was commandant of a notorious prison camp near Mulmein, where many allied prisoners perished during the construction of the infamous Burma to Siam Railway.

That was all. The cutting was no more than about two inches long, but it meant a great deal to Bert, as it would to anyone who had suffered under Colonel Osako.

'It were too good for him, Freddy. Shootin', I mean. He'd plenty under him who'd a lot to answer for but, when all's said and done, he were in command, an' it's up to t' main man to carry the can.' He lifted his tankard and drank thoughtfully.

The silence that followed was so lengthy that Freddy imagined the reminiscence to be over. It seemed that Bert had said all he was going to say, at least for one evening. Harry, the landlord, came round with a taper, lighting the gas mantles and acknowledging Bert's silence with a knowing nod.

After a while, Grace put another log on the fire and, with a quick smile for Freddy's benefit, returned to the bar. The sound of the log settling in the grate seemed to act as a prompt, because, almost like waking from a doze, Bert spoke again.

'I can't really tell you what it were like, Freddy. You've some idea, I know, but out there, it were like nowhere else. Working in that heat....' He shook his head. 'And the humidity. It took it out of us, even before t' guards started on us.' He drained his tankard. 'They weren't just Japs, you know. Some of them were Koreans, and they were evil little buggers an' all.'

Freddy caught Grace's eye and motioned to the tankards. She came across the room and picked them up without a word.

'Same again, please, Grace,' said Freddy.

She nodded and took them to the bar. Elsewhere, men glanced furtively towards Freddy and Bert, looking away quickly, ashamed of their curiosity. The only occupant of the tap room who seemed oblivious to the two men was a border collie that lay on the stone-flagged floor, panting in the heat from the fire.

Freddy took the two pints from Grace and handed her two shillings and fourpence. She nodded her thanks before returning to the bar.

'Disease an' all.' Bert carried on as if there had been no interruption. 'There were no end to what fevers you could catch in that bloody valley.' He began to list them, counting on his fingers. 'Malaria, pellagra, beriberi, dengue fever....' He hesitated, staring down at his hands. Then he continued. 'Black water fever, dysentery, cardiac beriberi.... That were a bugger. They said it were caused by eating polished rice. The husks had some vitamin or other in them, an' they were evidently too good for the likes of us. I expect the Japs kept 'em for 'emselves.' Suddenly he looked squarely at Freddy and said, 'This'll cap you, Freddy. Did you know that a man died for every sleeper that was laid? It's true.'

'I didn't know, Bert. That's horrible.' More to break the tension than for any other reason, Freddy pushed Bert's drink in front of him.

'Aye. Thanks, Freddy. It'll be my shout next.'

'Nobody's counting, Bert.'

'Even so.' Then, surprisingly, he asked, 'Did any of your lot escape, Freddy? I've been hearing about them escapes.'

'No, there was no time for that in the work camps. It was all work and sleep. I daresay we weren't physically up to it, either, although we must have been healthier than you blokes.'

Bert nodded his agreement. 'Some tried to escape. It were easy enough to disappear into the forest, but then what could you do? You either died of exhaustion or the Japs found you. Do you know what the punishment was for trying to escape?'

'No.' Freddy wasn't sure he wanted to hear it.

'They brought two lads back who'd made it as far as the nearest native village. Then they made us watch while they knelt 'em down and beheaded them.'

For a spell, they were both silent, and then, after a while, Harry called Last Orders. Grace came to them, and Freddy asked her for the same again. Bert appeared to have forgotten it was his round, but Freddy didn't care.

They drank together until Harry called Time, and that was when Freddy realised that Bert had drunk far more than he'd thought. He must have put a few away before Freddy arrived, and was now incapable of walking in a straight line.

'Come on, Bert,' said Freddy, hauling him to his feet. 'I'll see you home.' With Bert's arm around his shoulder, Freddy guided him towards the exit, stopping by the bar to speak to the landlord.

'Harry, will you do me a favour? Will you phone my wife for me, please?' He gave him the number. 'Just tell her I'm going to be late, will you? I'm seeing Bert home. He's a bit the worse for wear.'

'All right.' Harry nodded, seemingly preoccupied with the few drinkers who were slow to leave.

With some difficulty and less than coherent directions from Bert, Freddy helped him along the streets to his front door and applied the knocker. After a moment, the door opened, and Freddy addressed the woman who stood, surprised, in the doorway.

'Good evening, Mrs Whittaker. Bert's been relaxing, as you can see. I thought I'd better bring him home. I'm Freddy Hinchcliffe.'

'I know. Bert was talking about you earlier. You'd better bring him in.'

'I'll take him up to bed if you like.'

'Will you? It's upstairs, I'm afraid.' She looked careworn and apologetic.

'I'll manage. I'm a strong lad.' Even so, it was with some effort that he got Bert to the top of the stairs.

'Left off the landing,' called Mrs Whittaker, following them.

'Okay.'

The door opened on to a room with twin beds, and Freddy draped Bert gratefully across the nearer of the two.

'Thank you, Mr Hinchcliffe. I'm grateful.' Mrs Whittaker began unfastening her husband's collar and tie. 'I can manage now, thank you.'

Still regaining his breath, Freddy was relieved to hear it. 'Just tell me something, Mrs Whittaker. You said Bert had been talking about me. What was that about?'

'Oh, he said he had to tell somebody something, and you were the only man he could think of who would understand.' She shrugged dismissively. 'He's difficult to understand sometimes.'

'It was just pot luck I happened to go into the Shearer's Arms tonight. I think it might have been about something he read in a newspaper this morning.'

'Oh, that. Somebody had been murdered, I believe.'

'The commandant of the prison camp Bert was in,' prompted Freddy. 'He knew I was a POW. I think that's why he wanted to talk to me.'

'Oh, I didn't know that.' She walked out on to the landing and stopped. 'Would you like a cup of tea?'

Clearly, she wanted to talk, or she wouldn't be offering him tea at that time of night. 'All right. Yes, please.' Sylvia knew he was going to be late, so that was all right.

⊕◁╫◁╫⊁╫⊕

He let himself into the house quietly, stopping to stroke Thea and settle her in her basket. Then he crept upstairs, carefully avoiding the creaking stair. However, when he groped his way into the bedroom, he stopped when he heard Sylvia's voice. It was far from welcoming.

'There's no need to creep around. I've been waiting up for you. Freddy, where on earth have you been 'til this time? I've been worried to death.'

'Didn't Harry phone you?'

'Nobody phoned me. I thought you'd gone out for drink. I didn't expect you to drink the pub dry.'

'I didn't.' He sat on the bed to undress. 'I asked Harry to phone you. He obviously forgot.'

'Is that all you've got to say, that Harry, whoever he is, should have phoned me?'

'Listen, SP, I'll tell you about it in the morning. For now, just let me say that I'm sorry I caused you to worry. I will explain everything, but not now.'

'Well, I suppose that's something at least.' As she turned over to

97

face the wall, she said, 'And if you have anything else in mind, you can forget it.'

Freddy slipped into bed and pulled up the covers. 'Relax, SP. It's the last thing on my mind.' He laid his head gratefully on the pillow. 'The very last thing, I assure you.'

⸻

Sylvia must have been up well before Freddy, because his first sensation on waking was the welcome aroma of frying bacon. As the events of the previous evening returned, he pulled on his dressing gown and went downstairs to join her in the kitchen.

'Good morning, Freddy.' She looked up from the frying pan with an unexpected smile.

'Good morning, SP.' He kissed her lightly on the cheek, mindful that she was watching the bacon.

'Two eggs this morning,' she announced.

'Oh? Have Mrs Fearnley's chickens been laying away again?'

'Apparently, and I thought I'd give you a treat. I'm sorry I was so frosty last night. I thought about it, and you must have had a good reason for being so late.'

'I did, SP, and there's no need to be sorry. Let's both stop apologising, and I'll explain everything when we sit down.'

Later, at the table, he asked, 'Do you know Bert Whittaker?'

'Not really. I remember him at elementary school, but he was older than me, and I saw very little of him after that. I believe he came back from the Far East in a bad way.'

Freddy nodded. 'He was a POW. He was telling me about it last night. I had to take him home.'

'I thought he never spoke about it.'

'He did last night. He told me some terrible things. You know, SP, what Bailey and I experienced in Poland was nothing compared with what Bert and the others suffered on the railway. It wasn't just disease, hunger and brutality, either. There was mental torture.'

'I probably don't want to hear this, but what do you mean by mental torture?'

Freddy buttered a piece of toast, recalling the conversation that had taken place late that night. 'Do you remember how important the mail was to us, SP.' He waved the question aside. 'Of course you do. It was the basis of our relationship.'

'Did they get mail?'

'Not for about two years. Then, when it came, Colonel Osako, the Commandant, told them that because they hadn't worked hard enough he was going to punish them. To do that, he made a pile of the letters and made them watch while he set fire to them.'

Sylvia stared at him, open-mouthed. 'What a monster.'

'He was.'

'Was he brought to justice?'

'Yes, a few days ago. His body was found in a Tokyo hotel room.'

'What a horrible business.'

'I can't argue with that, SP, and it doesn't end there. Believe it or not, Bert and his wife have to sleep in single beds because of his violent nightmares. She woke up one night and he was trying to strangle her.'

'Horrible. I feel so sorry for both of them, and I'm glad you took him home.'

'Yes, it's as much as anyone can do.' Freddy laid his knife and fork on his plate, remembering his own state of mind after liberation.' It'll take more than a kindly father-in-law and a spot of fly fishing to lay Bert's demons to rest.' Illogically, another thought occurred to him. Speaking of which....'

'What?'

'I'm going to need a spell of fly fishing after tonight.'

'What's happening tonight?'

'I'm supposed to be speaking to Joan Curwen. Remember?'

16

Freddy had intended approaching Joan after the rehearsal, when they could speak privately and, hopefully, in a civilised way, and that had remained his intention up to the moment when fate unexpectedly seized control of the proceedings.

Having established his *bona fides* as a man of creativity, Erik the Not Quite Ready was revealing a new dance of his invention.

ERIK   This is not one of your preening, courtly frolics, ladies, but a dance for ordinary folk. I have called it 'The Folk's Trot,' and I believe people will dance these steps for centuries to come.

ELGA   What a perfectly silly name. I doubt it will be remembered beyond the year, never mind the century.

ERIK   At least give it a try, good lady. Put your right hand in mine, and your left on my right arm. Now move backward on your right foot.

At this point, Joan broke away, clearly displeased. 'Bailey,' she demanded, '*must* you dance so close to me?'

'Of course I must, you infuriating harpy! It's not a mincing minuet, you know. It's a fucking foxtrot!'

'You really are the limit, Bailey. All you seem to do when you're not posturing is to leer at me like a lascivious schoolboy!'

'Oh, give your imagination a rest, Joan. You really do have an exalted opinion of your feminine charm, and goodness knows where you've been hiding it. As for lusting after you.... Frankly, my dear, I wouldn't touch you with... with Freddy's, never mind mine!'

Before Freddy could derive any comfort or relief from that disclosure, the cast, who had been following the exchange in wonder and disbelief, now reacted to Bailey's protestation with immoderate laughter, a development that proved to be the ultimate insult.

'I've had enough of you all!' Joan swung around with one hand outstretched in accusation. 'I'm sick of you all talking behind my back. I've heard you! Well, let me tell you, I have more ability than the rest of you put together! I came into this show because you needed a leading lady. I took pity on you, and now, all I can say is....' At this point, she appeared to be at a loss for a suitably wounding insult. Instead, she said, 'You can carry on without me!' With that, she made her exit.

Freddy watched her go. 'I don't suppose she'd change her mind,' he said.

'You could go after her,' suggested Sylvia without discernible enthusiasm.

'I should,' agreed Freddy. 'It would be polite, after all.'

He found her in the cloakroom, buttoning her coat.

'Joan,' he began, 'I've come to say....' But one look from her persuaded him to leave the rest unspoken.

'No, Freddy,' she said with barely-contained anger, 'you will not persuade me to take any further part in your show.' Waving him aside and mustering what dignity remained, she left the building, closing the door firmly behind her.

He re-joined a cast that clearly expected him to say something, so he motioned everyone to listen.

'I imagine you all spotted the moment when the scene departed from the script,' he said, making a palms-downward gesture to discourage laughter. 'I can tell you now that Joan has confirmed that she will no longer be available.' He waited for them to settle again, and went on. 'Finding a new leading lady will be up to Sylvia and me, and I'll let you know as soon as we have anything to report. Meanwhile, this evening's disturbance has been unsettling, to say the least, and I think the best course is to end the rehearsal now and reconvene on Monday. Thank you all for attending.'

Eventually, only Freddy, Sylvia and Bailey remained. Bailey was humbly apologetic.

'Freddy, old friend, I'm beside myself. I simply lost my composure. It's unforgivable.'

'It wasn't your fault, Bailey. I had it in mind to say something to her tonight that might easily have had the same result.'

Bailey's guilt was only partly assuaged. 'Even so,' he said, 'I apologise too, 'for referring to your personal equipment, your faithful friend, in that cavalier manner. It was a spontaneous outpouring, I assure you. I prefer to rehearse my tantrums, as you can imagine, for maximum effect, but she caught me at an unguarded moment.'

'Bailey,' said Freddy, laying a hand on his friend's shoulder, 'you are cleared of all blame. And, for what it's worth, my faithful friend agrees with me.'

'Very decent of you both, old man.'

'Not in the least.' The two men shook hands.

Meanwhile, Sylvia had been thinking.

'We're relieved of a problem,' she said. 'Let's be honest about that, but where do we look for an Elga. I wonder if Marjorie Bentham could do it.'

'I'm afraid not.' Freddy had also wondered about Marjorie, but had reluctantly dismissed the idea. 'She's a mezzo-soprano. She hasn't the upper register that's needed for Elga.'

'Wait a minute, folks.' Now absolved of blame, Bailey was once more his ebullient self. 'What about Elaine? She has the soprano range and everything else that's needed, and you could cast Marjorie as Ardith.'

Freddy had only to give Bailey's suggestion a second's consideration. 'Bailey,' he said, 'every now and again you pour forth pure and indisputable wisdom.'

'My dear old thing.'

'No, I mean every word.'

'Good,' said Sylvia, keeping the conversation practical, 'so that's settled.'

'It will be,' said Freddy, 'with the co-operation of Marjorie and Elaine. Let's not take that for granted.'

17

The Dalesmen's services were required the next evening at a twenty-first birthday celebration in Northallerton, so it wasn't until Sunday that Freddy was able to speak to Elaine and Marjorie. Thankfully, they both agreed to the arrangement. Marjorie was particularly enthusiastic, unlike Elaine, who seemed somewhat reserved, a matter that continued to puzzle Freddy until that evening, when Bailey joined Sylvia and him for dinner.

'I'm afraid I'm indirectly responsible for that,' he confessed.

'How are you responsible? I thought Cupid had the drop on you two.'

'It only happened yesterday, Freddy. Basically, Elaine wants some time apart from me so that she can decide how she feels.'

Freddy put down the steel and the carving knife he'd been sharpening and asked, 'How she feels about what?'

'About an ex-con who hadn't quite got around to telling her about his chequered past. I was going to tell her. I just got the timing wrong.'

'So, how,' asked Sylvia, putting a tureen of potatoes on the table, 'did she find out?'

'There's an unsavoury blighter, a rotten turnip called Geoffrey, who's carrying the torch for Elaine....' He went on to tell them about the collision and about Geoffrey's repeated and unwanted attentions.

'Surely not.'

'I'm afraid so, Sylvia. And that's not all. As a copper, he has access to certain information and he's used that to bring Elaine up to date about my lurid past.'

'Six months on the Isle of Wight and that sort of thing?'

'Actually, it was twelve months in Borstal, Sylvia. I know I told you I did a spell in prison, but, I mean to say, a chap can't cut much of a dash with a sentence in a place that's not even for grown-up criminals.'

'If you say so, Bailey. Do help yourself to more runner beans, by the way.'

'You disappoint me, Bailey,' said Freddy, passing the runner beans. 'Do you mean you never opened the batting for "D" wing in Parkhurst?'

'Don't be cruel, Freddy. Bailey's having a crisis, and it's up to us to be sympathetic and helpful.'

'I'm used to it, Sylvia, and I was the one who wove the tangled web in the first place. No, Freddy, there probably isn't an exercise yard in any prison in this country that could accommodate a cricket match. I did open the batting, however, in Borstal. I mean to say, punishment or not, I felt obliged to do it. After all, it doesn't do to hide one's light under a bushel, you know.'

'I can't see you ever doing that, Bailey.'

'But what's to be done about Elaine and Bailey, Freddy?' As ever, Sylvia was inclined to be practical.

Freddy had been looking thoughtful, and now he said, 'I have an idea.'

'Trot out your idea, old man.' Bailey was instantly receptive.

'Yes, Freddy, don't keep us in suspense.'

'All in good time. Now, Bailey, I can see a way of bringing this Geoffrey character to heel. I need to speak, first, with Sylvia's father, but will you leave Elaine to me?'

⚜

Freddy turned from the piano and said, 'You know these numbers already, Elaine.'

'I've heard Joan sing them often enough. It's just the libretto I need to learn.' The two were alone, the rehearsal wasn't due to begin for another forty-five minutes or so, and it seemed to Freddy a good opportunity for a chat with Elaine, who was still withdrawn.

'Elaine,' he said, 'I know there's a problem between you and

104

Bailey, because he's upset about it too, and before you tell me to mind my own business, let me say that if it affects the show, it is my business.'

'I suppose it is.'

'Yes. He told me about this friend of yours, the one who filled you in about Bailey's past.'

'Geoffrey? He's no friend of mine.'

'I'm glad to hear it. Look, Elaine, what is the problem, exactly? Is it simply that Bailey has a record, or is it that you feel he should have told you about it before now?'

She took a seat by the piano, silent for a moment. Then she said, 'I really don't know. Every time I think about it I seem to go round in circles.'

'But the fact that you keep thinking about it suggests that you still have feelings for Bailey.'

'Of course I do. It was just such an awful shock.'

'Which is, presumably, what this Geoffrey character intended?'

'I suppose so. I've never met anyone quite like him, and I hope I never shall again.'

'Good. Let me tell you something, Elaine.'

'I'm listening.' She gave him a half smile, which was encouraging.

'I first met Bailey during the war, when we were prisoners in Poland, but I really got to know him on a five-hundred-mile hike across Poland and Germany.'

'Was it really as far as that?' There was incredulity in her eyes.

'No, it was a little further than that, but I was talking in round figures, not that it was the distance alone that made it so awful. We were hungrier than you can imagine, and it all happened during the severest winter anyone could remember. Now, the reason I'm telling you this is because it's in such circumstances and conditions that you really get to know someone. No one can maintain any kind of pretence when hunger, cold and exhaustion are his main preoccupations.'

'And you got to know Bailey?' Her tone suggested that she was keen to hear him out.

'Absolutely. I learned about his past and his spell in... penal servitude. He'd had an awful start in life and he'd made mistakes, but if one thing came through with total clarity, it was his intention to lead an honest life. I believed him then and I still do.'

'I just wish he'd told me.' She looked down at her hands.

'He was going to. If your informant hadn't spoken first, Bailey would have told you. I know that.'

'How can you know that?'

'Because I know Bailey better than I know anyone, except perhaps Sylvia. He couldn't tell you earlier, because you didn't know each other well enough. It would have put you off straight away.'

'It probably would,' she agreed.

'He has a wonderfully generous nature, you know.'

She nodded.

'When Sylvia and I were about to meet, having only ever communicated by mail, Bailey knew our date might be precarious, and he helped me organise it to the last detail.'

'So you and Sylvia got to know each other through writing letters?'

'Yes, I'd lost my family in the Blitz, I'd been taken prisoner, and I was at rock bottom when I got Sylvia's first letter. Pretty soon, her letters were making life worth living, and she's been doing the same ever since.'

'That's the most romantic thing I've ever heard.'

'I'm glad. And, you know, that first date was made perfect by Bailey's intervention. He even left a request with the bandleader at the night club. It was the song that Sylvia and I had come to think of as our own: "All the Things You Are", and it put the finishing touch to the most magical evening ever.'

Elaine was blinking hard, so Freddy handed her the handkerchief from his breast pocket.

'Thank you.'

'Bailey came home from his five years in Poland to find a summons against him. It was nothing serious. Apparently, at the time he left for France, he owed some money to the taxman.' He shrugged. 'It wasn't a particularly large sum; maybe four or five pounds, but he had to attend the City Magistrate's Court, and I spoke up for him as a character witness. As I recall, I told the magistrate that I would trust Bailey with my life. I meant it then, and I mean it now.'

Elaine stood up and asked, 'Will you excuse me?'

'Of course.' The cast would start arriving soon, anyway, and he reckoned he'd put Bailey's case quite convincingly. He turned again to the score and took out his pencil. There was something he needed to remind the chorus about, but before he could mark the score, he found Sylvia at his elbow.

'Freddy,' she said, 'I've just seen Elaine with tears in her eyes. What have you said to her?'

'Oh, I just told her to sort her ideas out and stop giving Bailey a hard time.'

She stared at him for a moment, and then shook her head despairingly. 'I don't believe you, Freddy.'

After the rehearsal, they were careful to avoid the cloakroom that served as the male dressing room. Bailey and Elaine had slipped in there when the rest of the cast had gone and, as Sylvia pointed out, there had to be a result of some kind.

Eventually, the two emerged: Elaine red-eyed but visibly happy, and Bailey with his usual aura of self-assured bonhomie. Freddy and Sylvia were also relieved.

⚜

Now reconciled, Bailey and Elaine arranged a meeting with Geoffrey, who arrived at Elaine's cottage both surprised and inquisitive. He hesitated, however, when he saw Bailey.

'Relax, old man,' Bailey assured him. 'I'd be a fool to engage in fisticuffs with the law. No, I simply want a chat.'

'Why?'

'Why not, old thing? I mean, there's absolutely no harm done.' He beamed at Elaine, who returned the gesture.

By this time, Geoffrey looked less apprehensive but still disinclined to be friendly. 'What do you want to talk about?'

'Relationships, old sport. I mean, for instance, how well do you know your superiors, your senior officers?'

'What do you mean?'

'It's a fairly easy question, surely. How well do you know your inspector, your superintendent or, for that matter, the Chief

Constable? How might they react, for example, if you turned up at the station with a record number of bookings for motoring offences and maybe the occasional Driving under the Affluence of Incohol?' He smiled at Geoffrey's bewilderment and went on. 'More to the point, old boy, how might they react when informed that a certain junior officer had used Criminal Records for his own nefarious purposes? Hardly the done thing, what?'

Now that he understood the purpose of the meeting, Geoffrey's attitude hardened. 'Would you really expect them to listen to an old lag like you?' He glanced at Elaine but, getting no reaction, concentrated on Bailey.

'Not for one moment, old soul, but just suppose the information were supplied by a respected citizen, say, a Justice of the Peace? How then, my hapless, flat-footed friend?'

'But how...? I mean, how you come to know a JP?'

'I refer to the father of a good friend, who considers your behaviour reprehensible, to say the least.'

'Have you spoken to him?'

'Of course I have.'

'Have you named me?' Geoffrey was now rattled.

'Not yet, old thing, but who knows?' He chuckled briefly. 'Now, the rest of the North Riding Force apart, how do you think your colleagues, the bobbies on the beat, as 't were, might feel about a man who insists on pestering a lady who cares naught for him and would prefer whole-heartedly to be left in peace? I'm talking about a man who appears frequently on her doorstep, even though the message would be clear to anyone less fixated that he is as welcome as an icy blast in a nudist camp.'

Geoffrey's resolve appeared to have vanished. In a more subdued tone, he asked, 'What are you suggesting, Bailey?'

'Only that you're in a precarious situation. If you don't want the good Justice of the Peace and me to spill the beans, I suggest you leave now and make this your last visit. I promise you that if you don't, you will soon be handing in your warrant card, notebook, whistle and truncheon as a prelude to swelling the ranks of the unemployed.'

It was a telling argument and one that bore the desired result.

When the door closed behind Geoffrey, and they were alone, Elaine wrapped her arms around Bailey and said, 'You were magnificent.'

'You're too kind, dear one, but all credit must go to Freddy. It was he who planned this, after all.'

'Suddenly we owe a lot to Freddy.'

'I've been in his debt for some time.'

'What do you mean?'

'I'll tell you about it one day, when conversation is flagging.'

'That'll be the day, Bailey.'

18

'I've been thinking, Freddy. We really should take Thea to see Mr Womersley again; at least, one of us should. I don't mind taking her if you're too busy.' Sylvia dropped two more slices of toast into the rack and sat down, casually awaiting his response.

After a pause, he said, 'It's good of you to offer, SP, but I'm free this afternoon, so I could do it.'

'Good. Let's both go.'

'Yes, let's. It's much better that way.' He took a slice of toast and buttered it before voicing his unease. 'I just hope he won't be upset all the time,' he said. 'You know what he was like last time we went.'

She nodded. 'It's bound to affect him, seeing Thea again.' She was smiling at him, knowing what was going through his mind. 'It really bothers you, doesn't it? I'm quite happy to take her on my own.'

'No, no,' he insisted, 'I'm not going to dodge the column, but it will be better with you there.'

'Why?'

'You're much more at ease with him than I am. I feel sorry for the poor old boy; of course I do, but I still find it difficult.'

'But you spent an evening in the pub with Bert Whittaker pouring his heart out to you. Why was that so different?'

'You weren't there, SP. Bert didn't pour his heart out at all. I think he's lost the ability to do that, as anyone might who'd experienced the same. No, SP, all he did was deliver a catalogue of horror, and all in a monotone, scarcely more than a whisper.'

Reaching across the table and taking his hand, she said quite seriously, 'Men don't cry in Hull, do they?'

'Not so as you'd notice.'

'As a general rule, they don't in Wensleydale, but Mr Womersley is a frail old man who's had to give up his home, he's made to feel unwelcome by his son-in-law, and he's lost the loving companion who meant so much to him.'

Freddy nodded. 'You're absolutely right, SP. I'll work on it.'

'I knew you would.'

'Of course you did. You're my personal Jiminy Cricket, my official conscience.'

Her fingers tightened on his hand. 'I'm not criticising you, Freddy. I'm only trying to help you.'

'I know.'

'Oh, by the way.' She released his hand as she remembered something. 'Bring a camera.'

'Why do I need a camera, SP?'

'It could be useful as a diversion. You never know.'

⟳⟳⟳

On the road to Hawes that afternoon, Freddy slowed down and parked at the side of the road.

Sylvia asked, 'Why have we stopped?

'Look up there,' he said, pointing to a prominent hill on the right. 'That's Lady Hill.'

'Why is it called that?'

'Search me. It's been called that for ever.'

'Well,' he said, releasing the handbrake and moving off again, 'it looks to me like a special kind of place. You know, I think it's been there since before the ice age, and when the glaciers moved down here they swept past it, leaving it untouched. It has to be pretty special to have been spared like that.'

'How do you know that's what happened?'

'I don't, but when things happened so long ago, you can make them anything you want them to be. I mean, no one's going to say, "You're quite wrong. I was there, and it didn't happen at all like that." '

They drove a little further, and he said, 'I wonder what kind of trees they are.'

'Which trees?'

'The trees on Lady Hill.'

'Oh, I can tell you what the very tall ones are. They're Scots pines.'

'What on earth are they doing in England?'

'They used to grow all over the British Isles at one time. I know that because one of my class teachers at junior school was a whale on flora and fauna.'

'You know, SP,' he said, slowing down to enter Hawes, 'you're a fund of information. I must remember to keep asking you about things. I could learn a lot that way.'

'As you grow older, you'll find that grown-ups are not infallible, Freddy,' she cautioned. 'I don't know everything.'

'Oh, heck.'

'But I do know that we've passed Mrs Jagger's house.'

'That's another thing, SP. You know the way to places much better than I do.'

'Mm. Can we turn round?'

'Yes, just as soon as the traffic clears ahead.' He waited until two vehicles had passed in the opposite direction, and turned in the road. 'Maybe that was a what-do-you-call-it, a Freudian slip, driving past the house,' he suggested.

'I prefer to think it was just your terrible sense of direction, Freddy. It's the next street on the right, by the way.'

With Sylvia's help, he located the house and parked outside it. Sylvia opened her door and stepped out with Thea.

After a short time, Mrs Jagger answered Freddy's knock.

'I hope it's convenient, Mrs Jagger. We have to arrange these things when I have a quiet spell and, as you're not on the phone....'

'It's fine. My dad's always here, anyway, and it's him you've come to see. Come in, both of you.'

Mr Womersley was in his armchair, smartly dressed as usual. When he saw Thea, he held out his arms to welcome her and the familiar tears of joy came to his eyes.

'How are you, Mr Womersley?' Sylvia knelt beside his chair as Thea came forward to greet her old master.

'I'm very fair, love, an' thanks for bringing Thea. It's a right treat to see her again.' He leant forward to stroke his old friend and scratch her behind her ears.

'She's a very happy dog,' Freddy told him. 'I thought you'd like to know.'

'Aye, she's found a good home with you an' your missis. I'm right pleased about that.'

'Mr Womersley,' said Sylvia, 'would you like Freddy to take your photograph with Thea, and then you can keep it with you all the time?'

He looked at Freddy, seeing the camera for the first time, and then back to Sylvia. 'Oh, that'd be grand, love.'

'Well, you'd better dry those tears and look happy for the photo.' Turning to Freddy, she asked, 'Do you want to take it in here or outside?'

'Outside would be better, if that's all right with you, Mr Womersley.'

'Aye, I can come outside.' He prised himself out of his chair, panting with the exertion.

'Are you all right, Mr Womersley?' Sylvia took his arm to support him.

'Aye, I'll be all right.'

'I'll get you a chair, Dad,' said Mrs Jagger, picking up an oak dining chair.

'Now, I'll just let you get your breath back,' said Sylvia, helping him on to his chair.

'Eh,' he panted, 'I'll be all right.'

'Do you want Thea on your lap for the picture, or sitting beside you?'

'Nay, I can't lift her up.'

'I can. Just a minute.' Sylvia picked up Thea by her chest and hind quarters and laid her gently on Mr Womersley's lap.

Freddy waited and, when Thea raised her head, as she inevitably would, to look Mr Womersley in the eye, he took the photograph.

❦❦❦❦❦

'That was magical,' said Sylvia. 'He'll have a lovely picture to keep beside him.' She waited for a response and found Freddy unusually silent. 'Don't you think so, Freddy?'

'Sorry, SP, I was miles away.'

'What were you thinking about?'

'I was just congratulating myself on marrying a remarkable woman. You were wonderful back there.'

'Oh, that.' She waved the compliment aside, saying, 'It's a woman thing.'

'I believe you.'

'You should. I'm a fund of knowledge, after all.'

'Agreed.'

After a while, she said, 'Freddy?'

'What?'

'Didn't you tell me that your training as a telegraphist/air-gunner included navigation?'

'Elementary navigation. It was in case the observer was killed or wounded.'

'Hm.' The information appeared to afford food for thought. 'Did they ever have to rely on your navigational skills?'

'No.'

'It's perhaps as well. I'd been wondering if that was how you came to ditch in the Med., but evidently not.'

'Oh, very funny, SP. That was below the belt.'

'I'm sorry, darling.'

'It'll take more than a glib apology. My feelings are in tatters. I'm going to exact a penance for that. Just see if I don't.'

'And I've a pretty good idea what that penance will be.'

'Well, you can consider your card marked.'

As they approached Lady Hill, Sylvia was suddenly reminded of something. 'I just remembered, Freddy, about Lady Hill—'

'It's no good changing the subject.'

'I'm not; at least, I am, but it's something genuine.'

'All right, let's hear it.'

'Well, as far as I can make out, Lady Hill was terraced at one time, so that peasant farmers could have a share of the land. It couldn't have been much fun, though, trudging up there every day to labour and toil.'

'How very prosaic. I prefer to think of it as something altogether more mystical, like the Enchanted Place in *The House at Pooh Corner*.'

'As I remember it, the Enchanted Place had "sixty-something trees" and, whilst Lady Hill has quite a lot, they can't possibly add up to sixty-something.'

'You're being too literal, SP. This has nothing to do with Christopher Robin and Winnie-the-Pooh. I only said it was *like* the Enchanted Place, but it can actually be *our* enchanted place. I mean, we had the new moon, didn't we? And our special song: "All the Things You Are". We had our special trysting place, as well, in Trafalgar Square, so why not an enchanted place? We could bring a picnic and Thea, and we could climb up there and see what it does for us.'

'If you insist.' She was silent for a moment, and then she asked, 'Is that the penance you had in mind?'

'No, it's purely for enjoyment.' He added hastily, 'So is the penance I have in mind.'

'I had an idea it might be.'

Further along the road, he said, 'SP?'

'I'm still here, Freddy.'

'Good. Do you imagine these visits might be unsettling for Thea? I mean, seeing Mr Womersley and then being taken away again.'

'No, I think you're worrying unnecessarily. She's simply being taken by two of her favourite people to visit another of her favourite people. It's a treat.'

'Are you sure?'

'I'll ask her, if you like.'

'I thought you didn't talk to her.'

'Of course I talk to her.'

'Really?'

'You'd be surprised at some of the things we discuss when you're in your darkroom or away on your adventures.'

It was a comforting thought, although Freddy had plenty to think about, including the proposed picnic on Lady Hill.

19

Of the three photographs Freddy had taken of Mr Womersley with Thea, one appealed to him particularly. It was because they seemed to be looking at each other so intently that they might have been in conversation. He found it so engaging that he enlarged it to ten inches by eight and mounted it on card for framing. It was just frustrating that he wouldn't be free to deliver it until the end of the week.

Sylvia was almost as impatient as he was, although she knew the week ahead was a busy one. Even so, she couldn't help asking, 'What are you doing this afternoon?'

'I'm photographing a tortoise, and I need time for that.' He'd only done it once, and the frustration had lingered in his memory long after the event.

'Good luck, Freddy. You'll need lots of patience. I once had a tortoise, and he did absolutely everything in his own time.'

So, with that encouraging advice, he set out for Leyburn, where the Garside family and, more importantly, their tortoise Jerry lived. He'd chosen to make it a visit rather than have Jerry come to him, because he reckoned that, being on his own territory and therefore, hopefully, more confident, Jerry might be inclined to co-operate.

Surprisingly, he found the house with little difficulty, and Mrs Garside, a pleasant young woman of about thirty, welcomed him in.

'Come through and meet Jerry, Mr Hinchcliffe. By the way, would you like a cup of tea?'

'Yes, please, I'd like that very much, Mrs Garside.'

'Right, I'll take you through to Jerry and put the kettle on while you're getting acquainted.'

She led him through the house to the garden shed, where she reached into an enclosure and retrieved the subject of the photo session, setting him down on the lawn.

'Hello, Jerry.' Freddy addressed the protruding head, which gave him a quick look of appraisal before withdrawing into the shell. 'Jerry,' coaxed Freddy, 'don't be shy. I've made a special journey to meet you.' He felt quite ridiculous, reasoning with a camera-shy reptile, but they were alone, so at least he wasn't embarrassed. He tried again.

'Come out, Jerry. I can see you. I know where you're hiding.' On reflection, that probably wasn't a wise thing to say. In hiding, the tortoise no doubt imagined it was out of sight and therefore safe from predators, annoying children and intrusive photographers. He tried another approach.

'I wonder where that Jerry is. I'd really like to meet him.' Again, there was no response. 'Jerry,' he said finally, 'stop playing games. I haven't got all bloody day.'

'Is he holding out on you?' Mrs Garside appeared with the tea things on a tray, which she set down on the lawn. 'Milk and sugar, Mr Hinchcliffe?'

'Just milk, no sugar, thank you, Mrs Garside.' It was unfortunate that she'd heard him swearing at her tortoise. 'Yes, I'm afraid he's quite resolute.'

'He'll come out again. We mustn't hurry him. Tortoises take their time over everything.'

'Mrs Garside, If you don't mind my saying so, "Jerry" seems an unusual name for a tortoise.'

'It must seem so,' she agreed. 'My little girl gave him that name. She thought he looked like an upside-down chamber pot.'

'Quite understandable.'

'We have to be open-minded about these things.' She poured the tea and added milk, saying, 'Don't look now, but we have a development.'

Out of the corner of his eye, Freddy could see Jerry's head emerging gradually and slowly. Its gaze seemed to be fixed on the tea things.   Freddy took a light reading and set the exposure.

Suddenly, Jerry seemed to develop a sense of urgency. All reticence forgotten, he journeyed towards the tea tray, like a battleship about to engage the enemy.

'I think it's the teapot he's after,' said Mrs Garside, steadying it with her hand.

'What has he got against the teapot?'

'He thinks it's a rival tortoise.'

'Surely not.'

'Watch him. He'll butt it.'

'What?'

'It's how they fight, Mr Hinchcliffe. They butt their enemies, like rams and stags.'

'Well, I never.' Freddy lay on the lawn and photographed his subject laying down the law to the upstart teapot. Jerry really believed it was a rival reptile, and he'd reasoned with him as if he were an intelligent creature. The only consolation was that the pictures would be good.

'He's never done this with the teapot,' said Mrs Garside. 'It's as well it's got the cosy on it. I wouldn't want him to burn himself.'

'What sort of thing does he usually attack?'

'Oh, gum boots, the children's toys…. You should see him with a football. My husband says if he was a bit faster, Middlesbrough would sign him.'

It had been a fascinating session, and Freddy had learned a great deal about the species. One question had occurred to him, however, that he'd been reluctant to ask Mrs Garside, and so he saved it for Sylvia on his return.

'SP,' he asked, 'how is it possible to tell a male tortoise from a female? I mean, everything's usually tucked up inside the shell, isn't it?'

'I suppose so, but the female has a hollow in the back of her shell. It's to accommodate the male when they… when….' Inspiration came to her. 'If the female upsets the male, maybe by making fun of his sense of direction, and she has to serve a penance….'

'So it's for the purpose of mating.'

'Yes.' She smiled self-consciously.

'You know, SP, we need to find a word you can use without tying yourself in knots with embarrassment.' He thought for a few seconds and asked, 'What about "nooky"?'

She eyed him unsurely. 'Is it a proper word?'

'Is that important?'

'Yes, it needs to be a word that's in the dictionary. Nothing smutty.'

'As single young men,' he assured her, 'we used it frequently. Of course, as kriegies, we tried not to think about nooky. That would have amounted to masochism, but yes, it's a proper word used in the highest echelons of society, I'm told.' As an afterthought, he said, 'We could call it *Geschlechtsverkehr.*'

'Now you're making fun of me. Is that the German word for you-know-what?'

'Yes, but it's not what they call it.'

'I don't want to know. I'll settle for "nooky".'

'Bravely done, SP.'

<hr />

By Friday evening, Freddy had decided to take the picture to Mr Womersley. His son-in-law would most likely be at home, but that couldn't be helped. He would leave Thea in the car so that Mr Womersley could see her. If Mr Jagger didn't like it, it was just too bad.

Loyal as ever, Sylvia went with him, with Thea travelling, as usual, between her feet.

Since his conversation with Sylvia, Freddy had given Mr Womersley's predicament much thought and, when they arrived at the Jaggers' home, he walked up to the door composed and ready to deal with the kind of emotional scene he'd come to expect.

Neither of them was prepared, however, for what happened next because, instead of Mrs Jagger, her husband opened the door.

'Oh, it's you,' he said. 'You'd best come in. I expect you want to pay your respects.'

'Our respects?' Freddy was thrown for the moment.

'I thought you must have heard. The old man died on Tuesday. Isn't that why you've come?'

'No, we'd no idea. Look, we don't want to intrude. We came to deliver this photograph of Mr Womersley and Thea.'

Mrs Jagger's voice came from inside. 'Who is it, Arthur?'

'It's them as took your father's dog. They've brought a photo for him. They didn't know about Tuesday.'

'Oh, bring them in.'

'We'll just have a quick word,' said Freddy. Stepping inside, he found Mrs Jagger in her father's old armchair. Her eyes were red and swollen.

'It were good of you to do this,' she said, accepting the photograph. 'He were right looking forward to seeing it.'

'We don't want to intrude on your grief, Mrs Jagger,' said Sylvia, 'but if there's anything I can do, any cooking, perhaps, I'm only too ready.'

'Nay, I can manage. Thank you all the same.' She looked at the photograph and it brought fresh tears to her eyes. 'It were his heart, you know. He could never have taken Thea for walks, but I could have done that if it hadn't been for '*im*.' She inclined her head towards the far end of the room, where her husband sat reading his newspaper. 'It meant a lot to my dad that she was happy and settled with you.'

'When's the funeral, Mrs Jagger?' Freddy had a reason for asking.

'It's next Friday at St Peter and St Paul's. Ten o'clock, if you can make it.'

'We'll certainly do our best.'

As they passed Mr Jagger on the way out, it took all Freddy's self-control to bid him a civil good night.

They drove into the Main Street, and Sylvia asked, 'Do you want to go to the funeral?'

'Yes, I do, but I'll speak to the vicar first, and get his permission to take Thea. I think Mr Womersley would have liked that.'

'I'm sure he would.'

They were so preoccupied that neither of them commented on Lady Hill as they passed it, even though it was still high on Freddy's agenda.

20

Accordingly, Freddy, Sylvia and Thea paid their last respects to Mr Womersley, both in church and at his graveside. Their attendance gave some comfort to Mrs Jagger, at the same time causing her husband obvious irritation, a development that Freddy noted with mischievous satisfaction.

'What I can't understand,' said Sylvia afterwards, 'is what she saw in him in the first place.'

'You could say that about a great many couples, couldn't you? I suppose people don't always know the extent of what they're getting.'

'They don't all know each other as well as we did,' she agreed.

It was the Monday after the funeral, and they had taken advantage of a free afternoon and a welcome break in the weather to visit Lady Hill.

'We can't be far from the bridge.'

'What bridge is that, SP?'

'The footbridge across the river. You'd forgotten about the river, hadn't you?'

'I've been looking at the wider plan. I leave the details to you, SP.'

'You *had* forgotten about it, hadn't you?'

'Yes.'

'I thought so. Well, if you can find a good place, you need to pull in and park.'

Obedient as ever when Sylvia was in charge, he drove on to the grassy bank and switched off the engine.

'Right. I'll bring Thea if you'll carry the food and the rug.'

'Yes, m' lady.' He followed her across the road, across the meadow, over the stile and down to the wooden footbridge, which he'd never noticed before. It seemed to be strong enough, however, so he led the way, and was partway across when Sylvia said, 'Thea doesn't like it, Freddy. She won't set foot on it.'

He wondered for a moment if Thea knew something they didn't, but then he dismissed the thought. She had her qualities but she was no structural engineer. 'If you can take the food,' he suggested, 'I'll carry Thea and the rug.'

'If you're sure.' She took the bag from him and handed over Thea's lead. He slung the rug over his shoulder and picked up Thea.

'By Jove, Thea,' he said, 'you're going on a diet tomorrow.' Even so, he carried her to the far bank, where he set her down again.

'If we're lucky,' Sylvia told him, 'we may see a black rabbit. They used to catch them here for the Tsar of Russia. Mind you, I suppose they'll have mated with the other wild rabbits by this time, and the strain will be lost.'

'What did the Tsar want them for?'

'Their pelts, I imagine. I'm sure it wouldn't be for food. I mean, I can't think they tasted very different from any other rabbit.'

'I'd never eaten rabbit until I stayed with your mum and dad after I was repatriated.'

'I don't suppose there are many rabbits on the streets of Hull.'

'There's no shortage of fish,' he told her defensively.

'Lovely.' Clearly, she was saving her breath for the ascent. Eventually, however, she felt compelled to say, 'I don't know why I allowed you to talk me into this, Freddy.'

'You'll appreciate it when we get to the top,' he assured her.

'I'm glad you told me that,' she panted.

'Stop and have a breather. Give me the bag and take Thea. She can pull you up the hill.'

Sylvia stopped gratefully and exchanged loads. 'Go on, Thea,' she urged. 'Pull me up the hill. You could find a black rabbit.'

Eventually they reached the crest of the hill, and Sylvia subsided on to the ground. 'It's wonderful now we're here,' she admitted. 'You know, these Scots pines were planted for Queen Victoria's Diamond Jubilee or Golden Jubilee, or one of those things.'

Freddy nodded. 'Life was a string of jubilees for her. I wonder she ever got anything done.'

Sylvia was searching the bag. 'Ah, here it is.'

'Here what is?'

'Thea's bowl.' Having found it, she poured water into it, and Thea lapped gratefully.

'That's a good idea. Let's have a wet, SP.'

'All right.' She took out two enamel mugs, a Thermos flask and a medicine bottle containing milk. 'Can you take the cork out of the milk bottle without spilling it?'

Freddy eyed it speculatively. 'It sounds like an initiative test,' he said.

'If I do it, the milk goes everywhere.'

'Hm.' He held the bottle against the ground and eased the cork out.

'That was clever, almost as good as when you opened the champagne that night in London.'

'Yes.' His thoughts went back briefly to that night. 'A lot of things have happened since then.'

'Lots of things,' she agreed.

'You were a virgin then.'

'I was a virgin when I stood at the altar, small thanks to you.'

'And for the following week, as I recall.'

'You'll never forget that, will you?' The thought seemed to lead to another, because she smiled bashfully and said, 'My mother gave me a little talk the night before the wedding. It was really embarrassing. You know, I've wondered, sometimes, how Audrey and I ever happened.'

'Was it Audrey who told you about the birds and the bees?'

'No, it was Ruth, a girl I met on the voyage to Malta. She'd... you know... in an Anderson shelter in Dulwich.'

'I wonder how many girls did, and not just in Dulwich.'

'I don't know, but Joyce told me things as well.' Suddenly, she remembered something. 'Oh yes, I've had a letter from Joyce. They're thinking of coming to see the show.'

'It'll be good to see Len again.' Freddy's old kriegie chum and his wife lived in London. 'I don't see how we can put them up, though.'

'No, she says they'll find accommodation.' Thinking again, she said, 'Maybe Dorothy and Alf would like to come. The harvest will be in by then, so it'll be easier for him.'

'You'll have to remind me about them.'

'Dorothy and I served in Dover and Malta. She's the girl from Liverpool. You met her at our wedding.'

'So I did. I remember her hubby, now I think of it. He was the huge fellow, wasn't he?'

'That's right. He's a farm worker.' She opened a box of sandwiches and offered it to him. 'Spam or cheese,' she said, wincing. 'They were all I could find, but I don't suppose you're worried about that.'

'Not in the slightest.'

'It's been five years now, and you still eat anything I put before you.'

'Be thankful I'm not finicky, SP. Some blokes are, but I'll bet they were never behind barbed wire.' He smiled at a memory. 'There was one ex-kriegie I heard of,' he said, 'whose wife was helping to organise an old folks' treat. There was entertainment followed by a buffet supper, except it didn't seem to be following quickly enough for some of the old people, and they were getting restive. Anyway, one of the organisers said they had to wait a little longer, at which the ex-kriegie went berserk, shouting, "Don't you *dare* tell these people when they can eat!"' He smiled again, visualising the scene. 'I imagine there'll be many more struggling to make the adjustment, and some never will.'

'Oh yes. Did you hear about Albert Whittaker? There was a terrible scene at the Shearers' Arms on Tues... no, it must have been Wednesday, because it was Mrs Thompson who told me, and I saw her on Wednesday afternoon.'

'Never mind that. What happened?'

'A visitor, a holidaymaker, I suppose, was showing off his camera to anyone who'd listen, and it was one of those new Japanese cameras. I forget the name.'

'Nikon or Canon, maybe?' They were the new post-war excitement for some people.

'Nikon, I think. Anyway, they had to hold Albert down, or else I don't know what he'd have done to the man with the camera.

Grace, who works there, said he was furious.'

'Poor old Bert. I hope Harry didn't bar him for it.'

'No, Grace said Harry took Albert's side and chucked out the man with the camera instead.'

'Good for him.' Freddy lay on his back, gazing up at the trees. 'SP,' he said, 'let's forget about the war and just enjoy this place.'

'I'm game.' She stretched herself out beside him on the rug.

'This a wonderful spot,' he said, watching the tops of the towering Scots pines sway in the breeze. Raising himself to peer through the trees at the distant landscape, he continued to voice his wonder. 'It's as if we're on top of the world.'

'You really think it's enchanted, don't you?'

'Yes, I do. I think we were drawn here.'

'By an irresistible, invisible force?'

'Yes, I'm talking about destiny, and please don't mock me when I'm being poetic.'

'All right. So we were drawn here, but why?'

'For a special purpose.'

'So, what are we supposed to...?' Realisation came to her. 'Freddy, you've got that look in your eye. Not here, surely. Not out in the open.'

'No one can see us, SP, and you can make as much noise as you like. There's only the birds, the black rabbits and Thea.'

'That's another thing. We've never done it in front of Thea.'

'She won't mind. She's watching the birds and the black rabbits.'

'Freddy, you're impossible.'

'But just think, SP, 'It's our own enchanted place. What a place to make a baby.' He emphasised his point by kissing her forehead, the tip of her nose, her lips, her chin and her throat, stopping briefly to unfasten the top three buttons of her blouse so that he could extend his downward journey.

'All right,' she said, 'but let's do it quietly and not attract attention.'

'No one will know,' he assured her.

They lay together for a while, until a chilly breeze caused them to gather their things and make the journey down the hill.

'Those clouds are looking very ugly,' said Sylvia. 'I hope we can make it to the car before the rain starts.'

'At least it's downhill all the way, SP. We should be all right.'

It was true that it was a downhill journey, but they were far from all right. The first drops of rain fell as they reached the footbridge and, by the time they crossed the road to the car, they were comprehensively soaked.

'You and your precious enchanted place!' Sylvia put Thea in the back with the rug while Freddy stowed the picnic bag in the boot. 'I'm soaked to the skin!'

'But until that happened,' said Freddy, 'it was a pretty good afternoon, wasn't it?'

'Don't talk to me. Just don't talk to me.'

'Okay.'

Thea shook herself, creating a miniature shower in the back of the car, but that, the rumble of the engine and the swish of the wipers were the only sounds as they drove home.

Eventually, Freddy parked the car and took Thea into the porch to dry her while Sylvia ran a bath.

'She'll be all right when she's had a bath and changed her clothes,' he assured Thea, rubbing her with a towel. He hoped so, anyway.

'Freddy.' Sylvia called from the landing.

'Am I allowed to speak?'

'Don't be silly. Of course you are. Will you bring up the bath towels? I left them drying in the kitchen.'

He took the towels from the clothes horse in the kitchen and carried them up to the bathroom, where Sylvia was filling the bath. She had undressed and was very wet.

'Here are the towels.'

'Thanks, Freddy.' She tested the water and turned off the cold tap. 'Are you going to join me?'

'I thought you'd never ask. I'll take the tap end,' he offered chivalrously. He waited until she was settled before joining her.

'You were right,' she said, smiling in belated agreement. 'It was a lovely afternoon until the rain came.'

They sat together, luxuriating in the warmth and each other's company. It was a perfect end to an afternoon that, if they viewed it in the right perspective, had been only slightly flawed.

Common sense could wait another twenty-four hours, after which they would have to face the last month of rehearsals before the show. One matter that had been on Freddy's mind was that of ticket sales. According to Walter, they were mounting steadily, but they had yet to cover the hire of the Town Hall. What they really needed was some good publicity.

21

Bailey was a city dweller, born and left to grow up in London, with its attendant attractions and temptations, some of which, it was true to say, had led him, on occasions, to stray from the ways of rectitude. Moving to the North Riding, however, had given him a chance to view the world with fresh eyes, and the novelty so far showed no sign of abatement.

One of his new-found pleasures was to saunter among the stalls of Northallerton Market. It was true that London boasted several markets, some of them world-famous, but rural fare now beckoned more invitingly and, as his day off coincided with market day, he was at liberty to indulge himself on a regular basis.

He was taking his usual stroll that Wednesday, enjoying the drifting aromas of pies, pasties, fish and chips, pie and peas, pease pudding and an assortment of sausages, that emanated from the vending vehicles. Elsewhere, stallholders offered for sale second-hand tools and kitchen utensils, galvanised buckets and bathtubs, working apparel, kittens, rabbits, puppies, books, gramophone records, knitting wool, bolts of fabric, towels, sheets and pillow cases, baby clothes and towelling nappies. Beyond them were the food stalls that held fresh fruit and vegetables, where stallholders advised shoppers in stentorian volume of the excellent quality and bargain prices of their merchandise.

Bailey was drawn towards a stall where the trader appeared to be selling Victoria plums at an astonishing rate. Certainly, the plums looked very enticing, and he decided to buy some.

He took his place next to two women and a man who fascinated him in an odd way. The man's eyes seemed to be everywhere, as if he expected something to happen at any moment. His features were sharp; even his chin was pointed, and Bailey couldn't help disliking him.

The woman at the head of the queue paid for her purchase and made room for the next customer, a short, grey-haired woman with a handbag that seemed to have been intended for someone twice her size.

The trader weighed a pound of plums, dropped them into a brown paper bag and waited. She opened her bag and, in one deft movement, the man behind her seized her purse. At that moment, Bailey grasped his wrist.

'Not a good idea, old man. If I were you, I'd leave that purse where you found it. Yes, dear lady, do take it. It's yours after all.'

The woman stared at him in astonishment. Eventually, still shocked, she said, 'Thank you.'

'You're welcome, madam. Now,' he said, addressing the crowd, 'would someone be kind enough to alert a member of the constabulary?'

In desperation, the purse snatcher aimed a punch with his free fist at Bailey's head. Bailey blocked it with his left and drove his right into the man's solar plexus. His antagonist collapsed, making a noise like a steamroller approaching retirement.

'Will someone please find a handy rozzer,' prompted Bailey, 'while I contain this blighter?'

Within a short time, the constable on market duty arrived at the scene of the crime.

'A purse snatcher,' Bailey explained. 'He took this lady's purse.'

'That's right,' the woman told the policeman. "E pinched me purse an' this gentleman stopped 'im.'

'Oh, yes,' said the policeman, addressing the purse snatcher, who was still struggling for breath, 'I know you, don't I? Well, you're under arrest.' He proceeded to inform the miscreant of his rights and handcuffed him. 'Now,' he said, taking out his notebook and pencil, 'I have to get this character to the station, but first I need the names and addresses of the lady whose purse it was, and the gentleman who intervened.' He proceeded to write the lady's and Bailey's details laboriously in his notebook, stopping occasionally to keep an eye on the handcuffed purse snatcher.

'Don't worry,' Bailey told him, 'I won't let him get away.'

The purse snatcher looked at him nervously, but the policeman dismissed any hint of renewed violence, by saying, 'No more fisticuffs, please, Mr Bailey. You've done enough.'

'I'm very grateful to him for what he did,' the lady reminded him.

'Aye,' said a bystander, 'I wouldn't want my ear'ole brayed by this fella. He's got a punch like Rocky Marciano.'

'It's decent of you to say so, old chap,' said Bailey. 'As a matter of fact, I was Royal Artillery Light-Heavyweight Champion before the war.'

The purse snatcher, now breathing normally, winced at the memory of the blow.

'That's as maybe,' said the policeman, addressing the bystander. 'Are you saying you witnessed the incident?'

'I'll say I did. The thief came at him with his right, and then, quick as a flash, the posh bloke blocked the punch with his left an' let him have a right jab to the body. It were a treat to behold.'

'I meant,' said the policeman patiently, 'did you see this man seize this lady's purse?'

'Aye, I did, an' I saw what he got for it. You should have seen that punch.'

'So that's three of you who need to make a statement.'

<hr/>

Bailey finished reading his statement and nodded approvingly.

'Are you happy to sign it, Mr Bailey?' The policeman, a colleague of the officer who had attended the scene of the crime, offered him a pen.

'Thanks, I prefer to use my own.' Bailey unscrewed the cap of his fountain pen and signed the document.

'Thank you, Mr Bailey,' said the constable. 'You've been most helpful.'

'Only too happy to assist the forces of law and order.' Bailey shook his hand, smiling inwardly at the irony of the situation. 'Goodbye.'

'Goodbye, sir.'

As Bailey made for the exit, he heard the desk sergeant call his name.

'Mr Bailey, there's a reporter hanging around outside. He says he'd like a word with you, but that's up to you.'

'Thank you, sergeant.'

'It's no trouble, sir.'

He found the reporter in the porch. He was young and seemed eager.

'Mr Bailey?'

'Yes. You must be the reporter,' he said, opening the outer door.

'I'm from the *Gazette*, Mr Bailey,' he confirmed. 'I wonder if you can spare me a few minutes of your time.' He looked even younger in sunlight.

'How old are you?'

The boy frowned uncomprehendingly. 'I'm twenty,' he said.

'Done National Service?'

'Yes, in the Green Howards. I was demobbed in May.'

'Splendid. I like to know that a chap's pulled his weight. Look, old man, shall we find a place where we can have a cup of tea and a civilised conversation?'

❦

Freddy opened his copy of the *Evening Gazette* that Friday and smiled. 'Listen to this, SP,' he said. 'The headline is: "BOXER FOILS PURSE SNATCH." It says, "On Wednesday, 6th September, an habitual thief, who, for legal reasons, cannot yet be named, attempted to steal a shopper's purse in Northallerton Market, but he reckoned without Royal Artillery Heavyweight Boxing Champion Gerard Bailey. No sooner had he lifted the purse, than Mr Bailey punched him to the ground and recovered the purse before sending for the police." '

Freddy put the paper down to butter a piece of toast.

'Go on, Freddy,' urged Sylvia. 'What else does it say?'

'Patience, SP. It says, "Mr Bailey won the regimental heavyweight title in 1939. 'My boxing career might have gone further,' he told our reporter modestly, 'had the war not intervened.' He is now employed as Sales Manager by Blackwell Brothers, the motor dealers." '

Freddy was shaking with laughter. 'Can you imagine Bailey being modest?'

'Go on, Freddy,' said Sylvia. 'Don't keep it all to yourself.'

'All right.' Freddy wiped his eyes with the back of his hand and continued to read. ' "And that is not the limit of Mr Bailey's talents. He is currently preparing for the starring role in a new musical: 'Viking High Jinks', with Yoredale Players, based in Easingthorpe. 'It's a marvellous show,' he said, 'a comedy about our Viking past, written, composed and directed by Freddy Hinchcliffe.'

"He and Mr Hinchcliffe met when they were prisoners-of-war in Poland. Mr Bailey is also excited about the female lead, played by Elaine Stafford from Thirsk. 'She's absolutely brilliant,' he said. 'You'll be amazed.' The production will be held at Easingthorpe Town Hall, week commencing the 9th October. Tickets are available in all parts of the house from Charlesworth and Buckley, Chartered Accountants, 14 – 16 High Street, Easingthorpe. When applying for tickets, please include a stamped, addressed envelope." '

'What bliss.' Freddy continued, wet-eyed, with breakfast.

'You never know,' said Sylvia. 'He may have done the show some good.'

⊷╫᛫3᛫╫᛫Є᛫╫⊷

On Sunday afternoon, Freddy found the cast in a frivolous mood.

'They'd all been wondering about Bailey's first name,' Sylvia told him, 'and now, thanks to the local paper, the cat's out of the bag.'

'That's not all,' said Freddy. 'Ladies and gents, your attention, please.' He waited for silence and continued. 'I had a phone call from Walter this afternoon. He told me that, thanks to Bailey's interview with the *Gazette* reporter, his office spent the whole of yesterday morning dealing with requests for tickets for the show. He also told me that we have now broken even. We all owe our thanks to Bailey.'

There was general applause, and then Bailey spoke.

'I'm overwhelmed,' he told them, 'but I would ask that you all forget about my first name. I stopped using it years ago and, celebrity notwithstanding, I'm still simply "Bailey" to you all.'

22

When Sylvia came into the studio, she spoke in a careful, level tone.

'There are two pieces of news,' she said. 'The first is that they've taken soap off the ration.'

'Good news, then.' Seeing her falter, Freddy asked gently, 'What is it, SP?'

'Audrey's having another baby.' Her voice was beginning to waver. 'I should be pleased for them but it's not as if they wanted this one.' Her eyes filled with tears. 'It was an accident.'

'I know,' he said, opening his arms to her. 'It seems unfair. They have two already, and now there's another on the way, and we're still peeing into the wind.'

She broke away from him to blow her nose and said, 'I wouldn't have put it quite like that, but yes, that's how it seems.'

'Having said that, SP, none of it's their fault.'

'All the same, you'd think a doctor and a nurse would know better.'

'Be fair, SP. There's no such thing as fool-proof contraception.'

'I'm not so sure. Whatever we're doing seems to fit that description.'

'Was it Audrey who phoned you?'

Sylvia nodded. 'She said she wanted to tell me before anyone else did. She wanted to spare my feelings.' She dabbed at her eyes with her handkerchief. 'Oh, Freddy, I feel so mean-spirited when I'm like this.'

'I don't know how you came over to Audrey on the phone, but I'm sure you can make things right with her.'

'I suppose so. Anyway, I'll let you get on with your work.'

'I'm always available, SP.'

'I know.' With a brave attempt at a smile, she left him and went upstairs.

⁂

Cleaning the dark room gave Freddy an opportunity to consider Audrey's announcement and its effect on Sylvia. It was simply bad luck, and there really was no other way to look at it. He was sure Audrey and David would soon adjust to the situation and make the most of their new baby, but Sylvia's problem was a different matter. Motherhood was becoming an obsession, and it worried him.

He brooded a little longer until, having finished the cleaning, he went to wash his hands, and that reminded him of the other piece of news Sylvia had brought him. When he'd dried his hands, he took out his copy of the *Viking High Jinks* script and turned to Act 2, because he'd had an idea. It would be no more than a throw-away line but he reckoned it would still get a laugh.

⁂

He had shown Mrs Woolliscroft and Tigger to the door that afternoon, and was about to unload the camera, when the phone rang. It was Walter.

'Hello, Freddy. How are you?'

'Exhausted. I've been photographing an exuberant Jack Russell and trying to be diplomatic with his harassed mistress.'

'Yours is a multi-faceted profession, isn't it? How's Sylvia?'

'I imagine that's the reason for this phone call?'

'How did you guess?'

After a moment's deliberation, Freddy said, 'Resentful, introspective, self-demeaning, and otherwise downright miserable.'

'I'm sorry to hear that, Freddy. I went home for lunch but I didn't linger. Audrey's there, filled with woe because she upset Sylvia. I'm ashamed to say I left Jessie to perform the parental function alone. She didn't need me and, in any case, I felt distressingly unequal to the task.'

'It's the cross we have to bear, Walter. The sad truth is that there are things women do so much better than we ever could, and they know it. I blame the war for making them aware of their latent abilities.'

'Yes.' Walter sounded preoccupied. 'I imagine those two will sort things out between them,' he said. 'I just hope they'll do it sooner rather than later.'

'I'll encourage at my end, Walter.'

'Good man. I'll do what I can.'

'Okay. Bear up, Walter.'

'Yes. I'll be in touch. 'Bye.'

Half-an-hour later, the phone rang again.

'Hinchcliffe Photography.'

'Mr Hinchcliffe? This is Section Officer Wilkinson of the local Auxiliary Fire Service. I wonder if you'd consider photographing a fire appliance.'

'A fire engine?'

'Well, yes. You see, we've had "Betty", as the lads call her, since before the war, and they're all very attached to her, but she's going to be replaced this Friday. They've only just told me.'

'I see. When would be a good time?'

'Ah, well, the best time would be during one of our training sessions, and then the section will be there to be photographed with her. There's one tonight,' he added on what sounded like a hopeful note.

'I'm afraid I'm very busy with rehearsals most evenings this month.' It would have been an unusual job and they were always welcome.

'Of course, you're involved with the Players, aren't you? What time do you start rehearsing?'

'Seven-thirty at the school.'

'We muster at six-thirty, if that's any help.'

'I could be with you for six-thirty.'

'Excellent.'

Something else had occurred to Freddy. 'Tell me,' he asked, 'are you ex-Navy?'

'No, I served full-time in the fire service throughout the war.'

'It's just that you said "muster".'

'Oh, that. It's in regular use in the fire service. It comes of having so many ex-sailors, you see. The influence is everywhere. We even have red and green watches.'

'Really?'

'Are you ex-Navy, Mr Hinchcliffe?'

'Yes, I was in the Fleet Air Arm, telegraphist/air-gunner.'

There was a pause, and then Wilkinson asked, 'I don't suppose you'd consider joining the AFS, would you? It'd be just two nights a week and weekends.'

'I'm afraid I'd have great difficulty fitting it in.' He added quickly, 'But I'll be with you at six-thirty tonight. At the fire station, I imagine.'

'That's right, Mr Hinchcliffe. I'll look forward to seeing you then. Goodbye.'

Freddy worked on until he realised it was almost five-forty, so he locked the studio and went upstairs, expecting to find Sylvia there. Instead, the flat was empty. He was still looking for a note when the phone rang.

'Freddy, it's Walter. Sylvia's on her way home. I thought I'd better tell you. I came home and found Audrey and her hugging each other. I'd say things are all right now.'

⊷⊷⊷

Freddy called the rehearsal to order and said, 'I'd like you to turn to Act Two, Scene Two, if you will. It's where Elga is trying to interrogate the captured Pict. Elga, take it from "This is hopeless. I can't understand a word he says".'

ELGA   This is hopeless. I can't understand a word he says. Anyway, bring him back to me when he's clean. (Indicates war paint and tattoos.)

ARDITH   Come on, girls. Let's get this blue stuff off him. Rub harder.

FIRST GIRL It won't come off, Ardith. It's as if the blue stuff is under his skin.

ARDITH   Nonsense. Use more soap.

'Stop there,' said Freddy. 'Ardith, will you write into your script after "Use more soap", "It's not as if it's in short supply. Heaven forbid that soap should ever be rationed".'

'Will do, Freddy. That should get a laugh.'

'I hope so. I could use one after today. Okay, folks, let's run that scene again.'

⸙⸙⸙

Sylvia found him at the end of the rehearsal.

'I'm sorry I wasn't there to cook dinner, Freddy. Did you find something? You weren't there when I came home.'

'I was photographing a fire engine and a dozen heartbroken firemen.'

She looked incredulous. 'What?'

'It's a long story. Don't worry about dinner, SP. The main thing is that things are all right between you and Audrey.'

'They're fine. I'll cook you something when we get home.'

'No, we'll call at the chip shop on the way.'

The idea evidently appealed to Sylvia, who said, 'We haven't had fish and chips for ages.'

'Let's call it a treat. I think you're due for one, and we need to stoke up, anyway. We've a lot of hard work ahead of us.'

23

Freddy sat upright, gasping, first with the horror that had been so real up to that moment, and then with the relief that came with wakefulness.

Sylvia was instantly awake. 'What's the matter, Freddy?'

'Sorry, SP.' It was little more than a croak.

'Was it a nightmare?' She put her hand on his arm, which was covered in perspiration.

'Yes. I'm sorry.'

'Don't keep apologising, darling. It's not your fault.' She lifted the covers and slipped out of bed. 'I'll run you a bath - there'll be enough hot water - and then I'll go down and put the kettle on for tea.'

Freddy lay for a while, listening to the sounds from the bathroom. When he heard the water stop running, he peeled off his sweat-soaked pyjamas and dropped them in the laundry basket before lowering himself into the bathwater. Then, for five or more glorious minutes, he luxuriated in soap-scented warmth and comfort.

Later, he and Sylvia sat downstairs drinking tea.

'I really thought I was finished with those damned things,' he said. 'I thought fishing and Redmire Falls had chased them away, but the buggers have come back again to haunt me.'

'I'm sure Redmire Falls will do it again, Freddy.' She took his arm and stroked it. 'What was it about this time?'

'Oh, the usual thing. There was a fall in the salt mine, you see. It derailed a truck, and one of the Russians was trapped beneath it. I tried to persuade Vogel, the sergeant, to get his men to help right the truck so that we could get him out. Instead, he had him shot.'

'And is that what you dreamt about?'

'Bits of it. It was very disjointed.'

'I wonder if it was hearing about those Scottish miners in the news that started it off for you.'

'Very likely.' He'd kept wondering about them. Apparently, more than a hundred miners had been trapped for two days in a pit in Ayrshire. 'It's awful. You know, I never thought much about miners until I worked in the salt mine.'

'They got some of them out today.'

'Yes. I just hope they can get the rest of them out alive, because it'll be a living hell for them until they do.'

'More tea?' She reached for the teapot.

'Please.' He held his cup and saucer while she poured it.

'That was when they beat Bailey so savagely, wasn't it? I remember now.'

He hesitated for a moment until he realised she was referring to his experience in the salt mine. 'Yes,' he said. 'I was knocked unconscious after that. When I came to, I really thought they'd killed him.'

'But you both came home. Thank goodness for that.'

'You're quite fond of Bailey, aren't you?'

'It's difficult not to be. He's too kind and good-natured not to be liked.'

'That's true.' He sat for a while in silence, soothed by the tea and Sylvia's presence. Eventually, he said, 'Some good came of that episode, you know.'

'I don't believe it.'

'It didn't make up for two deaths. Nothing could do that, but one little bit of good did come out of it.'

'Don't keep me in suspense.'

'Okay. The next day was Sunday, our day off, and I was so sick of the brutality in the mine, I wanted to do something good and decent, so I decided to tell you something I'd wanted to say for a long time. That's when I wrote that song about how you made everything better.'

'Oh, Freddy, I'd no idea. It's a lovely song as well.'

'I thought once about arranging it for the band and getting the lads to play it, but it's very private, isn't it? Best kept between you and me.'

'I think so.' She drank the rest of her tea and asked, 'Are you ready to go back to bed or do you want to sit for a while longer?'

'No, the hammock beckons.' He picked up the tray to take it into the kitchen.

'Leave it, Freddy. I'll wash those things in the morning.' She stood up to follow him, and asked, 'Did you ever sleep in a hammock?'

'On board ship, yes.'

'What was it like?'

'Cosy, comfortable, restful. Much better than a bunk in a POW camp.'

As she switched off the light, she said, 'I know what will help you forget those wretched things.'

'What's that?'

'You know.' She kissed him enticingly.

'No, I don't.'

'You do,' she said, kissing him again.

'Not until you tell me.'

'All right,' she said impatiently. 'I'm talking about... *nooky.*'

'You know,' he said, 'it might just be worth a try.'

<hr />

With a free morning ahead, there was no need for Freddy to be up early, and Sylvia let him sleep later than usual. Consequently, he was rested and ready for his rehearsal with the band. He had set aside the evening to run through the music for the show, and everything seemed to be going well until Wilf Bennett, the bass player, stopped playing and waved to him with his bow.

Freddy gave the 'cut' sign to the band and asked, 'What's the matter, Wilf?'

'It's this four bars' unaccompanied *recit*, Freddy.'

'Yes?' He was referring to the short line of sung dialogue that led into Erik's song. 'Some of you said it made the show more like an opera than a musical. You seemed to like it.'

'Aye, we do. There's nowt wrong with it as long as we know where we are in the score.'

'That's right,' said Derek Littlewood. 'All we've got is four bars' tacet, and you need to beat them so that those of us that are count-ing thirty bars or more know that four of the buggers have gone by.'

'Aye,' said Wilf, 'we can't read your mind, Freddy.'

'Just give us a downbeat for each bar,' Derek advised him, 'until you get to the fourth bar, then one and three, and wait for the singer to catch up. Then, when he does, give the upbeat, and we're back in business.'

'Right,' said Freddy. 'I never thought about that. I'm sorry.'

'You weren't to know,' Derek told him gently, 'but you needed to, so we told you.'

'Thank you. Let's try that again from rehearsal mark "C".'

He led them into the *recitative*, gave four downbeats followed by the third beat of the fourth bar as he sang, *'Good lady, I implore you, let me speak and make you understand....'* Then he led the band into the next number.

'That's right,' said Wilf at the end of the number. 'You've got the idea.'

Derek said, 'We told you we'd look after you, didn't we?'

'You did, and it seems I need looking after.'

'Nay, you'll pick t' job up soon enough.'

'It's just as well. The leading lady's going to join us later, to go through a couple of her songs. She's the one I told you about, the girl who took on the part at short notice.'

'Ah well,' said Derek generously, ''appen we'll be able to help her an' all.'

'I shouldn't be at all surprised. Now, let's go from number five. Straight in.'

They worked for the next half-hour, until the door opened and Bailey came into the room, followed by Elaine.

'Ah,' said Freddy, 'welcome, you two.' Turning to the band, he said, 'This is the lady I told you about, and the bonus is that the bloke who's with her is Erik the Not Quite Ready.'

'Yes,' said Elaine. 'If we could run through our first duet, we'd be very grateful.'

'It's no trouble,' said Freddy. 'Music Number Three, please. "Brutes and Ravishers".' He started the number, and Elaine took up her cue.

'Brutes and Ravishers! Foul invaders! Yet again, you come to raid us!'

Bailey made his entry, and Freddy was particularly thankful that the business of the recitative had been dealt with earlier. He listened to Bailey and Elaine in duet and decided that fate had provided him with the ideal partnership.

At the end of the rehearsal, George Clay surprised everyone by saying, 'I can't help wondering if we've found a pair of band singers. These two would do very nicely, wouldn't they, Freddy?'

'It's a lot to ask, George. They're working hard enough already on the show.'

'And I'm certainly not what you're looking for,' Bailey told them.

'You're maybe a shade operatic for what we need,' agreed George, 'but the lady is a natural, if you don't mind me sayin' so, love.'

'I wouldn't mind doing something with the band,' said Elaine.

George hesitated. He asked, 'Can you sing published keys?'

'I don't know.' She looked at Freddy for explanation.

'Published keys are the ones used most often in band music,' he told her. Turning to George, he said, 'Elaine's fine with F, E flat and A flat, C is probably okay, but she might struggle with B flat. We could get around that, though.' Realising that a *fait* was about to become *accompli*, he asked her, 'What would you like to sing, Elaine?'

'I don't know.' She thought for a moment and asked, 'Have you got the music for "Somebody Loves Me"? I think it's by George Gershwin.'

'It is, and I think we have. Harold?' He addressed a serious-looking clarinettist.

'Just give me a minute, Freddy.' Harold, the band's librarian, left his place and went to the locker set aside for the band. After a brief search, he pulled out a set of band parts. 'Here it is, Freddy.' He squinted at the piano/conductor part that lay on top, and said, 'It's in concert A flat.'

'Excellent. Will you give them out, please?'

Harold passed the band parts around, and the musicians looked expectantly towards Freddy and Elaine.

'In this arrangement,' he explained to Elaine, 'you have just eight bars' intro, and then I'll cue you in.'

She nodded, and he turned to the band. 'A-one, a-two, a-one, two, three, four.' The band played the eight bars' introduction and Freddy looked at Elaine. She smiled and came in on cue.

He'd heard her sing often, but never anything like the Gershwin, and he was impressed. At the end of the number, she agreed enthusiastically to join the band for their next gig. Freddy could only hope she wasn't trying to do too much.

24

Freddy was surprised to find Sylvia in her coat and hat, about to leave the house. The rehearsal wasn't for another hour.

'Aren't you coming tonight, SP?'

'No, I told you at the weekend. It's something the W I are trying out, a home-made wine evening.'

'It doesn't sound like your kind of thing.' Sylvia drank very little as a rule.

'I know, but they need me all the same.'

'All right, I'll see you later.'

'Okay. 'Bye. Have a good rehearsal.'

'Thanks.' Something occurred to him as she was leaving. 'Oh, SP.'

'Yes?' She was halfway out of the door.

'Be careful with that home-made hooch. Some of it's like aviation spirit.'

'Okay.' She closed the door behind her, leaving Freddy to wonder why on earth the Women's Institute had chosen to spend an evening tasting and comparing the fermented produce of the wayside.

He thought no more about it, however, as he had to prepare for the evening's rehearsal. He wanted to work on the chorus items; he'd been aware of some raggedness since floor rehearsals had begun, and he wanted to address the problem before standards slipped any further.

With that stern thought in mind, he arrived at the school and set out the chairs for the chorus, some of whom were beginning to trickle in. By 7:30, his male chorus amounted to ten men, which was excellent. Their female counterparts, however, numbered only four. He decided to wait a little longer to see if any more turned up.

After five minutes, no one else had made an appearance.

Ernie Holmes said casually, 'You know where they are, don't you?'

'No,' said Freddy, 'I've no idea. Please enlighten me, because I'm rapidly losing patience.'

'They're at the Women's Institute meeting down the passage. They're having a wine-making competition,' he added wistfully.

'Seven of them,' said Freddy, 'and not one with a sense of urgency. We open in three-and-a-half weeks' time, and they're tasting dandelion plonk.'

'Some of it's not bad,' Ernie told him. 'Mind you, you have to be a bit careful. That parsnip wine of Esme Whittaker's is a bit strong. It's 'ad me under t' table afore now.'

'Never mind that, Ernie. I think we'd better make a start.'

'An' you'd think Albert would raise an objection. They're his prize parsnips, after all.'

'Ernie, please. Let's forget about parsnip wine and get on with the rehearsal. Now, ladies' opening chorus, please.'

He did what he could with three sopranos and one alto before turning to the men's chorus. After half-an-hour, he decided to call on the W I to see if he could entice some of his female chorus away from the noble if ill-timed demands of their committee, and bring them back into the fold.

Inviting the faithful few to take a break, he followed the sound of feminine laughter, which seemed to be issuing from a classroom at the end of the corridor.

When he reached the room where the merriment was loudest, he peered through the glass and then shook his head in total despair because there in the classroom were his missing chorus members, all helpless with immoderate laughter. Entreaty was pointless; even if they had been willing to join the rehearsal, they could have contributed nothing, inebriated as they obviously were on home-made wine.

He was about to return to the rehearsal when Sylvia saw him and beckoned him into the room.

'It's awful,' she said, drawing him inside. 'They're all plastered. They'd tried most of the bottles before they started on Mrs Whittaker's parsnip wine, and that was the last straw.'

'I've heard about Esme Whittaker's parsnip wine,' he told her, 'but I'd have preferred the sound of a full chorus tonight.'

'I know.' She looked penitent.

'It wasn't your fault, SP. They know their own minds.'

'People have loyalties that go back a long way.' It was an excuse that lacked conviction.

'I've noticed.'

A tall woman with a determined look zigzagged towards them.

'Mrs Hi… shcliffe,' she said, 'why have you bro…brou…. Why has your husban' come to a meeting of the Women's Inst…ute… Inst… the Bubl U I?'

'He was looking for his chorus, Mrs Parkinson.'

'Excel… exc…. Good idea. Let's all join in th' chorus.'

There was no need, because the faithful chorus members, no doubt tired of waiting for Freddy's return, were now at the door.

'Let them in,' said Mrs Parkinson. 'They can join th' chorus as well. Wha' are we singing?'

A plump lady with dark-rimmed glasses said, 'I'll sing a solo. Le' me sing a sol…. I always sing the solos.'

'Oh, glory,' said Sylvia. 'She'll be in trouble when she gets home.'

'I imagine they all will.' Freddy didn't really care.

'No, her especially.'

'What's special about her?'

'She's the Methodist minister's wife. She probably signed the pledge at some time.'

'While she was still sober, presumably.'

Ernie Holmes said, 'I told you about Esme's parsnip wine, didn't I, Freddy.'

'So you did, Ernie.' Freddy watched with detached interest as one of his chorus bent helplessly over a table before subsiding beneath it. Meanwhile, Mrs Whittaker replaced the cork in a quarter-full bottle, somewhat belatedly removing further temptation.

'I won't bring it another time,' she said. 'This lot can't hold their drink.'

Freddy could only wonder about Mrs Whittaker's personal limit.

'I don't suppose there's any harm in having a taste,' said Edith Foster. 'We're W I members after all. It's just that some of us have different priorities.' She picked up a glass and approached the row of bottles. One by one, the others followed her example, to be joined in turn by the male chorus.

'It's an epidemic,' said Freddy.

Sylvia nodded sadly. 'It won't be repeated.'

'Not if Mrs Whittaker keeps her word.'

'I mean the wine tasting won't be repeated. It was only a try-out.'

'It certainly was,' said Freddy. 'They all tried it, and most of them are out for the count.'

As he spoke, Mrs Parkinson viewed the male chorus members at the wine table and seemed about to demand an explanation, but closed her eyes instead and joined the minister's wife on the floor.

'I suppose we should leave,' suggested Freddy, 'before the irate husbands arrive.'

'We can't just leave them.'

'There's nothing we can do for them, SP. It's better to let their husbands scrape them up and take them home.' He couldn't help adding, 'It would be interesting to hear the minister's sermon on Sunday.'

'Don't be cruel, Freddy. The poor woman didn't know what she was doing. She probably thought she was drinking fruit cordial.'

It sounded like a good excuse, and Freddy filed it away for possible future use. He was still annoyed with the errant members of the female chorus, but he had to move on. In time, he would see the lighter side of the incident and his admiration for the W I and its produce would remain undiminished, but he would only ever refer to that august body as 'The Bubble You Eye.'

25

Happily, the minister's wife had time to recover from her condition, if not her embarrassment, for the following Sunday and the Harvest Festival. It was always a splendid occasion that drew large congregations to all the churches in the Dale and doubtless beyond, but harvest was also celebrated in other places, albeit on the eve of the festival and on a largely bacchanalian level. One such venue was the Shearers' Arms in Easingthorpe.

Fortunately, the landlord had a licence for music and, as many of those attending the Harvest Supper were members of the Yoredale Players, it wasn't long before the singing began.

Oklahoma! had opened in London three years earlier but the show was still so popular that before long none of the locals present was in any doubt as to the spelling of its name. There were those, however, who grew impatient as the Players sang the opening song.

'I don't care if the corn is as high as a giraffe's earhole,' said Nathan Parker. 'That's in Oklahoma. We're in Easingthorpe, and it's our harvest we're celebrating, not theirs.'

Accordingly, the Players switched to something more traditional, and Bailey regaled the gathering with 'The Farmer's Boy.'

Nathan Parker was known to be a hard man, but Freddy could see he was visibly affected by the song, especially when the lyrics told of the boy's dead father and his hard-pressed mother with five children to rear. For his part, Freddy could only concentrate on playing the piano, because picturing Bailey as a diminutive farm boy was beyond both his imagination and his composure.

When Bailey reached the end of the song, Nathan Parker called out, 'Sing it again, lad. It's a grand song.' So Bailey obliged, with the Players this time joining in the refrain.

'Eh,' said Nathan, 'I'll ask thee to sing it again afore t' night's out.'

Another patron asked, 'Does anybody know "The Lass of Richmond Hill"?'

Someone asked, 'Do you want *all* the words?'

'Of course I do. There's no point in singin' it otherwise.'

Elaine said, 'I know it.'

'It's a lad's song,' objected the patron.

'Well,' said Elaine, 'you'll have to use your imagination or go without. It's one or the other.' She gave Freddy an enquiring look, and he nodded. It was one of many songs he could play by ear. He also knew that his father-in-law, now seated with Jessie and Sylvia, would appreciate it, as it had been the regimental quick march of the Green Howards since the eighteenth century.

The applause that followed the song demonstrated that Walter wasn't the only one who had enjoyed it. Typically, Nathan Parker called for an encore, and Elaine and the Players' chorus indulged him. Then it was time to eat.

Walter peered at the dark liquid in Freddy's glass and asked, 'What's that you're drinking, Freddy?'

'Dark mild. They only started brewing it earlier this year. I like it.'

'I wonder if you've been spending more time here than I thought,' said Sylvia, looking around her at the unfamiliar surroundings. The Harvest Supper had created a mixed clientele for that evening. Otherwise, women were seldom seen in pubs.

Freddy raised his hand to greet Albert Whittaker, who was standing at the bar, waiting to be served. Albert lifted his empty glass in reply.

'I wonder if he drinks his wife's parsnip wine,' said Sylvia.

Freddy shook his head. 'I had to help him home after five pints of dark mild,' he said. 'I doubt if he could handle her high octane stuff.'

Jessie was looking mystified, so Freddy explained. 'Easingthorpe W I organised a home-made wine tasting evening, and most of them got blotto on Esme Whittaker's parsnip wine.'

'Oh, Freddy,' said Jessie in her 'you'll tell me anything' tone.

'It's true.'

Jessie now looked sternly at her daughter.

'I didn't have any,' protested Sylvia.

'It's true.' Freddy backed her up. 'Sylvia and Esme were the only two who were sober.'

'It must have been a good night,' said Walter, ignoring a sharp look from his wife.

Adroitly changing the subject, Sylvia said, 'I wonder if Albert Whittaker would like to come to the show. It might take him out of himself. You never know.'

'It'll take more than an amateur show to give Bert some peace of mind,' said Freddy.

'I didn't mean in the long term. I just thought he might enjoy a change and maybe a distraction for one evening.'

'I'll ask him and Esme.' He realised that Walter and Jessie knew nothing about Bert, so he told them, 'He was a POW in Burma. It's affected him badly.'

'Poor devil,' said Walter.

'I spent an evening in here with him, and he told me some horrible things.'

'And he nearly killed a man who came in boasting about his Japanese camera,' added Sylvia.

Lightening the mood, Walter asked, 'What do you know about these new Japanese cameras, Freddy?'

'Apparently their lens quality's good, but I'll stick to my German equipment for now. It's served me well and I'm happy with it.'

'Someone in the Rotary Club told me the Japanese are pursuing a particularly aggressive marketing and sales policy.'

'I gather so,' said Freddy. 'Apparently Canon's top man has told his employees to overtake and destroy Leica.' He pondered that for a moment before saying, 'You know, bombs can create horror on an unimagined scale, as we've seen, but the basic characteristics of human nature emerge unchanged.'

'That's very true,' said Sylvia uncomfortably, 'but let's eat.'

Mercifully, Freddy was able to rehearse the chorus as he'd intended before the W I event had intervened, and he could now press on. His next rehearsal was with the full cast.

'Act Two, Scene Six,' he announced. 'Elga.'

Elaine took centre stage.

ELGA The Picts could be here at any time. What are we going to do? Somebody, think of something quickly!

Everyone adopts a thinking pose.

ELGA Well? Has anybody thought of anything?

ERIK I have an idea that may work.

ELGA Well? Don't keep it to yourself. Tell us before the Picts massacre us all.

ERIK Do you remember when we tried to feed the Pict we captured, and he screamed and leapt over the battlements?

ELGA Yes, but that was only one Pict. We're threatened with hundreds of them.

ERIK Yes, but what was it that horrified him so much? I'll tell you. It was the curd tart we gave him. Picts can't abide curds or whey. They believe that curds are bogeymen's brains.

ELGA And whey?

ERIK Bogeymen's blood.

ELGA Brilliant, but why didn't you tell me this earlier? I've been going frantic.

ERIK   I don't know. Somehow, I forgot.

ELGA   If I know you, you were probably miles away, composing one of your odes. Anyway, everyone, there's not a moment to be lost. We need curd tarts and buckets of whey. Let's start acidifying, coagulating and baking!

Freddy clapped his hands. 'Excellent. Thank you, Elga and Erik, and well done the chorus as well. Don't forget to look as if you're listening, and keep reacting. Don't upstage the principals, for goodness' sake, but be natural.' It seemed the Harvest Supper had relaxed everyone and done them all a power of good. If the remaining rehearsals went as well, they would have an excellent show.

26

Rain lashed against the window panes, causing Elaine to snuggle further beneath the covers.

'Bailey,' she said, 'are you awake?'

'Of course I am, old thing.'

'It was a silly question,' she agreed. 'You're not one to lose consciousness immediately after the main event, and I'm thankful for that, but must you call me "old thing"? I'm only twenty-five, you know.'

'I'm sorry, dearest one. It's an appalling habit, I know, and I'm trying to break it.'

She patted his shoulder in an encouraging way. 'You can do it, Bailey, but I wouldn't want you to become too ordinary.'

'I really wouldn't know how. I haven't been ordinary for... I don't know how many years.'

Elaine was looking thoughtful. 'Tell me about your childhood,' she said. 'I know absolutely nothing about your life before....'

'Before my criminal career took off? I'm sure you don't want to know about my early life.'

'I'm unshockable, Bailey. You can tell me anything.'

He hesitated for a moment. 'All right,' he said, rolling on to his back and slipping his arm around her. 'I was born in Stepney in nineteen-seventeen. My father was killed before we could be properly introduced, and my mother always seemed to have pressing business that was, let's say, unrelated to the normal duties of motherhood. I seem to remember a number of honorary uncles passing through the house during my early years and, judging by their readiness to dash upstairs, and by the creaking sounds that came from my mother's bedroom, they were all keen to play competitive games on the bed. I often heard her cheering the blighters on to greater efforts.'

'Oh, Bailey.' She hugged him out of helpless sympathy.

'My dear girl, brace yourself. It gets worse.'

'Is that possible?'

'You'll see.' He continued to hold her close as he continued with his story. 'I went to school occasionally, when I felt like it, so that after a while the truant officer could find his way to my house blindfold, but then, when I was fourteen, I left school and made the dear old boy's job so much easier.

'I had a succession of jobs, mainly around the market. Somehow, I managed to stay on the straight and narrow, at least most of the time, but then, when I was sixteen, I got into White Hart Lane Stadium, home to Tottenham Hotspur Football Club, posing as a messenger boy. I did it more than once; in fact, I made a habit of it, but I also made the mistake of pinching a pie on the last occasion, and I was caught. The stall keeper called the forces of law and order, and I was taken into custody. With no one to speak up for me, I was sent to a Borstal Institution for twelve months.'

'And that's why Geoffrey called you an "old lag"?'

'That's right.'

'You didn't deserve that. It's not as if you went to a proper prison.'

'No, but he was right about my having a criminal record.'

'Oh, Bailey.' She kissed him like a mother comforting an unhappy child. 'Getting into a football match without paying, and stealing a pie doesn't amount to serious crime.'

'It was the number of times I'd done it that upset the judiciary. They considered it downright cheeky.'

'It was very harsh of them.'

'They didn't think so. They thought it would teach me a lesson and turn me away from crime.'

'And did it?'

'Not immediately. I have to confess that I learned other skills in Borstal.'

'Oh, no.'

'Oh, yes. It was like a technical institute. It was where I learned how to steal headed notepaper and forge a testimonial. That was how I got into the motor trade.' He patted her arm. 'Don't worry, I only did it once. Since then, my references and testimonials have been completely *bona fide*.'

'I believe you, Bailey.'

'Then that's all that matters.'

'It is, but there's one thing I don't understand.'

'Name it, dear girl, and I shall reveal all.' He grimaced. 'I may as well after telling you all that.'

'I'm sorry, Bailey. I didn't mean to put you under pressure.'

'You're not putting me under pressure,' he assured her. 'Ask away.'

'It's only that, with no education to speak of, how did you become so articulate, and how did you acquire this aura of sophistication? I don't understand it.'

'Ah, you see, selling motor cars to the leisured and privileged few, I had an opportunity to adopt their ways. It's not difficult. You see, education comes in various guises.' He reflected on that for a moment, and said, 'The important thing is that I joined the straight and narrow path. I have to say, also, that meeting and getting to know Freddy encouraged me no end to go straight. There was an American on the March as well, called Randy, would you believe? He was a stout ally, but it was Freddy who really influenced me.'

They lay for a while in thought, and then Elaine said, 'We both owe Freddy a great deal.'

'Hm?'

'There's what you've told me and, of course, the Geoffrey thing.'

'My dear, good girl, must you bring that rotten tomato's name into the conversation?'

'I'm sorry, Bailey. I'm just making my point.'

'Of course you are, and I agree that we're indebted to Freddy.'

'I just wish we could do something, albeit something small, a gesture.'

Thoughts of the Long March sounded a chord in Bailey's memory. 'There is something we could do, old thi... dearest. At least, it's something *you* could do that would give pleasure to both Freddy and Sylvia.'

The band's next engagement was a gala opening night at the County Hotel in Northallerton, a booking that meant a great deal to Freddy because it was a huge compliment for a band formed only three years earlier.

'I'll have to leave you with Bailey again, SP,' said Freddy as he parked the car.

'Oh good. I didn't know he was coming. How did you wangle the ticket for him?'

'He's here as Business Manager.'

'Oh, I daresay he'll carry that off easily enough,' she said, following him into the hotel.

'I think he already has.' Freddy inclined his head towards the ballroom, where Bailey stood in the doorway in a characteristic pose, looking about him with benign approval, as if he'd just acquired the place. He saw them and walked over to greet them.

'My dear old things. How are you both?' He kissed Sylvia's cheek and shook Freddy's hand. 'I've spoken with the manager,' he told them. 'He's attending to some matter in the kitchen, so let me show you the band room while he's doing that.'

'You're taking your duties as Business Manager seriously, I see,' said Sylvia.

Bailey coughed modestly. 'I try to give satisfaction.'

'And, as usual,' said Freddy, 'you do much more than that.' He looked around and asked, 'Where's our new band singer?'

'Elaine is powdering her nose.'

'I think I'll follow her example,' said Sylvia.

'Outside the ballroom and second left,' said Bailey, pointing helpfully in the general direction.

'Thank you, Bailey.'

'I'm going to start the proceedings,' Freddy told him, 'and then I'll leave quite a lot of it to Jimmy. He's keen, so it makes sense.'

'Jimmy?'

'Jimmy Benson.'

'Oh, the pianist chappie, of course. Good idea, Freddy,' said Bailey, sounding like someone who had just received a vital piece of information. It puzzled Freddy, but not for long, as he had a few things to organise before the gala began.

The evening's entertainment began, as usual, with the band's signature number 'Zip-a-Dee-Doo-Dah,' and then Freddy came to the microphone.

'Good evening, ladies and gentlemen. Welcome to the gala opening of the splendid, new County Hotel. Let's begin with a waltz, an old favourite. It's "By the Sleepy Lagoon".'

Sylvia gave Bailey a discreet nod and watched him lead Elaine on to the floor. Her turn would come when Freddy handed over to Jimmy but, for the time being, she would enjoy watching them. Tall and graceful, Bailey was quite natural in the waltz, and Elaine was no less elegant. Together, they made a charming picture. Their relationship was young, but Sylvia still found herself wondering if they might have found their ideal match. She hoped so because she liked them both.

The number reached its close, and Freddy introduced Jimmy Benson before joining Sylvia.

'You're on after this number,' he told Elaine.

'I know. I'll go now.' Shyly, she stroked Bailey's hand and left him to go to the band room.

'The next dance is a foxtrot,' announced Jimmy. 'It's "The Nearness of You".'

'That sounds like us, SP,' said Freddy, taking Sylvia's hand. He looked around him as he led her on to the floor. 'They're a good crowd,' he said. 'They don't need to be encouraged to dance.' He took her in hold and they danced without speaking until Sylvia said, 'I've been watching Bailey and Elaine. They make a lovely couple.'

'SP,' he admonished, 'you're matchmaking.'

'I can't help it on a night like this. The music, the dancing and the occasion demand it.'

At the end of the number, Jimmy came to the microphone to announce the next dance. 'Just to liven things up,' he said, 'let's have a quickstep and a new singer as well, ladies and gentlemen. Here to sing "I Got Rhythm" is Elaine Stafford.'

Bailey, Sylvia and Freddy stayed at their table to hear Elaine's first public band performance. She looked magnificent in a long, emerald-green dress, and her voice blended perfectly with the band. If she were nervous, she gave no indication of it but sang confidently and with great commitment. The applause at the end of the number was a fitting accolade.

Freddy returned to the platform for a spell, during which Sylvia danced once with Bailey, and spent the rest of the time simply enjoying the music and the occasion.

Eventually, he returned just as Elaine was heading for the band room. He wished her luck, and joined Sylvia and Bailey at their table.

'I'll get the drinks in,' he offered.

'No,' Bailey told him, 'I'll get them. You and Sylvia stay here.'

It seemed an odd thing to say, but Freddy sat down just as Jimmy announced the next number.

'This is a special song,' he told them, 'for two people in particular. It's Jerome Kern and Oscar Hammerstein at their very best. Here's Elaine to sing "All the Things You Are".'

Freddy and Sylvia took to the floor, not trusting themselves to speak. It symbolised their relationship, and Freddy knew he hadn't put it into the programme. That was clearly again down to Bailey and, very likely, Elaine, who was now singing it beautifully.

More than five years had elapsed since that night at the Glass Slipper, when Freddy, still struggling with the bewildering strangeness of freedom and his long-awaited meeting with Sylvia, had finally realised that the obstacles of the past were no more and that their future was secure.

For Sylvia, it had been the culmination of months of anticipation, conjecture and longing, and the perfect outcome after a nervous and tentative meeting in Trafalgar Square.

It meant as much as that and it made Bailey's gesture, with Elaine's able assistance, the welcome gift they had presumably intended it to be.

27

The first half-hour of Monday's rehearsal was scheduled for a costumes try-on, which meant that, exceptionally, Freddy and Sylvia had no need to hurry and could enjoy a leisurely meal. When they did arrive at the rehearsal, however, they found the cast less than content.

'It's not the fit,' one of the chorus told Freddy. 'That's fine. It's the colours that are wrong.'

Freddy looked around him, making an allowance in the circumstances, for the curious blend of theatrical costumes and twentieth-century accessories. One Anglo-Saxon woman's costume was complemented by fully-fashioned nylon stockings. Elsewhere, a Viking warrior sported sock suspenders and polished brogues.

He asked, 'What's wrong with the colours?'

'They're all different,' Herbert Brook told him. 'They've all been dyed different, 'stead of all t' same.'

'Good. That's the effect I want.'

'What do you mean, Freddy?'

'Herbert,' he said gently, 'do you really imagine there was a dye house in ninth-century Britain that turned out thousands of garments all dyed to exactly the same shade of brown? Those people must have done their own spinning, weaving and dyeing. It was a time of individualism, and it's a safe bet that no two women would ever turn up at a function wearing the same dress.'

That last observation earned him a welcome chuckle from members of the female cast, and Herbert Brook shifted uncomfortably.

'Well,' he said, 'I just thought they looked daft.'

'But you see my point, don't you, Herbert?'

'I do now, now you've explained it.'

'Excellent.' To the rest of the cast, he said, 'I think you all look very much the part.' Then, as an afterthought, he added, 'Maybe I should say the *parts*, because I'm looking forward to seeing you all on stage and in costume.' Herbert Brook was entitled to his own ideas, but it would be better if he kept them to himself and stopped upsetting other members of the cast. 'Now,' he said, 'I'd like to run the last scene, when the Vikings and the Daleswomen are preparing to repel the invaders. Are you ready, Elga?'

Elaine moved to centre stage for her song. The chorus arranged themselves tidily around her.

'No,' said Freddy, 'you can't do it like that. Some of you even have your backs to the audience, and you're supposed to be preparing for battle, not a lesson in nature study.'

Marjorie Bentham looked mystified. 'We don't know what to do, Freddy. You seem to forget we're women who do the typing and cooking when men go to war.'

'No, you're not, Marjorie. You're doughty amazons, daughters of tough Dalesfolk, and you're not going to be pushed around by painted marauders at any price. Now, I'm going to give each of you a position on the stage and, when Elga calls you to her side, I want you to go straight to that place. If you have to push one of your comrades-in-arms out of the way, fair enough. That will look authentic.' He looked around for the male chorus, and said, 'Vikings, I'll start with you. You will stand behind Elga as you were briefed in the previous scene. Okay, tallest stage right, shortest stage left.' He waited for them to sort themselves into the line he'd described. 'Good. Now the women's chorus....'

He spent the next ten minutes setting the music number, and then had the cast practise taking their places. They repeated the process several times before he was satisfied.

❦

'They have absolutely no sense of urgency,' he told Sylvia the next day. 'Show week is almost upon us and they're behaving as if next year is soon enough.'

'What are you doing to Thea, Freddy?'

'I'm looking at her teeth. Tooth decay is always a risk with Aberdeen terriers.'

'I thought so, but what can you do about it? You can't brush her teeth with toothpaste. It might make her ill.'

'Yes.' He gave Thea a stroke and considered the problem. 'I'll ask the vet about it,' he said.

'That's always a good idea.'

'In Italy and Poland, when we had no tooth paste, we used soot.'

'Soot?'

'Ordinary soot from the flues.'

'Ugh.'

'It worked very well, but I can't use it on Thea.'

'I certainly wouldn't want my teeth cleaned with soot.'

'Not even if I gave you a biscuit and tickled you behind your ears?'

'Not even then.'

'You've no sense of adventure, SP.'

Returning to the original subject, she said, 'You can't blame the cast. They haven't taken part in a show for more than ten years, and another thing to remember is that, in a rural community like this, people have their own priorities.'

'I suppose so, and I can't change them, so I'll just have to take them as they are.'

'That's right.' Sylvia was looking at Thea, who, despite her recent dental examination, was sitting faithfully beside Freddy, the rule about dogs on furniture having been somehow forgotten. 'You know,' she said, 'it's amazing the way Thea takes everything in her stride. If you held my mouth open and stared into it, I wouldn't speak to you for a week.'

'Ah, but I don't need to as long as you go on using toothpaste.' He closed his eyes at the thought of it. 'I love it when you taste of toothpaste.'

'I know. You keep telling me.' The thought seemed to lead to another, because, after staring at the floor for several seconds, she shifted her gaze to Thea, and said, 'Is there room for me on that sofa, or would I be intruding?'

'Not a bit of it. Move up and make room, Thea.' He pushed her gently to the other end of the sofa. 'No, you don't need to get down. Just make room for SP. Good girl.'

Sylvia took the place Thea had vacated. 'It's nice and warm,' she said.

'I've been training her to warm the seat.'

'Oh? What happened to the no dogs on furniture rule?'

Freddy shook his head sadly. 'Good intentions, SP. I did my best, but I was up against forces beyond my control.'

'The big brown eyes, eh?'

'Well, you try looking into her little face and being stern and forbidding, when all she wants is to be accepted as one of the family.'

Sylvia gave him a meaningful look.

'It comes of being an air-gunner, you see. Isolated and alone in the after cockpit, I've known what it is to feel excluded.'

'Nonsense. You're just soft-hearted. Still, I'm glad you mentioned family, because that's what I want to talk to you about.'

'Talk away, SP. I'm listening.'

'All right.' She hesitated for a second before saying, 'Would you be prepared to consider adopting a baby?'

For a moment, he was taken by surprise. 'Crikey, SP, you came at me out of the sun with that one.'

'Well, what do you say? Is it something you'd consider?'

'I'd consider it....'

'You don't sound convinced.'

'You've only just asked me, SP. Give me a chance to think about it.'

'Okay,' she admitted, 'I did spring it on you.'

'Mm. I couldn't make an immediate decision....'

'Don't be silly. I don't expect you to.'

'The thing is, you see, I haven't completely given up on doing it the old-fashioned way.'

She nodded. 'I'm being impatient.'

'Only because it's so important to you. You're allowed to be impatient, SP.'

'But we've tried everything.'

'I know.' They had too. They'd tried harnessing gravity: the pillow under the bottom, the post-coital handstand, and they'd tried focusing on ovulation…. Freddy always thought of that as the repro-ductive equivalent of firing a pistol at a moving target. It seemed to him much better to do it whenever the urge came upon them, to fire at will, so to speak. He was naturally careful not to use the shooting analogy when discussing the problem with Sylvia or, for that matter, with the gynaecologist, who was a precise and refined man unacquainted with levity.

'We could consider it,' he said. 'I'm certainly not dismissing it.'

'Perhaps we can find out more about it,' suggested Sylvia. 'Who should we ask?'

'The county council, I imagine. It's worth an enquiry.'

'Maybe they have leaflets at the doctor's surgery.'

'Very likely.' He felt as if he were humouring her but, as always when dealing with frustrated motherhood, he knew better than to present obstacles.

She surprised him then, by saying, 'I shan't do anything until after the show. We must concentrate on that.'

It was true. Show week was looming, and there was still a great deal to be done.

28

Freddy picked up the two pints of dark mild he'd bought, and joined Albert Whittaker on the oak settle. Albert looked up as he took his place.

"Evenin', Freddy. I'm obliged to you.'

'You're welcome, Bert.' He remained quiet for a while, knowing better than to hurry Albert into conversation. Eventually, he asked, 'How are things going?'

'Much the same, Freddy. How about you?'

'Well enough, Bert.' As conversations went, it wasn't too promising, so Freddy said, 'Some of us are putting a show on at the Town Hall next month. Maybe you've heard about it.'

'Aye, 'appen I have.' Albert appeared to consider the matter for a spell, and then asked, 'What sort of show is it, then?'

'A musical play. It's set in the ninth century, when the dale was plagued with Vikings and Picts.'

Albert nodded, as if digesting the information. 'It doesn't sound like a happy show.'

'Ah, but it is, Bert. It's a comedy; at least, I hope it is. I've been working hard on the funny bits.'

'When you say you've been working hard, Freddy, what do you mean? Where do you come into it, exactly?'

Freddy took a log and dropped on to the fire to save Grace the trouble. As he did so, he wondered how self-absorbed he was going to sound. 'I wrote it,' he said, 'I wrote the music and lyrics, and I'm Artistic Director as well.' In case Albert thought he'd collared every job, he said, 'I'm not doing the choreography. That's my wife's department.'

That seemed to nudge Albert's memory, because he said, 'You wedded Sylvia Charlesworth, didn't you?'

'That's right.'

'She were always a lovely lass. I knew her at elementary school.'

'I know.' He remembered Sylvia telling him.

'Even when she passed t' scholarship and went to t' grammar school, it didn't change her. Not like some of 'em. She always let on when she saw you, friendly as ever.'

Freddy was touched by his words, but he said nothing.

Albert asked, 'How did you two meet? You're not from round here, are you?'

'No, I'm from Hull. Another POW's wife worked with Sylvia and she persuaded her to write to me. It all went on from there.' He looked at Albert's glass and asked, 'Do you fancy another?'

'Thanks, Freddy. I'll get t' next 'un.'

It was a familiar story, but Freddy didn't mind. He knew Albert was out of work. He bought two more pints and brought them to the settle.

'Thanks, Freddy.'

'You're welcome.'

'So it all happened through writing letters, then?'

'It's surprising what you can learn about someone through letters, Bert.'

'Evidently.' He took a drink from his pint and returned to the original subject. 'What made you think of putting this show on, then?'

'Just the way things are, really, with rationing, austerity.... I know rationing means nothing to you and me, Bert, but it's been going on too long for some, and I just thought I'd do something to try and cheer them up.'

'Well, na' then.' Albert nodded to himself, and said, 'How much are these tickets, then?'

'They're free to war widows and returned POWs.' Then, seeing a look of suspicion in Albert's eye, he reassured him by saying, 'It was the producer, my father-in-law, who made that decision. I'll see you get the tickets, Albert.'

Eventually, he took his leave of Albert and left his empty glass on the bar. As he was leaving, Grace asked him, 'Have you heard about that dog of Bob Woolliscroft's, Freddy?'

'Tigger? No. What's he been up to?'

'Sheep worrying.'

'Oh, heck.'

'Aye, it'll be the long drop for him now.'

'I'm afraid so. Whose sheep were they?'

'Nathan Parker's.'

<hr />

When he arrived home, Sylvia was listening to the Ten o'clock News on the Light Programme, although there seemed to be very little happening, because she switched it off when he came into the room, and asked, 'Did you have a nice drink, Freddy?'

'Very nice, thanks. I saw Bert Whittaker.'

'Oh? How is he?'

'He seems to be in reasonable spirits. He was positively chatty tonight.'

'Really?'

'Well, by his standards.' Recalling the conversation, he said, 'He's coming to see the show.'

'Oh, good.' A moment later, she asked, 'What about the tickets? He's out of work, you know.'

'They're free to war widows and returned POWs.'

'Oh?' She looked puzzled. 'When did that happen?'

'It hasn't, but it will as soon as I can speak to your dad.'

'Good.' Looking up at the clock, she asked, 'Shall we have a cup of tea before we go to bed?'

'Why not? I'll make it.'

While he was in the kitchen, making the tea, he remembered his brief conversation with Grace, and decided to tell Sylvia. Then it would be out of the way.

Carrying the tea things into the sitting room, he said, 'There's bad news about Tigger, I'm afraid.'

'Oh yes, I heard about that. I was going to tell you.'

It always surprised Freddy that Sylvia got to know about things long before he did. Still, he had a lot to learn about rural life. 'I can't imagine Nathan Parker showing any mercy,' he said.

'You'd be surprised.'

'Go on. Surprise me.' In a perverse kind of way, he had a soft spot for Tigger, and any kind of reprieve would be good news.

'Mr Parker told Mrs Woolliscroft that he could either shoot him or cure him, and Mrs Woolliscroft opted for the latter, although she wasn't too pleased when she heard what he'd done.'

'Not a gentle training exercise, I imagine?' Freddy shook his head in anticipation.

'He put Tigger into a pen with a tup.'

'Surely not.'

'Oh yes. It's a well-tried remedy in sheep-farming circles and, suffice it to say, after a few minutes in the pen, Tigger began to see the situation from the tup's point of view. If he sees anything with wool on its back now, he'll either run for his life or close his eyes and pray for it to go away.'

❦

Two days later, Mrs Woolliscroft phoned to arrange a photo session and, as Freddy was free that morning, he agreed to the session.

He found Tigger surprisingly biddable, if not entirely docile, and put it down to his experience in the pen, but Mrs Woolliscroft was quick to enlighten him.

'I put me foot down, Freddy. I told my husband that if I was going to look after his dog, he'd have to be properly trained.' She looked down at Tigger, now sitting at her feet and awaiting orders. 'He found a retired police dog handler who does dog training, and booked him in. I'd say it was a good decision. Don't you think so?'

All things considered, Freddy did, although he had to admit, if only to himself, that Tigger wasn't quite so much fun as he'd been in the past.

29

'Freddy, Bailey's on the phone. It sounds important.'
'Okay.' He left the photograph he was mounting and went to the phone.

'Hello, Bailey. What's the problem?'

'Bad news, old man. Elaine's succumbed to the lurgy. She's sniffling, sneezing, complaining of a sore throat and, what's even worse, she won't let me near her.'

'Very sensible of her. We can't have both of you reporting sick on shore.'

'Well, it's very worrying. I've been wondering if she was over-doing things, you know, with the band as well as the show.'

'You can't catch a cold through overwork, Bailey. You just have to blame nature for that.'

'Oh well, I suppose I'll have to leave her to her bed and a bottle of whisky.'

'Port would be better.'

'Say again, old man?'

Freddy raised his voice, mindful of Bailey's partial deafness. 'Port,' he repeated. 'Produce of Portugal and all that.'

'All right, old man. I'm not completely deaf. I'll buy her a bottle of Port if you think that's better.'

'It's very good for the larynx, Bailey. Opera singers swear by it, and you can pick up a bottle quite cheaply nowadays.'

'Ply my beloved with cheap plonk? Perish the thought, Freddy. She's going to have a decent vintage if I have anything to do with it.'

'Okay, but keep your distance. With any luck, Elaine will be over it by show week, but we can't have you out of action as well.'

168

'I'll keep her at arm's length, much as it pains me.'

'That's the spirit, Bailey, and give her my best wishes.'

'Thanks, old man.'

Freddy put the phone down and spoke to Sylvia, who was waiting expectantly.

'Elaine's gone down with a cold,' he told her.

'Oh, no.'

'She should be all right for show week, but I've asked Bailey to keep his distance from her.'

'Quite right.'

He told her what Bailey had said about cheap port-style wine. She smiled broadly. 'Is that really what he called her? His beloved?' The thought evidently appealed to her.

'Honestly, SP, I'm in danger of losing my leading lady, and all you're interested in is matchmaking.'

'As you said, though, she should be all right for show week, although these things sometimes linger on, don't they? I mean bronchitis and that sort of thing.'

'That new penicillin stuff they use nowadays should take care of that. I just hope her doctor's sufficiently clued up to prescribe it.'

'Would it shorten a cold?'

'I don't think so. Cold is a virus, but they use it for secondary infections such as bronchitis.'

'They gave me something different for my ear infection. Whatever it was wouldn't dissolve in water, so I had to drink gallons just to flush it through my system.'

'I bet that kept you up and about.'

'Don't be awful.'

'No, I know you suffered, SP, but it brought you home, so it wasn't all bad.'

'It was bad enough.'

The situation with Elaine was also bad enough, as Freddy told Walter later. 'Fortunately, she's on top of the part, so I've no worries on that score. I just want her to be ready for show week.'

Walter nodded. 'If you give me her address I'll send her some flowers.'

'That's decent of you, Walter. With flowers from you and vintage port from Bailey, she'll feel quite spoiled. Still, it all helps, I suppose.'

Walter opened his folding stool and sat down. 'Bailey doesn't do anything by halves, does he?'

'No, but whatever he does nowadays is on the straight and narrow.'

'I'm glad about that, Freddy. Apparently, you were a reforming influence on him.'

'Oh?'

'When you were prisoners on the way back from Poland. He says it was your example that persuaded him to abandon his dubious activities.'

'Good grief. How did you hear that?'

'He phoned to thank me after the ugly incident with the policeman. We had quite a chat.'

'Evidently.' The news surprised Freddy, although, modest as ever, he had to set the record straight. 'His criminal past existed largely in his imagination, you know.'

'I know. As criminal acts go, it was small beer.'

Walter appeared to be studying a stretch of the river but, after a while, he asked, 'Considering the problems you've had to overcome so far, would you consider putting on another show for the Players?'

'As you're asking me now, Walter, with all that's going on, I don't think I would.'

Walter nodded understandingly.

'But ask me again next April or May, and my answer might well be different. I've enjoyed doing it – well, most of it – but I'll need a rest after this one.'

'Just as I thought.' He took out his pipe and lighter.

'So why did you ask me?'

Walter finished lighting his pipe before replying. 'You'd be surprised,' he said eventually, 'by the number of people who have remarked on the effect the show is having on the community, and I don't mean just the Players themselves; I'm talking about people generally. You told me you wanted to give these people a lift, and you've certainly done that.'

'In that case, Walter, you'd better ask me again next spring.'

'I shall.'

The two men sat for a while, enjoying the sounds of the birds overhead and the water tumbling over the rocks. Presently, Walter said, 'Tell me to mind my own business if you will, but Sylvia told Audrey that you're considering adoption.'

'Sylvia's considering it. I still haven't given up on Mother Nature.'

'Good.' Walter looked thoughtful before saying, 'She was always like that, you know. If something wasn't working for her, she would move on and try something else.'

'I must say, it's not a trait I've noticed.'

'Oh yes. She was the same at school. When she felt she was getting nowhere with sciences, she changed to classics.' He added with a hint of regret, 'Maths was always a problem for her.'

It sounded like the kind of distressing situation Freddy remembered discussing with his father. 'Walter,' he said, 'if you'd known me when I was at school, you'd have written me off as a non-entity. I got a School Certificate by the sweat of my brow, and it was the biggest surprise of all that I got a pass – not a credit, but a pass – in maths.'

'I'm sure we all have our strengths and weaknesses, Freddy. I'm only saying that Sylvia was always one for moving on.'

It was good of Walter to offer his counsel, but it wasn't what Freddy wanted to discuss. For one thing, Sylvia's latest whim worried him, and he was reluctant to talk about it.

'Let's catch some trout, Walter,' he suggested. 'By my reckoning, we have one more weekend before the end of the season.'

30

Rehearsals that week proceeded as well as they could without the leading lady, and it was a relief to see her that Friday. Unfortunately, that was the extent of the good news, as Freddy was soon to realise.

'Ernie Holmes sends his apologies.' Herbert Brook delivered the news in his usual precise way.

'Not another.' It was the fifth apology Freddy had received that evening. 'Do you know what this is about, Herbert?'

'Aye, there's an important meeting at the school about the Festival of Britain. There'll be regular meetings from now on.' He added sourly, 'Only, not everybody's important enough to be invited.'

'I'm thankful you weren't, Herbert. I need you here.' Turning to the members present, he said, 'Okay, let's run it from the end of the opening chorus. The ladies have made their exit. Enter Erik, Olaf and Dag.'

(Erik and his two henchmen make their entrance, looking warily from side to side.)

ERIK   There's no one about. The place is deserted (Looks around) Where's Nils?

OLAF   He's having one of his nosebleeds, Chief. He won't be long.

ERIK   (Pacing impatiently) By Thor's drawers, he's taking his time about it.

At this point, Freddy interrupted.

'He's taking far too long. Nils, where are you?'

'He's at the meeting.' Herbert delivered the information in his usual disapproving way.

'Oh, glory.' Freddy took a deep breath and asked, 'Sylvia, will you stand in for Nils, please?'

'Okay.' Opening her copy of the script, she entered stage right with a hanky clutched to her nose.

NILS   Sorry, Chief. By dose was bleedid. It's all right dow.

ERIK   Good. What's today?

NILS   Today, Chief? It's Woden's Day. (Consults his slate) Early Closing in Easingthorpe.

ERIK   That would explain why there's no one around. (Taps Nils on the shoulder.) When's Market Day?

NILS   (Consults slate again) Thor's Day, Chief. That's tomorrow.

DAG   (Clearly struggling to follow the conversation) Why do you want to know about Market Day, Chief? Are you planning a massacre in the Market Place?

ERIK   No, nothing like that. I need a pattern and some knitting wool.

Freddy clapped his hands. 'Let's stop there, folks. You're doing well in the circumstances, and thank you, Sylvia, but we're not going to do much good. Let's move on to the ladies' entrance.'

⊕⊢3⊹⊱⊰⊱⊢⊕

At the end of the rehearsal, he thanked those who had attended, and then sat down heavily on the piano stool.

'It's ridiculous,' he said. 'The Festival of Britain isn't until next

173

May. They've ample time to organise the town's contribution before then.'

Bailey asked, 'Who's in charge of this bally jamboree?'

'I don't know,' said Freddy. 'I'm just wondering about the commitment of the members who gave tonight a miss. Whoever's calling the shots seems to have more influence than I can exert.'

'As far as I know,' said Elaine, 'the Town Clerk is co-ordinating chairman. Maybe he's open to entreaty.'

Sylvia raised a cynical eyebrow. 'Mr Parker? That stuffy old bureaucrat?'

'Of all the times to spring something like this on us.' Freddy closed his briefcase and snapped the catches home. 'I'll get a list of their meetings, and then I need to think about it.'

⊷⊷⊱⊱⊰⊰⊶⊶

The list Freddy obtained from the Town Hall presented him with more bad news. The meetings that had been planned made utter nonsense of his rehearsal schedule.

One possibility he'd considered was that of postponing the show, but he dismissed the idea almost before it was formed. The hall was heavily booked in November, and December brought with it the threat of bad weather, making travel difficult. In any case, the Festival meetings would always be an obstacle however much he extended the rehearsal schedule. He also had to consider the effect a postponement would have on the cast, most of whom had been working on the show since midsummer. No, pushing show week back was out of the question.

He continued to think, his thoughts usually going round in circles, until a phone call on Saturday evening provided a welcome interruption.

'It's my dad,' Sylvia told him, handing the receiver to him. 'Maybe he'll cheer you up.'

'Hello, Walter.'

'Freddy, what's the matter with Sylvia? She sounded out of sorts when she picked up the phone.'

'That's probably my fault. There's a problem with the show, and

I've been in a foul mood ever since last night's rehearsal. I can't be much fun to live with.' A slow nod from Sylvia confirmed his theory.

'That's too bad of you, Freddy. I suppose I'd better drag you out of the house tomorrow for a spot of fishing, if only to give my little girl some peace and quiet.'

'It's a good idea, Walter. I'm glad you phoned.'

'So am I. You'll be able to air the problem to a fresh audience.'

As Freddy put the phone down, he said, 'I'm going fishing with your dad tomorrow.'

'I gathered that. Come back in a better frame of mind, won't you?'

'I'll try to. I'm sorry, SP, I've been impossible.'

'I won't disagree with that, Freddy.' Leaving her armchair, she joined him on the sofa. 'Don't forget that others are as upset as you are about this thing, and we're on your side. For what it's worth, I always will be, come what may.'

'I know that, SP,' he said, putting his arms around her.

'Just remember that your battle is with the Festival Committee, not the rest of us.'

He nodded contritely. Then, for good measure, he pushed out his lower lip.

'Don't be silly.'

'I can't help it. When you're being Leading Wren Charlesworth you intimidate me.'

'I never intimidated anyone.'

'Maybe you did, but none of them dared tell you.'

'Let me tell you something that's just occurred to me.'

'What?'

'Tell my dad about the problem when you see him tomorrow. He may just have some ideas.'

⚬┄❋┄❋┄⚬

It was a soggy day but the dogs didn't mind, and Freddy and Walter were suitably clad against the weather; Redmire Falls kept its appeal for all of them in all conditions, so everyone was happy. Freddy had even put his current problem temporarily behind him, and was ready to enjoy a day's fishing, whereas the dogs were prepared to enjoy anything that came along.

The two men fished happily, and with some reward, until Walter looked at his watch and suggested that lunch would be a welcome event.

'It's almost the end of the season,' said Freddy, 'but I'm afraid I'm going to need the remaining Sundays for rehearsal. That's if we're to give our audiences anything at all for their ticket money. How are ticket sales going, by the way, Walter?'

'Quite promising. The first night's almost sold out. Thereafter, it's quite good.' He opened a tin of sandwiches and said, 'I don't know what you've brought, but you're welcome to dive in.'

'Thanks, Walter.' Freddy opened his box and offered it. 'Likewise,' he said.

'Thank you.' He took a sandwich and tried it. 'My daughter,' he said finally, 'is remarkably inventive with fish. I wonder where she learned it.' He finished the sandwich with obvious enjoyment and then asked, 'What's this problem with the show, Freddy?'

'The Festival of Britain. It's eight months away, but our worthy Town Clerk had organised frequent and regular meetings throughout this month and, with only two weeks left, I'm working with half my cast.'

'Really?' Walter nodded slowly. 'Just the kind of thing we don't need.'

'But what can we do, Walter? Sylvia doesn't think there's even half a chance of persuading old Parker to play the game.'

'You and I must arrange a meeting with him, Freddy, as soon as we can.'

'Do you really think there's any point in appealing to his better nature?'

Walter considered the question and smiled briefly to himself. 'There are those who doubt that he has a better nature, Freddy. In any case, that's not the way to negotiate with Percy Parker.' As he uncorked his Thermos flask, he said, 'You'll have to trust me with this one.'

⊸═☧☖☧═⊷

With Thea dried and fed, Freddy soaked himself in the bath. Then, changed, dry and warm once more, he went downstairs to find Sylvia in the kitchen, preparing dinner. On hearing his foot- steps, she turned and smiled.

'Did you have a good day?'

'Very good.' He slipped his arms around her from behind and kissed her. 'The catch is in the fridge,' he told her.

'I've seen it. Well done.'

'Can I do anything?'

'No, thanks. It's all done.' Opening the oven, she put the stew inside and closed the door. 'You could put the kettle on for a cup of tea,' she suggested.

'That's a splendid idea.' He filled the kettle and placed it on the hob.

'I'm glad you're not miserable any more, Freddy. The fishing must have done you good.'

'As much as anything else, it was being with your dad that did the trick. You know, I don't know how he's going to do it, but he's confident he's going to solve the problem of the Festival meetings.'

'It wouldn't surprise me in the least.'

'Really?'

'Don't forget I lived with him for seventeen years and I know how he works.'

When the tea was made, they took it into the sitting room and sat together on the sofa.

'Welcome back, Freddy.'

'Was I really so awful?'

'No, you were worse than that, and I know it was for the best of reasons, but I'm glad you're back to normal.' She leaned forward so that he could slip his arm round her.

'It was such a body blow, and with two weeks before the show. None of us deserves that.'

'I know, and you've carried the whole thing on your back from the start.' She snuggled against him and turned her face up to his. He bent to kiss her, grateful as ever for her understanding, and re- lieved to be free of the awful dark cloud that had separated them since Friday evening. Then, what had begun as something gentle and affectionate grew into a searching, impassioned kiss that could have only one conclusion.

'Freddy,' she said breathlessly, 'let's go upstairs.'

⊷⊷⊰⊹⊱⊷⊷

Walter phoned shortly after nine o'clock the next morning.

'Freddy,' he said, 'can you be at the Town Hall for four-thirty?'

Freddy looked at his appointment book. 'Yes,' he said, 'I should be able to do that.'

'Good. I'll meet you in the entrance hall. Let me do the talking. All you need to do is agree or disagree as and when required.'

'Fine.' It all sounded very mysterious to Freddy, but he knew his father-in-law well enough to trust his judgement, which was just as well, as he was still devoid of ideas of his own.

He worked through his appointments: two rabbits, a Persian cat and one person requiring a passport photograph, an unusual request in parochial Easingthorpe, but one which was no less welcome for that.

Eventually, it was time to meet Walter at the Town Hall.

In the event, they arrived simultaneously, shook hands and reported to reception.

The receptionist recognised Walter at once.

'Hello, Mr Charlesworth,' she said. 'How are you?'

'Passing fair, thank you, Daisy, and you?'

'Oh, I'm all right, thanks, Mr Charlesworth.'

'And how is your mother?'

'Not so good, I'm afraid. She doesn't get out much nowadays, and when she does it's not very far.'

'I'm sorry to hear that, Daisy. Please give her my regards.'

'Thank you, Mr Charlesworth.'

'Now, Mr Hinchcliffe and I have an appointment with Mr Parker at four-thirty.'

'Just one moment, please, Mr Charlesworth.' She lifted the telephone receiver and spoke briefly to someone. Then, coming off the phone, she asked, 'Do you know where his office is?'

'Yes, if it's still on the first floor.'

'That's right. Goodbye, Mr Charlesworth.'

'Goodbye, Daisy, and thank you.'

As they mounted the staircase, Walter said, 'Daisy worked in our office for a while, but she soon realised it wasn't the job for her. She doesn't get on with figures. It pays to stay on good terms with people, though, especially in a small town like this, where they can be very helpful.'

Freddy wondered if there was anyone in the locality who didn't know Walter.

Soon, they came to a door with frosted glass panes. The sign on the door read: *Mr P. C. Parker, Llb. (Lond.), Town Clerk*. Walter pushed the door open and smiled at the secretary, who said, 'Go straight in, Mr Charlesworth. Mr Parker is expecting you.'

Freddy felt as if he were be taken into the headmaster's study. Everything about Parker's appearance suggested severity. His glance was severe, his morning dress tie was knotted tightly, his chevron moustache was trimmed precisely, and his pens, pencils and other stationery items were arranged on his desk with military exactness. He shook hands with Freddy, but returned his attention immediately to Walter.

With the initial greetings out of the way, Parker said, 'Well, Walter, I understand you wish to speak to me about The Festival of Britain.' He enunciated the title as he might refer to The Fate of Mankind or The Second Coming.

'In a word, yes.' Walter went on to describe Freddy's selfless bid to bring pleasure and entertainment, amid rationing and shortages, to the people of Easingthorpe. He went on to tell Parker about the preparation and work that had been put in by the cast since mid-summer. 'And now,' he said, 'all that has come to nought because of a series of ill-timed meetings called to plan an event that is to be held eight months from now.'

'You don't seem to realise, Walter, the scale of the Festival,' said Parker. Festivities will take place in every city, town, village and hamlet in the country. It has been planned nationally by no less a personage than the Deputy Prime Minister, Mr Morrison himself.' He sat back in his chair with the relaxed and confident expression of a gambler who has just played his trump card.

'I'm sure you and Herbert Morrison are in complete agreement about his importance, Percy. Unfortunately, I confess to being less than impressed.'

'You always were an obstinate tory, Walter, but Herbert Morrison has the right of it. Let me tell you that this is the biggest event to take place in this country since the end of the war.'

'And it's eight months away, whereas the Yoredale Players' production is scheduled for week commencing the ninth of October, just two weeks from now.'

'I can't help that, Walter. It's just unfortunate, the way things have turned out.'

'More than unfortunate for some, I'd say, Percy. "Tragic" might be a better description.'

Parker was unmoved. 'Well, you know, you can't make an omelette without breaking a few eggs.'

'In making your omelette, Mr Parker,' said Freddy, 'you're also going to break a few hearts. Is that your mission?'

Behind Parker's desk, Walter gestured minutely to Freddy to be patient.

'I think you're being melodramatic, young man.' In an unexpected attempt at humour, Parker added, 'That's the trouble with you dramatic people.' He laughed lightly at his joke.

By this time, Freddy was almost convinced that their argument was lost, but he listened nevertheless as his father-in-law tried a different approach.

'Percy,' said Walter, 'regarding this town's contribution to the Festival of Britain, presumably there will be some musical entertainment.'

'Yes, music is central to the whole thing. The Easingthorpe brass band will make an important contribution to the Festival.' He looked again at Freddy, and said, 'Am I correct in my belief that you lead a sort of band as well, Mr Hinchcliffe?'

Before Freddy could answer, Walter said, 'How marvellous it would be if both the Easingthorpe Brass Band and the Dalesmen could take part in so grand an occasion. Don't you think so, Percy?' As he spoke, he signalled Freddy again to keep quiet.

'That is what we have planned.'

'In fact it would be less than satisfactory without their input, I think you'll agree.'

'What are you suggesting?' For the first time, Parker showed signs of unease.

'I believe some of the Dalesmen also play with the Brass Band. Isn't that so, Freddy?'

'That's right, Walter.' Freddy was beginning to see a glimmer of light at the end of a very long tunnel.

'Let's just take an overview of the situation,' said Walter. 'The Dalesmen are providing the musical accompaniment for the production. Now, they're not going to be too pleased at having that snatched from them, are they, Freddy?'

'They'll be furious, Walter.' Freddy's heart was beating again.

'And, because of that, those members who are also in the Brass Band are unlikely to find much enthusiasm for the Festival of Britain.'

'Hardly any at all, Walter,' said Freddy.

The colour, such as it was, had drained from Parker's face. 'Are you telling me,' he asked weakly, 'that they'd refuse to take part in the Festival?'

'No one takes kindly to being ridden over rough-shod, Percy. You must see that.'

'Yes, I can see that.' He shook his head. 'This is a deplorable situation.'

'Most unenviable, I'd say, from your point of view.'

'It's dreadful. I never envisaged this.'

'It's a nightmare,' agreed Walter, still turning the screw. 'On the other hand, problems are there to be overcome.'

'What do you have in mind?'

'Well, I think you'll both agree that one good turn deserves another.'

'Yes?' Parker was almost pleading.

'Freddy,' said Walter, 'would you and the others be willing to take part in the Festival celebrations if Percy agrees to postpone his September and October meetings and lets you get on with your rehearsals?'

'I'm pretty sure the lads would agree to that, Walter, and I should be happy to take part on that basis.'

'What a blessing it is, Percy,' said Walter, 'that we can still count on men of goodwill. Don't you agree?'

'You're a rascal, Walter.' Parker's voice was feeble but in a last show of defiance, he said, 'You were a rascal when we were at school, and you still are.'

'Do we have your agreement, Percy?'

'Yes, you have my agreement.' Parker offered his hand, which Walter and Freddy took in turn.

As they stepped outside the Town Hall, Freddy said, 'Walter, I'm forever in your debt. How on earth did you think of all that?'

'It wasn't difficult. The most effective weapon you can have in such a case is that of knowing your enemy, and I've known Percy Parker since we were lads.'

'Yes, what was that he said about your being a rascal at school?'

'Oh, that.' Walter smiled at the memory. 'Percy saw some of us smoking behind the bike sheds, and he reported us to one of the teachers. We each got a caning, which was painful enough, but Percy's discomfort lasted much longer and it caused him more than a degree of embarrassment.'

'What did you do?'

'I smeared the inside of his football shorts with squashed rose hips.'

'I don't get it, Walter. What did that do?'

Forty years later, it still made Walter laugh. 'It's natural itching powder, Freddy. It nearly drove him round the bend.'

'It served the bugger right.'

'So it did.' Walter seemed about to bring the conversation to its close and go on his way, when he remembered something. 'I've been meaning to tell you something, Freddy. We've had two block bookings from old people's homes, actually, and ticket sales are looking very healthy.'

'Excellent. And you've just reminded me of something else, Walter.'

'Go ahead.'

'Can I make a request that tickets are free to war widows and returned POWs?'

'Of course. What prompted that?'

Freddy told him about Albert Whittaker, and Walter was in complete agreement. It had been a good day.

31

With the threat of public meetings lifted, rehearsals continued, chorus every other night and principals nightly. One scene was still to be set, and that was the one in which Elga was to realise the extent of Erik's feelings for her, and to confess hers for him.

'Right,' said Freddy, 'Erik, come downstage, please. This is where you're composing your ode to Elga.'

'Absolutely, old man.' Bailey took his place before the footlights and struck a pose with his slate.

ERIK   O Muses, where are you when you're needed? Can't you see I need your help? (Adopts a listening attitude and appears to hear something.) There you are, my dears. You've not forsaken me after all. Now, how to begin this ode. How to extol her. Ah! I have it! (Scratches on his slate, reciting as he does.)

    How best can I extol
    This fair ideal?

    (Thinks again.)
    Yes, I have it now.

    This paragon of all
    That man esteems.

    (Reads what he has written and nods approvingly.)

> If beauty were the one
> Essential deal;
> Would Elga still appear
> In all men's dreams?

Elga enters stage right. Erik continues, unaware of her presence.

ERIK   Indeed she would,
          And for much else besides;
          Her virtues are
          As countless as the stars.

ELGA   Erik, what are you doing? I suppose you're writing another of your odes. I've come to see if the ammunition is all in place.

ERIK   Yes, Elga, the curds and whey are waiting at the barricades.

At this point, Freddy interrupted them.

'Bailey,' he said, 'you're embarrassed by the interruption and anxious not to let Elga see what you've been doing. Hide the slate behind your back and look flustered.'

'Right away, old man.'

'Let's take it from "Yes, Elga".'

ERIK   Yes, Elga, the curds and whey are waiting at the barricades.

ELGA   (Reaching for his slate) You *are* writing an ode, aren't you? Let me see it.

ERIK   (Holding his slate firmly) No, it's not finished. There's still a lot of work to be done.

ELGA   Go on, show me.

ERIK   No.

ELGA   (In a tone of authority) Erik, show me your slate. Takes it from him and reads.) This is a strange poem.

ERIK   (Nervous and attempting to distract her.) It's in a new metre I've devised, a kind of pentameter. I haven't a name for it yet but the greatest poets may use it one day. You never know.

ELGA   (Still reading) Somehow, I doubt it. (Suddenly looks up in surprise.) Erik, this is about me.

ERIK   (Shamefaced.) Yes, but you saw it before I was ready to make my plea. (Visibly crumpling) I can only throw myself on your mercy, Elga.

ELGA   Nonsense. I wish you'd told me earlier how you felt.

ERIK   (Encouraged beyond belief) By Woden's whiskers, Elga, do you really mean that?

ELGA   Yes. I was wondering when you'd say something. The suspense has been awful. (Waits expectantly.) Well, aren't you going to say something?

ERIK   I'm at a loss. I don't know what to say.

ELGA   In that case, why don't you kiss me?

Freddy clapped his hands. 'Stop there, folks. This is where you clown it up, Bailey. Purse your lips and make a cow's arse. Sorry, Elaine, but it's the only way I can describe it.'

'It's just as well you don't write romantic novels, Freddy.'

'Agreed, but let's carry on. Take it from "In that case, why don't you kiss me?" '

ELGA   In that case, why don't you kiss me?

Erik purses his lips, closes his eyes and leans towards her.

      Not like that, silly. Like this.

'Okay.' Freddy clapped his hands to stop the rehearsal. 'You both know to ham up the rest of it, so I'll leave it to you.'

'This is dashed awkward, Freddy.'

'How's that?'

'Well… doing this before an audience. Baring our all, so to speak.'

Freddy resisted the urge to smile. 'It's a performance, Bailey, nothing to do with your private lives, and no one in the audience, or even the cast, will know what you told me earlier.'

'Scouts' honour, old man?'

'Your secret is safe with me.'

'You can tell Sylvia, of course.'

'That's decent of you, Bailey.'

'Don't worry about the scene,' said Elaine, clearly embarrassed. 'We'll work on it.'

'I know you will. Thank you both.'

⊕⊢ɜ⊣⊱⊱ɟ⊢⊕

'I've booked two double rooms at the Fox and Hounds, the only ones they have.'

'Well done, SP. Who are they for?'

'Oh, Freddy, I told you ages ago. Joyce and Len are coming on the ninth, and Dorothy and Alf as well. They've got tickets for the first night.'

'That's odd, coming to the first night. I'd have expected them to leave it until the weekend.'

'That was the original plan, but Alf couldn't have the weekend off, because one of the farm workers is taking a week's holiday then. Fortunately, Joyce and Len were able to change their plans to coincide with them.' She added wistfully, 'Joyce's mother is going to look after the little girl.'

'What little girl?'

'Oh Freddy, I wish you'd listen occasionally. I told you about Joyce's baby when she was born, two years ago.'

'Two years is a long time to remember something, SP.'

'For you it certainly is.'

'What about Dorothy and the big chap. Have they started a dynasty yet?'

'Not yet, but it's by choice. They're leaving it until after Alf's promotion.'

'Very sensible.' After a moment, he said, 'I hope they won't be disappointed.'

'Why should they be?'

'I suppose it depends on what they're used to, but I've never thought of amateur dramatics and suchlike as being for the audience's benefit. I mean, when all's said and done, it's the ultimate self-indulgence, isn't it?'

Sylvia caught his eye and hurled a cushion at him. 'Don't be awful. Anyway, Joyce says they've never seen a show, and Dorothy and Alf are usually too busy on the farm to go to anything.'

'Good.'

'How was this evening's rehearsal?'

'Pretty good. Bailey and Elaine are still a little bit shy about acting out something that's been happening in real life. It's the on-stage necking that worries them; they feel as if they're baring their souls to the public gaze, but I've left them to sort it out for themselves. They're grown-up enough to deal with it.'

'I can't imagine Bailey being shy about anything.'

'He's only shy where Elaine's concerned.' He stood up and asked, 'Are you ready for a cup of tea? I'll put the kettle on.'

'Not before you've told me about Bailey and Elaine, you don't.'

'You know all about them, SP.'

'I know, but why is he suddenly shy?'

'I thought you'd worked it out already, with your matchmaking.'

'Worked what out?' She was clearly impatient.

Freddy decided to end the suspense. 'For the first time in Bailey's life,' he told her, 'Cupid's arrow has found its mark, and I know for certain that they're going shopping at the weekend, but that's still classified information. You mustn't breathe a word to anyone. Promise?'

'All right,' she said impatiently, 'I promise.'

'Good girl.'

'So are they going shopping for a ring?' Sylvia was now animated.

'What else? I suggested a chastity belt, and Bailey considered it as a viable option, but they're hard to find nowadays. You can't find the locksmiths with the necessary skills, apparently.'

'How like a man.'

'Only kidding, SP.'

'I never thought you were being serious.'

'Good. There's something else as well, if I can only think of it.' He struck a thinking pose for a moment before saying, 'Ah, yes. I remember now. They're going to make the official announcement at the after-show party at the end of the week. That should be fun.'

'Oh, Freddy, you're hopeless.'

'Yes, it's not really a man's thing, is it?'

'I'll throw something at you in a minute.'

'In that case, I'll make the tea.' He was naturally delighted for the happy pair, and Sylvia knew that. Freddy just hoped their engagement wouldn't prove a distraction in the last days of rehearsal, although that was a fear he was careful not to voice in Sylvia's hearing. He suspected he'd tried her patience far enough for the time being.

32

The matter of Bailey and Elaine wasn't the only one occupying Freddy's mind in the week leading up to the dress rehearsal. It seemed that the musician's desks at the Town Hall were deficient in one important detail: namely the lamps, without which the musicians would be unable to function with the house lights down. The war, that had inspired so many acts of selflessness, had also given rise occasionally to licence and dishonesty. The lamps had no doubt been taken by opportunists for domestic use at a time when reading lamps were hard to find and ingenuity abounded.

Five years after the war, desk lamps were still almost unobtainable. Freddy could vouch for that, having tried every known source; in fact, in appraising Walter of the problem, he'd even declared them extinct.

'Leave it with me,' Walter had said. 'I'll ask around.'

Freddy could not imagine what Walter's line of enquiry might be, but he was content to hand over the problem, at least for the time being, as other concerns were claiming his attention.

Like the music desks, the dismembered stage had been stored in the Town Hall basement, and it soon became evident that it had suffered similar abuse, no doubt as a result of fuel rationing.

Sam Walker, Viking chorus member and proprietor of Easingthorpe Joinery and Funeral Service, had identified a number of missing components.

'I'll find what second-hand timber I can, Freddy,' he said, 'but it's all to be paid for.' His expression was bleak, but then it usually was. Freddy put it down to his calling.

'Just give me the bill when you collect the timber, Sam, and I'll see it's paid.'

'Right, I'll be in touch.'

Freddy could only wait and hope that there would be no further snags. He doubted his ability to cope with anything else.

Happily, work provided a distraction for much of the afternoon, and it was after five when Walter phoned him.

'You'll have your lamps by the weekend,' he said.

'That's marvellous, Walter. How on earth did you manage it? I thought I'd tried all the theatrical suppliers.'

'In a case like this, you have to think creatively, Freddy. All it took was a telephone call to Harold Watson.'

'The electrician?'

'The same, although he prefers nowadays to be called an electrical contractor.'

'Go on, Walter. I'm listening.'

'You're quite right that desk lamps are basically unavailable, but Harold knows where he can lay his hands on the requisite number of clip-on inspection lamps of the kind used, I believe, by motor mechanics. He assures me that they'll do the job very adequately.'

'You're amazing, Walter. Nothing ever stumps you, does it?'

'Oh, I wouldn't say that.'

Freddy would. Not for the first time, he had cause to be thankful to his father-in-law.

⸻

'I knew he'd come up with something,' said Sylvia that evening.

'You know, in a vague sort of way, I did too. He's becoming predictable.' He added, 'In the best kind of way.'

'It's an unusual relationship,' she remarked. 'Between you two, I mean.'

'We're friends, that's all.' He hadn't thought seriously about it until then, but now it made sense. 'In-laws don't usually have a relationship, but my friendship with your dad has nothing to do with his being my father-in-law. It's about mutual esteem, and it was cemented the day after VE Day, when he first took me fishing.'

The telephone rang, and Sylvia answered it.

'Just a minute.' She handed the receiver to Freddy. 'It's Sam Walker,' she said.

'Hello, Sam.' He hoped it was good news.

'I've found the timber we need. It's pretty horrible and full of nails, but it won't be visible to the audience, so who cares?'

'Sam, you're a hero. Thank you.'

'Not really, Freddy. There's a snag an' all.'

'Go on.'

'We have to collect it, and my wagon's off the road, having a new clutch fitted. And if that weren't all, the van's out tomorrow morning, picking a body up in Northallerton.'

'That's a bugger, Sam, because I sold my van some time ago.' He switched the receiver to his other hand, making calming signals to Sylvia.

'I'll tell you what we could do, Freddy. We could take the hearse. I'll need your help, though. There's quite a lot of timber.'

'I'll be glad to help you. When can we do it?'

'First thing tomorrow morning. I need the hearse for a funeral in the afternoon.'

❦❧

At seven-thirty, they left the cottage and drove thirty-some miles to the farm where the timber was stored.

'I've put a dustsheet in the back to protect the bier,' Sam told him. 'I don't make a habit of doing this sort of thing,'

'Quite.' They had received several odd looks from passers-by, and Freddie wondered what they were thinking.

Eventually, they entered a rutted farm track and jolted their way down to a ramshackle farmhouse, from which a shabbily-dressed man emerged. He waited for them to draw level and, after an odd look at their transport, said, 'T' timber's in t' barn.' He pointed to an equally ramshackle building that adjoined the house.

'Let's get loaded up,' said Sam.

''Old on a minute. We 'ave to agree a price yet.'

'I thought we already had,' said Sam. 'You said two quid, and that's a lot for scrap timber like this.'

'Aye, well, you want it in a hurry, and I might have a use for it, for all you know.'

Seeing that there was nothing to be gained by arguing, Freddy asked, 'How much?'

'Fifty bob.'

'All right.' Freddy counted out two pounds and a ten shilling note.

The farmer inclined his head towards the hearse. 'I bet you don't often carry timber in this,' he said.

'I can't afford to,' Sam told him. 'Not at the way prices are around here.'

'Aye well, I've got work waiting to be done, so you'd best get loaded up.'

Under Sam's supervision, Freddy helped load the timber into the hearse, a delicate business, as much of the timber was embedded with rusty nails, which had to be prevented from scratching the polished woodwork beneath. Eventually, they completed the task, and Sam folded the edges of the dust sheet over the timber to conceal it.

'It wouldn't make a good impression,' he said. 'People might think I was dealing in scrap timber.'

He was probably right, and the camouflage was good, because a number of pedestrians doffed their hats and bowed their heads as the hearse passed them.

'If they only knew,' said Sam.

Freddy could only feel relief that they now had the timber.

33

With the last-minute hitches now resolved, Freddy was ready for the dress rehearsal. The cast were assembled, the band was in position, Derek Littlewood's cushion was inflated, and everything seemed in order.

'We've been through the overture,' said Freddy, 'so let's take it from the opening chorus.' It all felt unreal, running the show in the hall, with the band and in costume. Also, the house lights were on so that Harold Watson and his helpers could carry out last-minute adjustments, and the voices of the stage hands could be heard backstage as they adjusted ropes and weights.

The opening chorus began on an upbeat, so Freddy signalled with his left hand to the musicians to draw breath before he brought them in.

They played through the first sixteen bars, and then Freddy raised his left hand again, the signal for Stage Manager Seth Atkinson to open the curtains. Unfortunately, nothing happened. Freddy motioned the band to stop playing.

'Seth,' he called, 'where are you? There's a chorus of Daleswomen all set to delight the audience, but the audience can't see them.' There was a titter from behind the curtains, but Freddy was unable to share in the fun. Hearing no response, he called, 'Where's Seth? Has anyone seen him?'

A voice said, 'I think he's in t' toilet. Someone said he had the collywobbles.'

A moment later, Seth appeared in front of the curtains, looking flustered.

'I'm sorry, Freddy.' He lowered his voice to a stage whisper. 'I've got the runs.' Sympathy could go only so far for the musicians, who were soon helpless with laughter.

'You rotten lot,' shouted Seth. 'You don't know what it's like, listening for cues and hauling on ropes when you're bursting....' The laughter of the female chorus drowned out the rest of his tirade.

'Seth,' said Freddy, 'if you're all right for the next few minutes, we'll start the opening chorus again, and then you'll have fifty minutes to find some kaolin and morph and be ready for Act Two. Right?'

'Right, Freddy.'

Freddy started the music again, cued the curtains, and the first number went without a problem. In fact, there was no problem until Freddy noticed some slipshod work with the main spotlight.

'Sweeping spot,' he called, 'try to stay with Erik, will you? You're trailing him.'

'Sorry, Freddy. I'm just getting the hang of it.'

'Good man.' Now that they were stopped, there was one more detail he had to mention. 'Ladies,' he said, 'some of you are wearing jewellery. I'm sure Anglo-Saxon women did, but not twentieth century jewellery. Also, two of the Vikings are wearing wristwatches, and they had definitely not been invented in the ninth century.'

One of the female chorus asked, 'What about wedding rings? My husband doesn't like me to take mine off.'

'Quite right, Amy, but you can cover it with sticking plaster.'

'What a good idea.' A murmur ran through the chorus, confirming the popularity of the suggestion.

'All right, let's carry on.'

'What is it they say, SP? Is it, "Bad dress rehearsal, good opening night" or "bad dress rehearsal, bad opening night"?'

'Oh, Freddy, take a step back and see it in perspective. It wasn't a bad dress rehearsal. All that happened was that there were three or four minor hitches.'

'I suppose so.'

'I gave Seth a bottle of kaolin and morph, by the way. He should be all right tomorrow night.'

'Well done, SP. We'd better get some more in tomorrow.'

'Why tomorrow?'

'Because with all these hitches, I'm going to need it.'

'Don't be coarse.'

'It was funny, though.' As he relaxed, he began to see the situation differently. 'He told us we didn't know what it was like. It wasn't the time for me to tell him I'd seen a thousand men on a five hundred mile march with dysentery.'

'I'll probably wish I hadn't asked, but what's dysentery?'

'Extreme runs. It's debilitating, dehydrating and, if it's not treated it can be life-threatening.'

'Poor Freddy. You must have seen awful things.'

'Mm.' He nodded soberly. 'A long row of bare bottoms crouched at the roadside, like an indecent chorus line, each gaining temporary relief while impatient guards urged their owners on to greater, or more abbreviated, efforts.'

She smacked him playfully.

'But don't you see, SP? It helps to trivialise these things. Many of those blokes died, but I'm not going to do them or anyone else any good by being pious about it and cringing whenever I think of it.' He looked up at the clock. 'Meanwhile, we have a show to put on.'

'And guests arriving tomorrow.'

'I'd forgotten about that.'

'You're allowed to, Freddy. You've plenty on your mind.'

It was true. He had a great deal on his mind, and it soon became apparent that sleep was impossible.

He'd lain awake for more than two hours, reliving the events of the dress rehearsal. As Sylvia had pointed out, it hadn't been a bad rehearsal; maybe he'd been somewhat unrealistic in expecting a flawless performance, but the show had become much more than the light-hearted diversion he'd first had in mind. Challenges, problems, frustrations and triumphs had made the show Freddy's compulsive fascination.

After a while, he slipped out of bed, careful not to disturb

Sylvia, and went quietly downstairs, where he picked up the score and script of the show and settled in an armchair.

Having made himself comfortable, he read through the music, lyrics and script, paying close attention to every detail until, finally prepared for the first performance, he reached the end, closed the books and fell into a belated sleep.

34

'Feeling better, SP?'

'Yes, thanks. The fresh air helps.' Nevertheless, it was an awful time to be stricken with a stomach upset.

'I wonder if your nerves got the better of you.'

'First night nerves? Yes, possibly.'

'Here it comes.' The engine became discernible beneath a column of smoke as it made its way along the line and eventually entered the station.

As the passengers descended, Sylvia spotted Joyce immediately. 'I'd recognise that ginger mop anywhere,' she said.

Oddly, Freddy didn't recognise Len immediately, although they'd not met for some time. When they drew closer, however, the broad grin on Len's face made him instantly familiar.

'Freddy, my old mate!'

'Len!'

The two shook hands before completing their greetings with Sylvia and Joyce.

They reached the station yard as a porter wheeling a barrow laden with cardboard packing cases reminded Len of a special event in their lives.

'Hey, Freddy, do you remember the time we put two cases of French letters on a train for the Russian Front?'

'It was one of our best efforts.'

Joyce had evidently overheard their conversation, because she asked, 'Are you two talking dirty already? Honestly, Sylvia, it always happens when men get together. You must have noticed.'

Len looked around appreciatively. 'The place hasn't changed since we came up for the wedding,' he remarked.

'It's only been a few years,' Joyce reminded him.

'Nothing much has changed in three hundred years,' Sylvia told them. 'We now have electricity, but that and the railway have been about the only changes in that time.'

Freddy opened the boot of the Vauxhall and put the suitcase inside. He'd been careful to take it casually from Len when he greeted him, unsure of how embarrassed his friend might be about the injury that had secured his repatriation.

'We'll take you to the hotel first,' he said, 'and then you can drop your luggage and check in before we come back to our place for a cuppa.'

All the conversation as they went to the hotel was small talk about current events and the journey from London.

'I think it's lovely,' said Sylvia as they turned into Easingthorpe, 'that we're all here now, and it was you and Len who got Freddy and me together in the first place.'

'And what a job that was,' said Len. 'Freddy was so bashful I nearly had to write the letter myself.'

Freddy made no response, but stopped the car outside the Fox and Hounds. 'This is the hotel, folks,' he said, taking their case from the car and carrying it into the lobby.

'This is a bit of all right,' said Len. 'Are all the pubs like this?'

'No, this one's the poshest by a long way. You can tell Sylvia chose it. If I'd done the honours you'd have been wading through sawdust.'

'Ah,' said Joyce, 'someone's seen us. Maybe we can sign the register and take our luggage to the room.'

Sylvia nodded enthusiastically. 'Yes, I don't know about you two, but Joyce and I have a lot of catching up to do.'

'I've no doubt you have,' said Len, 'but I'm looking forward most of all to seeing Freddy's show.'

'And Sylvia's,' added Freddy modestly, 'and lots of others are involved as well.'

'Yes,' said Len. 'Joyce said something about Bullshit Bailey being in it. Is that right, Freddy?'

'Len, watch your language! I may be used to that kind of coarseness, but I'm sure Sylvia's not.'

'Oh yes, I am,' Sylvia assured her.

'In answer to your question, Len, Bailey has one of the starring roles. He'll surprise you.'

'He always did. How did your paths cross again after the war?'

'Let's take your luggage up to your room and I'll tell you all about it.'

⚜

There was more catching up to be done when Dorothy and Alf arrived, although Alf seemed preoccupied at first.

Sylvia handed him a cup of tea and asked, 'What's on your mind, Alf?'

'It's all a bit strange for him, like,' explained Dorothy.

'What's strange?'

'I ain't never been to a theatre afore,' confessed Alf. 'I hardly know what to expect.'

Dorothy patted his knee reassuringly. 'You'll be all right, love. It'll be just like an ENSA show, but better.' As an afterthought, she added, 'And posher.'

'There's nothing posh about Easingthorpe Town Hall,' Freddy assured them. 'It's as down-to-earth as you can get.'

'You'll enjoy it, Alf!' Dorothy patted his knee again. 'Freddy's dead clever with songs and stuff. He wrote a lovely one for Sylvia instead of a valentine. It had us all in tears, didn't it, Joyce?'

'It put the rest of us in the shade,' said Len recalling the event.

'I hope you're not expecting too much,' Freddy warned them. 'I'm not Cole Porter, you know. I'm just an amateur bandleader who enjoys playing with words.'

'Well, we're looking forward to it anyway, an' we know it's going to be good.'

It occurred to Freddy that Dorothy would have been a useful ally when they were struggling to sell tickets, but she would be equally welcome as a member of the audience.

⚜

At twenty-five minutes past seven, the Fire Brigade arrived to inspect the temporary seating and the fire exits. One of the firemen leaned over the orchestra rail and asked Wilf Bennett, the bass player, what he would do if a fire broke out.

'I'd pick up me bass an' bugger off,' he said.

'No, that's the wrong answer,' the fireman told him. 'You should place your instrument on the stage and then leave the premises. You'll remember that, won't you?'

Wilf struggled to maintain a straight face. 'I'll remember it all right,' he said.

'Good.' Satisfied, the fireman went on his way, leaving Wilf to shake his head dismissively.

'I didn't pay a king's ransom for this thing,' he told his fellow musicians, tapping his double bass, 'to leave it on t' stage when t' building's afire.'

Unaware of Wilf's rebellious utterance, the senior officer told Seth Atkinson he was satisfied and that the performance might go ahead. Accordingly, Seth went backstage and found Freddy.

'Are you ready, Freddy?' The band were tuning in the pit.

'Yes.' His heart was pounding but he couldn't resist asking, 'Did the kaolin and morph do the trick, Seth?'

'Aye, I'm steady now.' He looked relieved as he said it. 'Right, Freddy.' He opened the door to let Freddy through to the pit.

There was a burst of applause as Freddy's head and shoulders appeared over the pit rail, and then he nodded to Stanley Wood, whose roll on the snare drum led into the National Anthem.

It was enough to settle Freddy's nerves. He started the overture, wondering a little how it would go down with the local audience, but his doubts were quelled by the applause that followed it.

Now buoyed up, he started the opening chorus, smiling to himself when the curtains opened to reveal the Chorus of Anglo-Saxon Daleswomen, all toiling away at jobs their late husbands would normally have done. Elaine was in great voice, too, urging them on to greater efforts.

They left the stage to enthusiastic applause, before a pair of horns followed by a helmet appeared above a painted boulder. Erik and his Vikings had arrived.

A voice behind Freddy said, 'It's yon posh lad that sang "The Farmer's Boy" at t' Harvest Supper. Now he *can* sing.' Without turning, Freddy recognised the voice of Nathan Parker. He hadn't expected him, but he was glad he'd come, even if his theatre manners lacked sophistication.

Bailey's rich, deep voice and droll presentation endeared him immediately to the audience, his first number winning Nathan Parker's unqualified approval. 'I told you he could sing, didn't I?'

Someone said, 'Hush.'

Nathan said, 'I haven't come here to be hushed. I've come to have some fun.'

His protestations were drowned out by the Viking chorus and then by the Daleswomen as they confronted the Vikings.

At one stage, Bailey's clowning caused a burst of hearty laughter from the front row, and Freddy turned briefly to see Albert Whittaker with tears coursing down his cheeks. Sylvia was right. The show was giving him an evening's relief, and that was precious.

All too soon, the Finale to Act 1 came to its dramatic close, with the Daleswomen and Vikings vowing to defend the Dale against the marauding Picts. Freddy waited for the applause to die down before leaving the pit to go backstage, where he found the cast excited and euphoric.

'Well done, everybody,' he told them. 'It's going down really well with the audience. Keep it tight and concentrate.'

Sylvia handed him a glass of light ale.

'Thanks, SP.'

'It's going really well, Freddy.' Her face was flushed with excitement.

'I know. I'm getting a running commentary from Nathan Parker. Bert Whittaker's enjoying it too.'

'If there was no other success, that would make it worthwhile.'

'Well said, SP, but I'll have to leave you. I need a pee before the second half.'

'And I need to see our guests. See you after the curtain.'

'Right. Oh, SP?'

'What?'

'I'd still like to have seen you as a Red Indian girl in *Rosemarie*. We must get a costume, and you can give me a private performance.'

'Keep your mind on the job, Freddy.'

'Okay.'

He managed to keep his concentration throughout Act 2, right up to the triumphant final chorus and curtain calls, when Elaine beckoned him on stage to everyone's applause, and he proudly waved the musicians to their feet.

When he'd congratulated the cast, he joined Sylvia, Joyce, Dorothy, Alf and Len in the lounge bar of the Fox and Hounds. Walter and Jessie were waiting for them.

'Excellent, Freddy,' said Walter, patting his back.

'A damned good show,' said Len.

'I really enjoyed it. I've never seen anythin' like that afore tonight.'

'Well done, Freddy.'

'Yeah, it was great. You must be really made up, Freddy.'

'Made up?'

'Yeah, really happy. It's what we say in Liverpool.'

'In that case, Dorothy, I'm "made up". Thank you.'

The door opened and Bailey walked in with Elaine.

'Bailey!' Len got up to congratulate him.

'My dear old soul! Elaine, meet another of my old kriegie chums.'

Freddy watched from his corner, delighted that the show had gone so well and, now he was more relaxed, pleased that the evening was going the same way.

35

After seeing off Alf and Dorothy, and then Len and Joyce, Freddy returned to the studio to do some printing. Sylvia took Thea for a walk down the lane. She wanted to think, and Thea was pleasant but unintrusive company, the ideal partner on such an occasion.

They walked for a while, Thea stopping frequently to investigate the profusion of scents that the grass verge offered, whilst Sylvia pondered, oblivious to her surroundings.

'Of course,' she said to her companion, 'it's never been a problem for you, Thea. When Mr Helliwell spayed you he took away any urge you might have had to reproduce.'

Thea continued to sniff.

'You know, it's a funny thing, but I never used to give motherhood a thought. From leaving school and then joining the Wrens, it never occurred to me; at least, not very often. It was only when I got involved with Freddy that it suddenly became important for us to have a family.' She watched Thea absently. After a while, she said, 'For various reasons, I wouldn't swap places with you, but I must say that dogs lead an uncomplicated life. I mean to say, unless the hand of man intervenes, they can have two litters of puppies every year.' She considered that briefly, and said, 'Well, sometimes more than that, and sometimes less. I think it depends on the breed and size of the dog, but the principle is the same. It's easy for you lot.'

A rustle in the hedgerow captured Thea's attention, and then a solitary thrush made its exit, and she returned her full consideration to the scents, which were infinitely more interesting. Birds might come and go, but scents, as a rule, were satisfyingly still. They gave a dog time to exhaust her curiosity.

Everything was so green. It was hardly surprising after such a wet summer, but it seemed wrong for October. Even so, Sylvia imagined, the leaves would soon begin to turn. It was another thing that happened quite naturally, part of nature's cycle. She mused about that and, as one thought gave way to another, something occurred to her. It began as the merest hint of a question, but it grew quickly into a matter of great importance.

'Come on, Thea,' she said, 'let's go home.' There was something she had to check.

❦❦❦❦

If, in spite of the deprivation and frustration, Freddy's experience as a prisoner-of-war had benefited him in any way, it was that it had taught him patience. It was a most advantageous quality because, without it, those years spent waiting for liberation would have been intolerable. It had also served him consistently in the years since his captivity, which made it particularly strange that, on that Tuesday morning, it appeared to have deserted him.

He dialled the number of Walter's office. After a few seconds, a woman's voice answered.

'Charlesworth and Buckley. Good morning.'

'Good morning. I wonder if I might have a word with Mr Charlesworth, please.'

'Hold the line a moment, sir, and I'll find out if he's available. Who shall I say is calling?

'Freddy Hinchcliffe, his son-in-law.'

'One moment, Mr Hinchcliffe.'

He waited, almost guiltily, realising that he was probably interrupting a busy man to ask him what must seem a trivial question.

The voice returned. 'I'm afraid Mr Charlesworth is with a client. If you'd like to leave a message for him I can put you through to his secretary.'

'Oh, that won't be necessary, although you may be able to help me with something.'

'What's that, Mr Hinchcliffe?'

'Do you know when the *Gazette* is usually delivered to the

shops?' He didn't want to admit he'd been about to ask Walter the same question.

'It's usually between three and half-past. They have to get it out in time for the paper boys and girls coming out of school.'

'Thank you.'

'I expect you want to read the write-up about the show.'

'Well, yes,' he admitted. 'A good review sells tickets, they tell me.'

'If what my sister says is anything to go by, you shouldn't have much trouble doing that. She saw it last night and she said it was excellent. We've got tickets for Friday night.'

'Well, I hope you enjoy it, and I'm glad your sister did.'

'She must have. She's going to see it again on Saturday.'

'Good for her.'

'Is there anything else I can help you with, Mr Hinchcliffe?'

'No, thank you. You've been very helpful. Goodbye.'

'Goodbye, Mr Hinchcliffe.'

It was good news, but Freddy would be happier when he saw the review in the *Gazette*. At least, he hoped he would.

A lunchtime appointment with a newly-purchased pony and its young owner was a welcome distraction, and he arrived home shortly after two-thirty to find a note.

Sandwich in fridge. Appointment with doctor. Back soon, SP XXX

She hadn't been at all well over the past few days, so he was glad she was seeing the doctor.

After a moment's thought, he took the Spam sandwich down to the studio, where he had a film waiting to be developed. It was two-forty. He had maybe half-an-hour to fill.

Eventually, he was able to lock the studio and walk down to Blunt's, the local newsagents. He arrived as the *Gazette* van was leaving and, feeling like a child expecting a treat, had to wait for Mr Blunt to cut the string on a bundle of newspapers before he could buy a copy.

'I expect you're keen to see what they've written about your show,' said Mr Blunt. Everyone seemed to know what was on his mind.

'Well, you know, reviews sell tickets.'

'All right, don't keep it a secret. What do they say?'

'Just a minute.' Freddy leafed nervously through the paper until he came to a half-page feature. There were pictures of Bailey, Elaine and a few others, the photographs he'd given the paper. Most striking, though, was the headline.

VIKING HIGH JINKS' A TRIUMPH.

'Go on,' urged the impatient newsagent. 'What does it say?'

'I'll read it to you.' Freddy read the headline and went on. ' "Yoredale Players are back in business. After eleven years' inactivity they returned to the footlights at Easingthorpe Town Hall, and delighted last night's audience with 'Viking High Jinks', a musical comedy by Freddy Hinchcliffe. The songs, choruses and ensembles are fresh and engaging, and the story, set in 9th century Wensleydale, is hugely entertaining. The character Erik the Not Quite Ready is played hilariously and sung masterfully by Gerard Bailey, whilst leading lady Elaine Stafford provides an excellent foil for him. Musical accompaniment is provided by The Dalesmen, and the choreography by Sylvia Hinchcliffe is polished and imaginative.

' "Readers will recall that only last month, Gerard Bailey was in the news after apprehending a bag snatcher in Northallerton Market." '

Freddy broke off to explain, but Mr Blunt was ahead of him.

'Aye, I remember reading about that. I expect you know him well.'

'Very well. We were both prisoners in Poland.'

'Well I never. You couldn't make it up, could you? Anyroad, well done.' He added, 'We'll be along to see t' show on Friday.'

'Good, I hope you enjoy it.' Freddy turned to leave, but Mr Blunt called him back.

'You may have your name up in lights,' he said, 'but you have to pay for your paper like everybody else.'

'Oh hell, I'm sorry. I wasn't thinking.' He felt in his pocket for threepence and handed it over.

'You mustn't let fame go to your head.'

'I'll try not to.'

Elated, he hurried back up the road to show Sylvia the review. He was sure she would be back.

When he entered the flat, she seemed to be waiting for him and she was beaming. It was as if she already knew about the review, but how that had come about was beyond him as he'd bought the first copy in Easingthorpe.

'I went to see the doctor,' she told him, still smiling, 'and I told him about the stomach upset.' Her smile grew wider. 'It's surprising how a thing like a show can drive things out of your mind. Do you remember the day we climbed Lady Hill?'

'Of course.' He wanted to show her the review, but she obviously had something to tell him.

'You thought it was an enchanted place, didn't you?'

'Well, yes, I did say that.'

'Let me tell you, it is. It's a *very* enchanted place.'

Freddy was floundering. 'You've lost me, SP. What did the show make you forget?'

'Only the fact that I'm more than three weeks overdue. I can't believe it had passed my notice. I didn't realise it until I looked at my diary this morning.'

'Three weeks?' No wonder she was excited.

'Nearly four.'

'Good heavens.' He remembered a time when Sylvia's cycle was more reliable than a calendar. She *had* been distracted.

'How long ago did we go up Lady Hill?'

'I don't know.'

'I do. It was six weeks ago, and morning sickness usually begins about six weeks after... you know.'

'Conception,' he prompted.

'I don't care what it's called,' she said, hugging him excitedly. 'All I know is that I'm going to have a baby!'

They hugged and kissed, and kissed again. Suddenly the review was old news.

Eventually, he said, 'I used to say you were a member of too many clubs.'

'Yes?' She seemed puzzled.

'The W I, the WVS, and now you've joined another.'

'What are you talking about, Freddy?'

'The pudding club.'

'You really can be coarse, you know.' But she still allowed him to hug her again.

THE END

www.ingramcontent.com/pod-product-compliance
Lightning Source LLC
Chambersburg PA
CBHW020838260626
47169CB00003B/1050